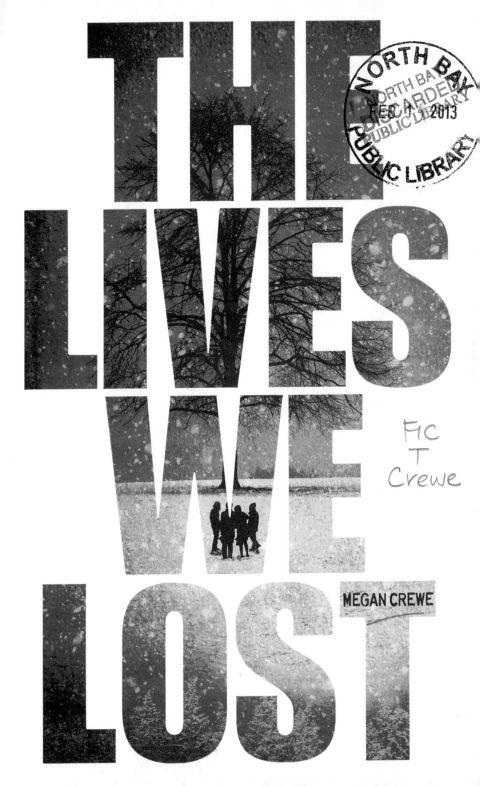

# THE LIVES WE LOST

## MEGAN CREWE

## ALSO BY MEGAN CREWE

**THE FALLEN WORLD**
# BOOK 1: THE WAY WE FALL

THE FALLEN WORLD
BOOK 2

# THE LIVES WE LOST

MEGAN CREWE

HYPERION
NEW YORK

Text copyright © 2013 by Megan Crewe

Printed in the United States of America

First Edition
10 9 8 7 6 5 4 3 2 1
V567-9638-5-13004

Library of Congress Cataloging-in-Publication Data

Crewe, Megan.
    The lives we lost: Megan Crewe.—First ed.
      pages cm.—(The fallen world; book 2)
    Summary: "In the second installment in this dystopian trilogy, the virus has spread beyond Kaelyn's island, and she and her friends must head to the mainland, carrying with them hopes for a cure"—Provided by publisher.
    ISBN 978-1-4231-4617-9 (alk. paper)
    [1. Survival—Fiction. 2. Virus diseases—Fiction. 3. Science fiction.] I. Title.
    PZ7.C86818Li 2013
    [Fic]—dc23                      2012032510

Text is set in 12-point Adobe Garamond Pro.
Reinforced binding

Visit www.un-requiredreading.com

To chances lost and
risks worth taking

# DEC 23

This is how the world ends: with the boy who used to be my best friend stepping off the ferry, hair shaggy and tangled, face too thin, looking at me like he isn't sure who I am. Like he isn't sure of anything.

I was so excited when I spotted Leo crossing the strait I didn't wonder how he'd gotten past the patrol boats that were supposed to be enforcing the quarantine. Or why he was alone. I just grabbed Tessa and dashed for the harbor.

Then he was limping down the ramp with the man who'd driven the ferry, and Tessa was throwing her arms around him, and he was staring at her with that uncertain expression—and an inkling of what it all meant rose up inside me. For a second I wanted to turn and run. As if I could outrun the truth.

But I stood my ground. A few people from town had gathered around us. "You made it from the mainland!" someone said. "Is the government sending help? The electricity's out, and the phones..."

"Did they find a cure?" someone else broke in, with a sort of desperate hopefulness.

Tessa stepped away from Leo, her gaze flickering to the opposite shore. "My parents," she said. "Did you see them?"

He looked at me again, even though I hadn't spoken, and this time a hint of recognition came into his eyes. Too faint to tell whether he was happy to see me, whether he was still stinging from our last argument, whether he cared at all.

Even before he spoke, my gut had knotted and my mouth had gone dry.

"There's no help," he said, with a rasp in his voice. "The virus, it ripped right through the country—the States—maybe the whole world. Everything... everything's fallen apart."

This is what I know: the doctors didn't control the epidemic on the mainland any better than they did here. On the other side of the strait, everybody's just as bad off as we are. No one is coming to fix the electricity or the water, to bring the supplies we need, or to bring about any of the other hopes I'd managed to hold on to.

I started writing in this journal for Leo, to practice saying what I couldn't say to his face. I kept going because I thought it was important to keep track of the awfulness we've been through, to have some sort of record for the rest of the world. But the world I was writing for—it's lost. The boy I started for looks lost too. So what is the point in writing? A journal isn't going to help me find them.

I have to believe there's something else that will.

# ONE

I decided before I came downstairs that I wasn't going to mention what day it was. I got choked up every time I even thought about it.

When I'd braced myself and made it down, Tessa was in the living room, pruning the bean plants on the window ledge. The smell of hot oatmeal was wafting from the kitchen. Gav stood over the pot with a wooden spoon, his tawny hair sleep-rumpled. I had to resist the urge to go over and run my fingers through it.

It was more than a week ago I'd suggested he crash on the air mattress here at what used to be Uncle Emmett's house, considering he was over all the time anyway and I couldn't help worrying when he went home to his family's empty house at night. In spite of all my other concerns, I still felt a little giddy finding my boyfriend here each morning.

"Hey," I said, and he glanced up and grinned.

"Good morning, Kaelyn!" Meredith crowed, bounding in from the dining room with an incredible amount of energy for a kid who'd just recovered from a deadly virus. I was starting to wonder if she was making up for all that time lying in a hospital bed by moving in constant fast-forward. But seeing the healthy flush in her dark cheeks made me smile.

She hopped up to peer into the pot of oatmeal. "Is there brown sugar?"

"Meredith," I said, my giddiness fading.

Gav held up his hand. "Not brown," he said, "but I can sprinkle on a little of the white stuff."

Meredith's lower lip curled, but she pressed her mouth flat before it could turn into a pout, and lifted her chin. "Awesome!" she said. "Thank you, Gav!"

"I picked up an extra bag from the storage rooms," Gav said to me as Meredith scampered over to the dining room table. "Figured if anyone deserved a treat, it was her."

"Thank you," I said. "And for breakfast, too."

"Hey, I know you only keep me around for my cooking," he said.

"And don't you forget it," I said. Slipping my arm around his waist, I leaned in for a kiss. Meredith snorted in amusement.

As I released Gav, he started spooning the oatmeal into the bowls on the counter. The floor creaked behind him, and Leo emerged from the tiny downstairs bathroom, where he'd been washing up. He looked at us for a second with the uncertain expression I'd first seen when he came off the ferry. Like he wasn't sure why he was even here. Then Gav turned, and the end of his serving spoon tapped Leo's arm. Leo flinched back, his hip smacking the counter's edge.

"Crap," Gav said. "I'm sorry."

Leo ducked his head and steadied himself with a hand on the counter. "I'm fine," he said. "Crazy reflexes." He laughed awkwardly, and my stomach twisted. The Leo I grew up with used to joke effortlessly. This Leo made it look like work.

His gaze lingered on me as I picked up my bowl, and my stomach twisted tighter. If anyone was going to notice the significance of today's date, it'd be Leo.

"Hold on a sec, Kae," he said, hurrying past us to the living room. Cloth rustled—the backpack he'd brought back from his parents' place, I guessed. His old home, like mine, didn't have a generator, so he'd been sleeping on the couch here.

Gav raised an eyebrow at me, and I shrugged. He knew the short story of Leo's and my friendship, an abbreviated version I'd told him and Tessa after we walked Leo back to the house two weeks ago. I'd said I hadn't talked about it before because I'd been so worried about what was happening on the island. Which was mostly true.

I hadn't brought up how Leo and I had argued and then stopped talking after I'd moved to Toronto for one of Dad's jobs. Not even to Leo. He'd seemed so messed up when he got back, I'd been trying to avoid all painful topics of conversation. Our argument hardly seemed significant, considering the friends and family we'd lost since. But then, on the fourth day, he'd said to me, "We're all right now, aren't we?" like he was afraid to ask.

All I'd managed to get out was, "I'm sorry, that whole fight was my fault."

"I'll take half the blame and we'll call it even," he'd replied, and hugged me so tight I lost my breath. And just like that, it didn't matter.

But even if *we* were all right now, I was pretty sure he wasn't.

As Gav carried his and Meredith's oatmeal to the table, Leo stepped into the kitchen with one hand behind his back.

"Close your eyes," he said, with a smile that looked almost real.

"Leo," I said, "I don't—"

"Come on," he said. "For old times."

I had the feeling that if I protested more, his expression was going to stiffen up again. So I closed my eyes, holding my bowl. There was a grating sound, and a clink, and the soft patter of something dropping onto the oatmeal.

"Okay," Leo said.

I looked down, and my breath caught in my throat.

He'd placed a dollop of blueberry preserves in the middle of the bowl. I recognized the angular handwriting on the label of the jar he held as his mom's.

"Happy birthday," he said.

I hadn't even had store jam in over a month. The juicy-sweet smell was making my mouth water. At the same time, my eyes prickled.

When we were little, Leo's family and mine used to go berry-picking together. I would watch for rabbits between the bushes, and Leo would practice leaps and tumble between the rocks. His mom gave my parents a couple jars of preserves every August, and Drew and I would polish them off by the end of September.

Back before the virus took all of them away. Gnawing through Mom's mind, making Drew feel he had to sneak to the mainland to try to find help. And Dad, struck down by the gang of islanders who'd wanted to burn the hospital and all the infected patients inside.

"I couldn't believe it," Leo was saying. "Our pantry was a mess, but this one jar was lying behind a box in the corner, like it was waiting for me."

"You should have it," I said, offering the bowl to him. "It's your mom's."

And she wasn't going to be able to make more, ever again. The virus had taken both of Leo's parents too.

He shook his head, nudging the bowl back toward me, but his smile faltered.

"I think she'd have wanted me to share it," he said.

He'd hardly spoken when he'd come back from their house, and I hadn't pried. He still hadn't even offered us more than a vague summary of how he'd hitchhiked and walked his way here from his dance school in New York. Most of what I knew about the mainland I'd heard from Mark, the other islander who'd been stuck across the strait and driven the ferry back with Leo. But what could I do except give him time?

As I hesitated, Gav poked his head into the room. "It's your birthday?" he said. "You should have told me."

"I didn't want to make a big deal about it," I said, carrying my breakfast over to the table. "Seventeen's not an important one anyway, right?"

"I think seventeen's pretty good," Gav said. "But then I might be biased."

"I forgot!" Meredith said. "I've got to make you a card!"

"You don't have to," I said, but she was already gulping down the last of her oatmeal and dashing into the living room, where construction paper and colored pencils littered the coffee table.

"Tess, breakfast is ready," Leo said, coming in after me. I sat down next to Gav, who hooked his ankle around mine.

"I'm going to think of something," he said.

"Really," I said, "you don't—"

"I know, I know. Still going to." He turned to Leo. "So, any other secrets of Kae's that I should know?"

Leo paused, as if taking the question seriously, and then put on a grin. "I think I should stop now. She might sic those vicious ferrets on me."

The teasing sounded weak to my ears, but it made Meredith spin around. "Mowat and Fossey don't hurt people!" she hollered, and the rest of us laughed, the tension breaking. But as Tessa slipped into the room and everyone started eating, my eyes kept prickling.

"No matter how busy we get," Mom used to say, "we shouldn't forget that family's more important than anything else." On my and Drew's birthdays, she and Dad had always arranged to go in to work late and for us to skip the first period of school if it was a weekday. We'd come down after sleeping in, to the presents Dad had stacked on the table and Mom making whatever we'd requested for breakfast the night before, and we'd all eat together.

I couldn't remember what breakfast I'd asked for when I turned sixteen last year. It hadn't seemed important at the time.

I swallowed a mouthful of oatmeal, the blueberries sliding in a sticky clump down my throat. The taste was both achingly familiar and completely alien to the lives we had now.

"Leave it in the sink," Tessa said as I finished. "I'll take care of the dishes."

I might have argued, but I needed to get away, just for a moment. "Thanks," I said. "I'll be upstairs."

Meredith's bedroom felt a lot smaller now that she was back from the hospital. I'd set up the cot, giving her the bed, and it took up nearly half the floor space. The cardboard box holding everything Dad had left at the hospital over the last few months sat in one corner. I'd collected it from his friend Nell, the island's only remaining doctor, on one of my trips to visit Meredith.

I sank down onto the cot and pushed open the flaps of the box. When I'd first brought it home I'd gone through it as quickly as possible. Now I pulled out the wool coat that was folded on top and pressed my face against the scratchy cloth.

It smelled like my dad, like oak and coffee and citrusy aftershave. Like being back in his study, talking with him about some curiosity of animal behavior or environmental phenomena.

Only three weeks ago he'd worn this coat. I wrapped my arms around it, willing back tears, and a hard shape dug into the underside of my arm.

I ran my hand over the lining and found the slit of an inner pocket. When I reached inside, my fingers touched a cool metal edge.

The two keys I pulled out hung on a delicate ring, with a plastic fob imprinted with the emblem of the research center where Dad had worked, a half circle split by a wavy line.

I stared at them. When I'd collected his possessions I'd been hoping I'd find the key to the research center, but I'd thought I was out of luck. I'd tried every one on the big ring Nell had handed over, and none had fit in the keyhole. They'd been here, separate and hidden, all along.

And now I had them.

I could finally check what he'd been working on all that time he'd spent there between his shifts at the hospital. If he'd been even partway through developing an experimental treatment, Nell could try it out. Or at least I could bring equipment from the labs over to the hospital. There had to be something we could use.

Gav's voice carried up the stairs faintly. If I told him where I was going, he'd want to come along. They all might. The thought of having to share my first glimpse of this last piece of Dad's life made me tense.

I folded the coat and laid it back in the box, then headed down to the front door. It wasn't far. I'd just pop in and look around. We could explore it more thoroughly together in the afternoon.

"I'm going out to stretch my legs a bit," I called as I tugged on my boots.

"You want company?" Gav asked from the living room doorway.

I shook my head. "I won't be long."

Outside, the air was cool but not brittle against my face. It was a thaw day, a couple degrees above freezing. The snow that'd fallen last week was disintegrating into a trickle in the gutters.

Otherwise, the streets were quiet. Last year there would have been people out shoveling or de-icing their walks. Now there was no one. Jagged glass glinted in the window frames and battered doors hung ajar, in the wake of the gangs' looting. The twenty or so volunteers who helped at the hospital mostly slept there too. Over the last two months, the few hundred houses Gav's group used to bring food to had dwindled to a couple dozen, where people who'd managed to avoid the virus were still hanging on. The rest were empty.

I skirted the hospital. Beyond it, a narrow stretch of pavement led me through fields spotted with fir trees and reddish crags peeking through the snow. Paw prints crossed my path here and there, mostly squirrel and coyote. On another day I might have stopped to examine them, but the keys pressing against my hip urged me onward.

Who was left who'd care what I observed anyway? There wasn't going to be much call for wildlife biologists for a good long while.

The research center stood amid a semicircle of pines, a broad rectangle of beige concrete. A few steps from the door, I stopped. Footprints marked the snow around the entrance—dozens of them, with the thick treads of winter boots. At least a few people had come around here since the last snowfall.

The thick glass in one of the windows looked chipped, as if someone had tried to smash it. Spidery scratch marks scarred the metal around the door's keyhole. The intercom mounted on the wall nearby had been broken open, the wires snapped. My hands clenched in my coat pockets.

So the gang had finally gotten interested in this place. As if they hadn't already taken enough.

The stream of footprints rambled off toward the trees in a line diagonal to the lane. No tire tracks, which meant the trespassers had probably been killing time rather than on an official mission. There was no sign of anyone else here now.

Shivering, I pulled out the keys. The larger one fit in the lock and turned easily. I pushed open the door.

The backup generator was still running—the lights blinked on in the hall when I tapped the switch. I guessed that wasn't surprising. Being the newest building around here, it probably had the best machinery on the island.

Past a row of empty mail cubbies, I found a kitchen, which held only a box of orange pekoe tea, and what appeared to be a meeting room, with a flat-screen TV filling most of the opposite wall. A thin crack ran down the middle of the screen.

A vague uneasiness washed over me, and I continued on to the stairwell.

Upstairs, the second room I peered into had to be Dad's office.

A framed photo of a younger me and Drew on the beach stood on one side of his desk, and the leather gloves Mom had given him our last Christmas together lay beside it.

The computer asked for a password I couldn't supply. I pawed through the drawers, finding only reports on marine bacteria and plankton populations, and then sagged back in Dad's chair.

How many hours had he sat here puzzling over the virus? Missing Mom? Worrying about me and Drew?

I blinked hard and pushed myself out of the chair. If I took too long, Gav would get concerned.

Three doors down, I came to a laboratory. When I flicked the light switch, the florescent panels flooded the room with flat white light. Microscopes and petri dishes dotted the shiny black tabletop beneath a wall of cabinets. A huge stainless-steel fridge stood in the corner, with an electronic display reporting the internal temperature. This was clearly where Dad had spent the rest of his time. A Styrofoam cup sat next to one of the microscopes, half full of cooled tea. Notebooks were scattered on the table beside it, one of them open to a page of Dad's loopy printing.

I picked up the notebook and my gaze snagged on one small word.

*Vaccine.*

I leaned over the table, skimming the page. *If I continue three more days without any side effects from the vaccine, I'll discuss the next step with Nell,* he'd written. And at the top of the page, *Project WebVac, Day 18.*

Heart thudding, I dropped into one of the chairs and flipped back through the book.

After several minutes of reading, I walked over to the refrigerator and opened it. On the second shelf, five sealed vials of a pale amber solution stood in a plastic tray. I closed the door before I let in too much warmth, and leaned against it. My hands trembled.

There they were. The samples of Dad's new vaccine.

He'd kept working on creating one even after his team had sent their original attempt over to the mainland; even when he was the only person left at the center. He'd recorded the whole process in the notebook. Trying new methods of inactivating the virus, incorporating proteins from its earlier mutation, he'd come up with a formula he was almost sure would be both successful and safe. But first he'd had to try it out. And being Dad, he hadn't felt right letting anyone else take that risk.

So without telling anyone, without telling *me*, he'd injected a sample into himself, eighteen days before he died. And he never got sick. Even though he'd been with infected people in the hospital every day.

We had a vaccine.

We had a vaccine that might work.

# TWO

The hospital was a lot less crowded than it used to be, but in the empty reception room I could hear every stage of the virus's progression. The coughs and sneezes and rasping of fingers chasing endless itches, in the rooms just off the hall. The bright babble of voices in the farther rooms, saying things the patients would have cringed to hear when they were well: a woman raving about her infatuation with a neighbor's husband, a boy gloating over how he'd broken his brother's favorite toys. And from the second floor, the screams and shouts of those the virus had gripped the longest. We had no sedatives left to chase away the violent hallucinations just before the end.

A couple weeks ago, Nell had told me they'd run out of face masks too.

"We're not really supposed to reuse them," she'd said, "but we'll still have the patients wear them—it does help protect us, and it can't hurt someone who's already infected."

The rest of us had been covering up however we could when out of the house. Because I'd been sick and so was now immune, I went to the doors first when delivering food around town with Gav or scavenging for supplies with Tessa, in case we ran into someone infected. Gav grumbled about it, but I wasn't taking chances. Catching the virus was all but a death sentence. I'd survived because I'd caught an earlier mutation that had given me partial resistance. Meredith had only made it because of an experimental treatment involving my blood.

I didn't see Nell on the ground floor, so I headed upstairs. A thin wail rose above the others, piercing the walls. I drew in a breath and climbed on. If I'd had enough blood to give, I would have tried to cure every patient here, but dying in the attempt wouldn't have helped anyone. Just saving Meredith had weakened me enough to put me back in the hospital for a day. If Dad's new vaccine did what he'd hoped, maybe it wouldn't matter. Because no one else would be getting sick.

When I came out of the stairwell, Nell was standing halfway down the hall, talking to one of the volunteers. They both had strips of fabric tied across their lower faces. Nell's was stark white above her stain-mottled lab coat. As I started toward her, she saw me and motioned toward the floor to say she'd meet me below.

The cries rattled in my ears as I hurried back downstairs.

Nell followed me a couple minutes later. She popped out her earplugs and tugged down her mouth-covering.

"Everything all right?" she asked wearily.

Her face looked worn, and her hair was falling out of its bun. I wondered how often she went home, slept, ate, even now that the hospital had only a fraction of the patients it'd held a couple months ago. She and two nurses were all that was left of the former staff.

"Yeah," I said. "I had to tell you—"

The lights overhead flickered. I looked up at them, startled. Nell smiled thinly.

"We're having a few issues with the generator," she said. "No one expected it to have to run this long. Howard thinks he'll have it back to normal in a couple days. What did you want to tell me?"

I pulled my gaze away from the ceiling, suppressing the nervous fluttering in my chest. "I found the keys to the research center today," I said. "I went to look around, and—Dad made a new vaccine, Nell."

She blinked at me. "A vaccine," she said. So he hadn't told her.

"For the virus," I said, as if that wouldn't be obvious. "He was testing it on himself, and when he was sure it was safe, he was going to make enough for everyone left on the island."

No more deaths. No more fear every time Gav or Tessa or Leo stepped outside the house. I felt like dancing, but Nell seemed firmly planted on the ground. She shook her head and gave a shocked little laugh.

"I knew he was trying to find a formula, but he never...He never said he was that close." She rubbed her forehead. "How much is there?"

"It looks like only five doses," I said. "He wasn't finished taking the data on himself, so I guess he didn't want to waste time making more until he was sure. But he had it in him for eighteen days and he was fine. That means the vaccine probably works, right?"

"There's a good chance it's safe, then," Nell said. "But he was taking all the same precautions as before—wearing a mask and gloves and a protective gown with the patients. To know whether it actually protects you..."

To know that, someone would have to take the vaccine and then allow themselves to be exposed to the virus. Was that what Dad had meant by taking the next step?

"But it might work," I said, and paused, a gnawing question

wriggling past all my other thoughts. "Why was he trying to make another vaccine, Nell? We know now from Leo and Mark that the first one, the one he made with the World Health people and sent over to the mainland, wasn't effective. But Dad didn't know that."

"He did know," Nell said softly. "His contact at the Public Health Agency reported back a few days before we lost satellite contact."

For a second, I couldn't speak. He'd known? Dad had known the virus was still spreading on the mainland, and he'd let me hope the world outside the island might still be okay, for weeks and weeks.

But that wasn't important now. "Well, now we have it," I said. "He left a lot of notes—could you use them to make more of the vaccine? Or, since the soldiers who were guarding the strait have left"—*or died*—"we could bring the samples to the mainland and find someone there who can. There's got to be *someone*." No matter how bad the situation had gotten, not everyone would have given up. We hadn't here.

"Yes," Nell said. "You're right. I wish I could do it, Kaelyn, but I don't have the training. I'd be more likely to make a mistake than replicate the vaccine properly. We'll have to organize a group to take it to the mainland and locate whoever's still working on the virus." She paused. "I wonder when they'd be able to go."

"They should go now," I said. "The sooner we can distribute a vaccine..."

"Kaelyn," she said, "we have to think practically. I've talked to Mark. The roads on the mainland aren't plowed; the gas stations are closed; there might not be anywhere to take shelter from the cold. There are at least two months of winter left. Sending someone now, it could be a suicide mission. And if something happened to the team, we'd lose the vaccine too."

"We could lose it *here* if we don't do something soon," I said. "What if the generator in the research center dies?"

"We can move the samples to the hospital," Nell said.

"Where the generator's already having problems," I said, and the lights flickered again as if to prove my point. Nell's mouth flattened, but I kept going. "And some people from the gang were already trying to break in—where can we keep the vaccine that'll be safe? What if something happens to us in the next two months?"

Nell touched my arm. "We're going to be fine until spring," she said. "I think we've proven we can withstand an awful lot. It's fantastic that you found the vaccine, Kaelyn, and we'll keep it safe, but I don't think we have any choice but to wait."

She said the words, but I didn't hear even a hint of joy beneath the exhaustion in her voice. Nell had been working in the hospital so long, and seen so much, maybe she couldn't believe in a vaccine appearing out of nowhere to save the day. Maybe it felt too much like a fairy tale.

Maybe it was. And she was right about the risks. But how many more people would get sick between now and the spring? If we even survived that long.

"We'll be fine," Nell said again, patting my shoulder. But as she turned away, the sense crept over me that she was saying it to convince herself as well as me.

The sun was glaring off the snow by the time I got back to the house, but the temperature had dropped, and the wind was grazing my face with icy fingers. I hesitated with my hand on the doorknob. As I'd walked from the hospital, the knowledge of what I needed to do had risen up on me. Now it sat like a stone in my gut.

I had no idea how to tell them. Tessa might support me, but I didn't know what to expect from Leo. And Gav...

I set my jaw and pushed inside.

Tessa and Meredith were sitting by the coffee table, Meredith muttering at the knitting needles she was stringing with yarn, and Tessa frowning at the faded instructions that had come with the old kit we'd found. Her gaze flickered toward me with a half smile of greeting, and then she said to Meredith, "I think maybe you wind it the other way...."

In the kitchen, Gav was sprawled on the floor half under the sink, while Leo crouched next to him with the toolbox. "Can't get a good grip," I heard Gav say as I slid off my boots. Leo cocked his head and then offered a wrench.

"Try this one."

There was a raspy metal sound, and Gav let out a breath. "Perfect! You done this before?"

The corner of Leo's mouth quirked. "My dad was always trying to get me into 'guy things'—tools, boats, guns—his idea of counteracting the dancing, I think. A few things stuck."

"Works out for us," Gav said. He knocked on the pipe and squirmed out. "My dad was a plumber, so this is about the only thing he did around the house. Guess I should have paid more attention."

Seeing them chatting together so easily warmed me a little. For a second I forgot the difficult conversation I was about to start. Then Meredith sighed and set down her needles.

"Kaelyn!" she said, snatching up a folded piece of construction paper from the couch. She dashed over, waving it. "I got everyone to sign it," she said. "And I'm going to make you mittens or a hat with the knitting stuff. For everyone else too, but you first. As soon as I figure out how."

She'd decorated the birthday card with shiny star stickers and a drawing of me with jagged hair and turned-out feet, surrounded by a ring of lines like the rays of a sun. *For the best cousin ever!* she'd written inside. The heaviness in my gut swelled with guilt.

I didn't want to get her overexcited about the idea of a vaccine, or worried about what I was planning to do, not while I was trying to explain it to everyone else and dealing with the arguments I knew were coming. I wasn't even totally sure what my plan was yet. But I'd talk to her when the arguing was over, when I'd figured out the details and could say exactly what was going to happen. Soon.

I wondered if that was what Dad had been thinking when he'd decided not to tell me about testing the vaccine. But Meredith was seven, and I'd been sixteen. It wasn't the same.

"Thanks so much, Mere," I said, bending down to hug her. "You want to take the ferrets outside for a bit? I've got some other things I need to do, but they could use the exercise."

"Sure!" she said, beaming at me. Any request having to do with the ferrets was pretty much guaranteed a yes. She scrambled up the stairs to collect Mowat and Fossey, and I went to the dining room window as she dashed with them into the backyard.

"You were gone for a while," Gav said, coming in.

"I stopped at the hospital," I said. The rest of the words stuck in my throat. I glanced out at Meredith again. I only had so long to do this before she came racing back inside. "Actually, I need to talk to all of you. Let's sit down."

When he, Tessa, and Leo had gathered at the table, I explained briefly how I'd found the keys and gone to the research center. When I mentioned the vaccine samples, their eyes widened.

Tessa spoke first. "It's so lucky you found them," she said, brightening. "If it works—"

"We could make sure everyone's protected," Gav jumped in, catching some of her enthusiasm. "It's worth a try, anyway. You went to the hospital to talk to Nell? Is she going to start making more?"

Leo just watched me, silent, a stiffness in his posture. As if he knew I wasn't finished.

"Nell can't," I said. "She doesn't know how. My dad was the only one left on the island who would have." I paused. "But there's got to be someone on the mainland who does. A scientist, or a doctor. People were still trying to find a cure over there, weren't they?"

Leo nodded. "Last I heard," he murmured.

"So she's going to send people over?" Tessa asked.

This was the hard part. "Not now," I said. "She thinks it's too dangerous for anyone to go during the winter. She wants to wait at least a couple months, until it warms up. But the generator at the hospital's acting up. The one in the research center could fail too. If the samples aren't kept at the right temperature, they'll be ruined. I don't think it's safe to wait."

Gav shrugged. "I know a few of the guys on the food run have been getting restless, especially knowing the army's abandoned the strait. I bet if I talked to them—"

"I don't think they'll listen," I said. Most of the remaining volunteers were adults, and while they respected Gav, I was sure none of them had forgotten we were teenagers. "Especially if we ask them to keep it secret. You know one of them will mention it to Nell, and she'll tell them not to do it, and then she'll probably insist on locking up the vaccine so no one can get to it until she decides it's safe to go."

"Maybe she's right," Tessa said, brushing a strand of carrot-red hair away from her face. "It is going to be dangerous. A couple months isn't that long."

Leo laughed weakly.

"In a couple months, the people who might be able to make more vaccine could die," I said. "In a couple months, who knows what will have happened to us here?"

"So what are you saying, Kae?" Gav said, but I think he'd already guessed.

I drew in a breath. "I'm going to take it. I'm not going to be able to think about anything else until I know the vaccine's with someone who can make more." Gav looked like he was about to argue, but I pushed on. "My dad was working on this vaccine up to the day he *died*. He risked his life to test it. I can't just let it sit in some fridge while more people die. I'm going to be careful, I'm going to make sure I'm prepared, but I have to do this. No one else is going to."

"You can't prepare for everything," Leo said.

My chest tightened. "Maybe not," I said. "But I'm going to try."

He met my eyes. A strange heat washed over me as I saw the look in his—startled but awed. Then he blinked, and the only thing I saw was fear.

"Kae," he said. His mouth stayed open, but no other sound came out. He jerked back his chair, standing up.

"Sorry," he managed, and walked out of the room. Tessa's face went even more pale than usual.

"He's just . . ." she started, then trailed off, obviously not knowing how to label what was going on with him any better than I did.

Gav cleared his throat, breaking the silence. "You shouldn't go alone," he said. "That'd just be crazy."

"But—" I said, and he took one of my hands.

"So I'll go with you," he said. "We'll do it together." He paused. "I mean, as long as you'd want me there."

The tension inside me released. "Of course," I said. "But are you sure? The food run, everything you organize here on the island—"

"The rest of the volunteers can look after the food run and the drop-offs for a while," he said. "I'm not going to be much use if I'm spending the whole time worrying about what might be happening to you."

I intertwined my fingers with his. "Thank you," I said, and glanced at Tessa.

She nodded before I even asked. "I'll look after Meredith until you're back. I don't mind at all. She's kind of like my cousin too, now."

"Thank you," I said again. A lightness filled me that could have been excitement or terror or both.

I was really going to do this. I was taking the vaccine off the island, into whatever waited on the other side of the strait.

# THREE

Gav found a car the next morning—an SUV someone had donated for the food runs, solid with wide snow tires. Rather than risk emptying the last working pump at the island's gas station, we took a rubber tube and siphoned out what was left in the tanks of the town's many abandoned cars. After a few failed attempts and a mouthful of gas for me that left me sputtering when I didn't move fast enough after getting the suction going, we managed to stock up an extra ten gallons in jugs that we stashed in the back.

"I'll see if we can find some heavy sleeping bags for the nights," Gav said as we closed the hatch. "And we'll want to have more than enough food, in case we run into trouble. How far are we going?"

"I'm thinking Ottawa," I said. "Since it's the capital—if the government still has scientists working on the virus anywhere, it'd be there, right?"

"Sure," he said.

"Or we could try Halifax first, since it's closer."

He shrugged. "What you said about Ottawa makes sense. If there's no one who can help in the capital, there probably isn't anywhere."

He said it so casually I stopped and looked at him. "You don't think we're going to find anyone?"

"We don't really know, do we?" he said. "Look at how quickly the government abandoned us here."

At my frown, he stepped toward me, resting his hands on my arms. "I get that you need to do this, Kae," he said. "And I want to go with you. I don't think anything else matters."

"I was always planning on leaving the island some day," he added when I didn't speak. "Me and Warren, we were going to travel the country, see what we'd been missing." A roughness had come into his voice mentioning the best friend he'd watched die, but then he tugged the collar of my coat playfully. "If I have to go with a pretty girl instead, I guess I can deal."

The warmth in his gaze made me flush. He leaned in to kiss me, and I pulled him even closer. In that moment, nothing mattered more than the tingling of my skin and the heat where his body touched mine.

Before dinner, Leo knocked on Meredith's bedroom door while I was refilling the ferrets' food dish.

"Hey," he said from the doorway.

"Hey, yourself," I replied, trying to keep my concern out of my voice.

"I'm sorry about yesterday," he said. "I wasn't judging you, or what you want to do. I just—when I even think about what things were like over there sometimes..."

"It's okay," I said.

"No, it's not, really." He dragged in a breath. "I wanted to see if I can help. With whatever you're planning."

I hesitated. As if sensing that I was evaluating his stability, he stood straighter. Though his body had always been lean, he looked too thin in his sweatshirt and jeans now. But his jaw was firm and his eyes clear.

"You're the only person I can talk to who's been off the island since the epidemic started," I said. "If I ask Mark too many questions, he'll probably mention it to Nell. I could use some advice figuring out the best route to take."

"Okay," he said. "I can do that."

So the next day I scrounged up a map book and sat down with Leo in the living room. He traced his finger from the grayed-out area of the United States across the spread that showed all of Canada.

"I came this way," he said, "through Maine and into New Brunswick. If you're going to Ottawa, I think you'll want to head up into Quebec and then down by the St. Lawrence River."

"How bad were the roads?"

"There wasn't too much snow yet. But there's definitely no one plowing anymore, and there won't be lights. You'll probably have to get around abandoned vehicles. I think some people just drove until they ran out of gas."

I bit my lip, studying the map. My grandparents on Dad's side had lived in Ottawa—we'd done the drive in a day and a half before. But that was on properly cared-for roads with working gas stations along the way.

"You must have gone through a few towns," I said. "What were they like? Did you see many people?"

Leo opened his mouth, and his eyes went briefly glassy. He lowered his head.

"It's okay if you don't want to talk about it," I said quickly. "If it's too hard thinking about it."

He exhaled, and then he looked back at me with a small, tight smile. "You know, I haven't thanked you," he said. "You've been trying so hard to make sure I'm okay—I know that. So, thank you."

He squeezed the top of my hand, where it was resting on the couch between us. Then the stairs creaked, and his arm jerked away. I felt my face warm as Tessa walked into the room, even though we hadn't been doing anything friends shouldn't, even though I hadn't thought of Leo as more than a friend in months. He'd reacted because the sound had startled him, that was all.

As Tessa bent to kiss Leo and then turned to the seedling tray she'd started setting up before breakfast, I thought of my old journal. All the feelings I'd poured into it—about Leo, about every horrible thing happening around me. I didn't know how I'd have stayed sane during the last four months without it. Maybe Leo needed more than time and space. Maybe he needed to get the memories haunting him out of his head.

"If you do want to talk about what you saw over there, I'll listen," I said. "It's not that I don't want to hear it. It's totally up to you—whatever you're okay with."

Leo ran a hand through his dark hair, which had been short and spiky since he'd taken Uncle Emmett's electric razor to it the day after he made it back to the island. His Adam's apple bobbed in his throat.

"It's not the roads that are really bad, Kae," he said. "It's . . . it's people. You can't trust them, even if they act like they want to help. You shouldn't talk to anyone if you can avoid it. Just keep driving."

"I know to be cautious," I said. "We've dealt with enough, with the gang and their craziness, here on the island."

He shook his head. "Everyone here is still mostly looking out for each other. Once you get to the mainland, it's not going to be like that." He paused. "You remember how you always told me, when we were kids, that the most important rule with wild animals is keeping your distance, making sure they don't feel you're threatening their home or their food? You have to treat everyone you see like that. They won't care that you're trying to save them from the virus. They'll just see a car with gas and food in the trunk that could keep them alive a little longer. And they won't care what they have to do to you to get it."

Tessa set down her watering can with a clunk loud enough that we both turned our heads toward her. "Do you really have to talk like that?" she said to Leo. "Kaelyn already knows it'll be dangerous."

"I think she needs to know just how bad it is," Leo said cautiously.

"She'll be careful," Tessa said. "She always is. How is going on and on about it going to help?"

A shadow passed over Leo's face. "Maybe," he said quietly, "I believe in telling people the truth. So they can decide how to deal with it for themselves."

Tessa stiffened. Without another word, she left her plants and headed back upstairs. I watched her go, baffled. Leo dropped his face into his hands.

"I shouldn't have said that," he said, his voice muffled by his palms. "I know why it bothers her. She still doesn't know what happened to her parents."

"I feel like I'm missing something," I said.

"We've argued a couple times," he said. "About—she was

writing e-mails to me, while I was at school, you know? Before the epidemic was big enough news that people were talking about it in New York. And she pretended everything was fine. Never mentioned people getting sick, or the quarantine, or any of it. . . . The last time I talked to my mom, I had no idea it might be the last time. We had a fight about whether she'd cook turkey or just a chicken for Thanksgiving. So that's my last memory of her."

I waited for the right words to come. When they didn't, I leaned forward and squeezed his hand the way he had mine.

"Tessa didn't know how bad it was going to get. No one did."

"Yeah," he said. "But you'd have told me. If everything had been normal with us, you'd have told me right away."

It felt like betraying Tessa somehow to admit it, but I wasn't going to lie. "I would have," I said. "I'm sorry."

He smiled at me for a second, less forced than before. "It's the past now," he said, reaching for the map book. "We've got the future to worry about. Let's get your route figured out already."

When I went upstairs a half hour later, Tessa was in the master bedroom.

"Hey," I said. "How're you doing?"

She turned, brushing her overgrown bangs away from her eyes. "I'm fine," she said. "I should probably finish up with those seeds."

"You know," I said, "I'll look for your parents on the mainland. Ask around. Maybe I'll be able to find them."

I didn't realize how much I wanted her to smile and say she was sure they'd make it back someday, until her face fell. "You don't need to, Kaelyn," she said. "I know they're dead."

"You don't," I protested. "They were smart—they knew about the virus early on—they'd have protected themselves. You can't assume they didn't make it. My brother Drew is still out there somewhere, and yeah, I know the chances aren't great, but I haven't given up on him."

"That's different," Tessa said, so calmly I felt suddenly cold. "Your brother could be anywhere. My parents were right there on the other side of the strait the last time I talked to them. They wouldn't have left, they'd have been there on the ferry if they were still alive. Which means they're not."

"Tessa..." I started.

"It's all right," she said. "I've known since Leo got back. I knew it might be true for weeks before that. Nothing's changed, not really. So it's better not to dwell on it."

That was Tessa. Practical, unemotional. Maybe she'd talked through the grief with Leo, gotten out all the pain she must have felt when neither of her parents stepped off the ferry that day.

Or maybe she was just pushing it down so deep she could almost forget it was there.

"If there's anything you want—or need—me to look into while I'm gone..." I said.

"I know." She touched my elbow as she walked past me into the hall; that was as close as Tessa got to hugging. "Thank you."

I drove out to the research center in the SUV, getting used to how it handled, the wipers swishing back and forth over the windshield with the gusts of snow.

Inside, I went straight to the second floor and rummaged

through the offices for books I thought might be useful. Unless we kept the samples in viable condition, there was no point in leaving at all.

One of the manuals had a chapter on vaccine transportation. After I read through it, I searched through the lab room until I found an industrial-grade cold-storage box in the cupboard beside the fridge. I grabbed a smaller plastic box too, to prevent the vials from touching the cold packs and freezing. Beside the cold box, I stacked the three notebooks of Dad's that were dated from after the virus appeared, and added a box of petri dishes, a container of syringes, and a pack of microscope slides I found in one of the cabinets. Who knew what supplies they'd still have on the mainland?

I set it all in front of the fridge, where I'd be able to grab it quickly as soon as the weather cleared up enough that we could safely take the ferry across the strait. Leo thought he'd be able to get it going, after watching Mark start it up before. Until then, the vaccine would be safer here than anywhere else in town, with the specially calibrated fridge and modern generator behind the unbreakable windows and the door that had already stood up to the gang's prying.

In the middle of the counter, where they would be easy to find, I placed the papers onto which I'd copied all of Dad's notes about creating the vaccine. I'd give the keys to Tessa when I left. If we failed, I didn't want Dad's work to be completely lost.

There were so many things he hadn't told me. He should have been prepared for the worst, for the possibility that he might not always be here.

He probably wouldn't have thought I could handle this. He would have said to wait, like Nell had. And he might have been right. The roads could be so bad Gav and I would get stuck. We could run out of gas in the middle of nowhere. We could get held up, like Leo said, because all people would see was a couple of teenagers with resources worth stealing.

But bigger than those doubts was the feeling that had been swelling inside me since I'd watched Nell turn away. That if I didn't do something now and we lost the vaccine, I'd spend the rest of my life regretting it.

# FOUR

The last things I packed in the SUV were two bags of sidewalk salt, which I thought to check the garage for after Meredith complained about the slippery front step.

The bags weighed forty pounds apiece. Despite the chill in the air, I was sweating under my coat by the time I'd carried them to the clear area by the door. But I'd also found a jug of winter windshield-wiper fluid, so I figured the effort had been worth it. I'd paused to stretch my arms when Leo stepped through the doorway.

"Hey," he said. "Meredith said you were out here. Looking for salt?"

"Yep," I said, nudging one of the bags with my foot.

"Ah!" he said. "That kind of salt."

The silence that followed felt awkward. I looked at him, and he looked back at me, his expression so serious my heart skipped a beat. Before I could ask why, he dropped his gaze.

"You want help bringing those to the SUV? They're for the trip, I guess?"

"Thanks," I said. "Grab one and we're good."

I hefted the first bag onto my shoulder and trudged along the snowy driveway. Flakes whirled around us.

"You're ready to go?" Leo asked as we shoved the bags into the back of the SUV.

"Completely," I said. He followed me as I headed back for the wiper fluid. "All we need now is a break in the weather."

We ducked into the garage.

"Kaelyn," Leo said. When I turned, he opened his mouth and closed it a couple of times, as if he'd forgotten what he'd wanted to say. Then he smiled crookedly. "You wouldn't believe how much I missed you when you left for Toronto, all those years back."

"Please," I said. "I bet it wasn't half as much as I missed you. You still had a gazillion other friends here, at least."

"Yeah," he said. "But it wasn't the same. You were the only one I knew really wanted me around."

"What are you talking about? Everyone liked you."

"Sure, they *liked* me," he said, and hesitated. "But they never stopped seeing this." He pointed to his face, and I knew he meant the shape of his eyes, the olive tone of his skin. "They never forgot I was adopted, different, not a real islander. I knew they couldn't help it, so I acted like I didn't notice. But with you I didn't have to act. You didn't judge me by where I was born."

He'd always seemed so happy. I'd never known he'd felt that way about the rest of the kids the whole time we were growing up. But he was probably right. I'd felt the same sort of judgment aimed at me. It'd been easy for me not to care that Leo was different, because I had parents who were of contrasting colors and a mainlander dad on top of that. I was different too.

"Leo," I said, but he kept going.

"I was so relieved when I got off the ferry, and you were there and you were *you*. When you moved to Toronto, you seemed to be getting so . . . critical, and closed off, and I started thinking you'd changed, or that I hadn't really known you as well as

I thought. Especially when you came back and it was like you were avoiding me. I can't believe I left for New York without trying to talk to you. And then the virus started wreaking havoc on everything. . . ." He swallowed. "But you're still the same person I remember. Even more that person. The way you've thrown yourself into helping the town—you're amazing, Kae. You know that, right?"

My cheeks warmed. "Lots of people are helping," I said. "It's Gav who really got everyone organized."

"You're the one who's decided to go to the mainland with the vaccine," he said. "You saw someone had to, and you're doing it, despite all the risks."

"I'm going to be fine."

"You can't be sure of that." He stepped closer. "Look, I know nothing's going to change; I know you have Gav and I have Tessa and that's—that's all right. But you're leaving, and I might not ever see you again, for real this time. I need you to know what that means to me, and how sorry I am that I didn't try harder to make things right with us before, and how much I really, really want you to get back safe."

Then he raised his hands to the sides of my face and kissed me.

It was a gentle kiss, but so steady and sure my lips started to part against his instinctively. I caught myself, stiffening. My brain stalled. Leo wasn't supposed to be kissing me. What was he doing? What was *I* doing?

I raised my arms to push him away, and suddenly the kiss was over. Leo shifted back, his hands falling to his sides. A tremor passed through his shoulders.

"I'm sorry," he said. "It won't happen again. Please be careful out there, Kae."

And then he turned and walked out into the snow.

The next morning, the wind had died down. We got a sprinkling of snow, but by the time we'd eaten lunch, that had cleared up too.

"We should wait until tomorrow and leave first thing if it's clear," Gav said. "We want to get as far as we can on the first day."

I could have left right then, but he made a good point. And it gave me a little extra time with Meredith before I said good-bye. We all ended up tramping out to the backyard with the ferrets.

The back of the house faced the strait, and the yard led down to the shoreline. Fossey scurried to the edge of the water, Meredith scrambling after her. I loosened my grip on Mowat's leash as he trundled over to join them. Behind me, Leo and Tessa stood together, Tessa's arm hooked through his. I was trying not to pay attention to them, but every time Leo moved, I felt it like a prickle over my skin, as if I had a new extra sense tuned specifically to him.

Since that moment in the garage, he'd pretended nothing had happened, so I'd pretended the same. Even though part of me was furious that he could lean into Tessa and peck her cheek so casually, like he hadn't been kissing someone else yesterday, like he hadn't betrayed her. Even though every time Gav smiled at me, guilt welled up inside me, as if I were the one who'd done something wrong. But my head was full of gnawing little questions I couldn't shake. How long had he wanted to do that? Had he been agonizing over me the whole time I'd had what I thought was a hopeless crush on him?

What would it have been like if I'd let myself kiss him back?

I closed my eyes, shoving those thoughts away. Leo had been through a lot. Maybe he wasn't thinking straight. I shouldn't be angry—I should just get over it, the way a girl who'd been kissed by her best friend, who promised it wouldn't happen again and for whom she had no romantic feelings whatsoever, should.

"It's funny how they don't get cold," Meredith said as the ferrets tumbled in the snow. She grinned at me, and a different sort of ache filled my chest. The thought of telling her I was leaving was almost as painful as remembering the night I'd had to carry her into the hospital. I couldn't even promise her I'd be back soon.

"There's someone on the water," Tessa said. She pointed to the opposite shore.

A small boat was pulling away from the mainland harbor. It veered a little north, then a little south, as if the driver wasn't used to handling it, but it was definitely headed toward the island.

*Tessa's parents*, I thought. *Drew. Someone from the government, finally.* "Hey!" I shouted, even though there was no way anyone could have heard me at that distance, and waved my arm. Meredith spun around. As soon as she spotted the boat, she started jumping up and down, waving eagerly.

"Come over here!"

"They'll go to the harbor where they can dock the boat, Mere," I said. As the boat drew closer, I saw it was a speedboat with no cabin, just a wide glass windshield with a lone figure behind it. My initial excitement dampened. It could be anyone. It could be a mainlander hoping the island would make for easy pickings.

"Maybe that isn't someone we want on the island," Leo said, echoing my thoughts.

"We could meet them at the harbor, be ready in case they try something," Gav said, and then paused. "Except I think they are coming this way."

The boat was bobbing on the waves, but it had definitely turned away from the harbor, toward us. I eased closer to Meredith, resting my hand on her shoulder. After a few minutes I could make out the man driving well enough to tell I didn't recognize him. He took his hands off the wheel to wave both his arms at us, the way Meredith had, but he looked more frantic than happy.

As the boat approached the shore, Gav stepped to the water's edge. "Everything all right?" he called.

The man drew the boat as close to us as the shallower water allowed. His face looked pale and thin, engulfed by the padded hood of his coat. "You have to get out of there!" he hollered, cutting the engine. "Tell everyone! You have to get off the island!"

"What?" I said. "Why?"

He might not have even heard me. "They'll be here any minute," he said. "They want to destroy the whole town."

The breeze brought a faint sound to my ears: the warbling rumble of a helicopter in flight. We hadn't seen a food-drop or a news chopper in ages. I made out a small dark shape in the northern sky, and when I glanced back at the man in the boat, my pulse stuttered. He was looking at the shape, too, and his expression was like that of a mouse in the shadow of a hawk. Pure, undeniable terror.

Whatever he was talking about, *he* obviously believed the danger was real.

"Who's coming?" I said. "What are they going to do?" But my words were lost as the boat's engine roared.

"I'll meet you at the harbor, for anyone who doesn't have a boat," the man yelled, reaching for the wheel. "Hurry!"

"Hold on!" Gav shouted. The boat turned toward the docks and sped away.

"Do you think we should listen to him?" Tessa asked.

"He could be in the hallucinating stage of the virus," I said, but I'd never seen someone that sick who'd still be capable of handling a boat. My heart started to thump. "But maybe we should do what he said, just in case."

"I can swing by the hospital and tell them something's up," Gav said.

"I'll go with you," I said. "Tessa, Leo, can you get Meredith to the harbor? We'll meet you there."

Tessa nodded, grabbing Meredith's hand. I scooped up the ferrets, let them leap through the back door, and closed it behind them before hurrying after Gav. He had hopped into the SUV. The growl of the helicopter's engine was getting louder.

"What do you think's going on?" I said as I scrambled into the passenger seat.

Gav hit the gas. "I don't know. Let's hope he's just a lunatic."

I hugged myself as we followed Tessa's tire tracks through the thick layer of snow on the road. Her car vanished around a turn up ahead. We were just rounding a corner, halfway to the hospital, when the shadow of the helicopter slid by overhead.

A second later, the block of houses next to us exploded.

I shrieked, clutching at the door as the ground rocked beneath the tires, the blast ringing in my ears. Beside us, roofs were crumpling, flames spurting through shattered windows. A sharp chemical smell filled the air. Gav drove on, faster, his jaw clenched, his arms trembling.

"Not a lunatic," I said shakily. "What the hell are they doing?"

Another explosion thundered somewhere to our right. I cringed. Gav leaned forward to peer through the windshield.

"I think it's a military helicopter," he said. "They're bombing us. After all the other ways the army's screwed us over, they're fucking bombing us!"

Tears I hadn't felt forming were leaking down my cheeks. I wiped my eyes and tried to breathe steadily. Then a single panicked thought jolted through my mind like an electric shock.

"The vaccine," I said. "Gav, what if they hit the research center?"

"Maybe they won't," Gav said. "We should go to the harbor— get out of here, like that guy said. I'm pretty sure no one in town needs to be warned that something bad's happening now. We'll come back when the chopper's gone."

"No!" I said. "We can't leave behind those samples. If we lose them..."

If we lost them, we were maybe losing our only chance to beat the virus, to get back the world we used to have.

"Kae—" Gav started.

"Please," I said. "We have to get them. If you won't drive there, I'll jump out of the car and run for it."

I was serious. He must have been able to tell. He swore under his breath, but at the next intersection he turned toward the research center instead of the harbor. We'd already missed the hospital. As the SUV careened down the lane, the ground shuddered with a third explosion. I clutched the keys in my coat pocket.

The research center was still standing when we reached it. The car skidded to a stop, and I leapt out. Gav left the engine running as I scrambled over a snowdrift to the door.

I fumbled with the keys and shoved the door open. My boots slid on the smooth floor inside. The cold-storage box and the supplies I'd set aside were all where I'd left them. I stuffed the sample vials and the packs from the freezer into the cold box, and dropped everything else in on top to make sure I didn't lose anything.

Smoke was billowing up over the trees as I dashed back outside, so thick the whole town could have been burning. *Not the hospital,* I pleaded silently. I hauled myself into the car.

The whole way to the harbor, I clutched the cold box on my lap, my eyes squeezed shut. The acrid smell of burning filled my nose. The helicopter rumbled by overhead, and I winced, bracing myself. I couldn't tell which of the tremors I felt were bombs and which were buildings collapsing or something else I couldn't even imagine. Gav's breath started to rasp as he yanked the steering wheel one way and then the other.

Tessa's car was parked by the harbor. We pulled up beside it and I tumbled out, dragging the cold box with me. The speedboat was bobbing by the far end of one of the docks, Meredith and the others sitting in it. Gav and I ran together, his hand on my back. Tessa took the box from me and helped us in.

"He wanted to leave without you," Meredith said, a sob in her voice, looking accusingly at the driver. "We said we'd throw him off the boat if he tried."

The driver—our savior—was too busy staring at the sky to look guilty. "We're going now," he said, grasping the wheel. "Before they notice us."

"But other people from town might come here to get away," I said. "The rest of the boats are wrecked. We have to wait and see—"

"No," the man said. "We're lucky we're not already dead."

He tugged the wheel, and the boat swerved away from the dock. As it sped toward the mainland, I turned. The town I'd spent most of my life in was hazed with smoke and flames, growing smaller as the strait stretched between us and the island.

# FIVE

When we reached the mainland harbor, we all scrambled onto the end of the longest dock, watching the strait in case someone else came. There was still the ferry, and those boats on private docks that hadn't been destroyed in the soldiers' rampage two months ago. But none of us could quite believe what we saw. So we stared, minds blank with shock.

That was our island burning. Our island flaring bright as the helicopter dropped another bomb. A faint glow flickered amid the distant shapes of the buildings. Billows of smoke were replacing the clouds. Meredith shuddered against me, and I wrapped my arm around her.

After what felt like ages, the helicopter turned and whirred north again. It dwindled into a dark speck and vanished. The waves smacked against the dock's supports. Drops of icy water splattered my already numb face. And still, I couldn't make out anyone in the island harbor or along the shore.

Maybe, despite the chaos, the most important places had gone untouched. Maybe Nell and the others were just fine and all we'd lost was a bunch of already abandoned buildings.

Or maybe we were the only ones who'd survived the attack.

It still didn't make any sense to me. Turning, I realized the man who'd driven us here had left. Anger sparked through the haze in my head. I picked up the cold box from where I'd set it by my feet and marched down the dock.

"Hey!" I shouted as I stepped onto the concrete loading area beyond the docks. "Hey, guy with the boat!"

The door to the harbor office opened, and our rescuer stepped out. He'd drawn back his hood, revealing a narrow face topped with a pale sheen of recently shaved hair. His lips were badly chapped, and his blue eyes twitched nervously. He couldn't have been much older than twenty. I wondered if he had any more authority here than we did.

"What's going on?" I demanded. "You knew that helicopter was coming—what it was going to do."

"I tried to get here sooner," he said. "I really did. The snow—the roads were just choked. And then I had to find the keys to one of these goddamned boats."

The others had come up behind me. "Who *are* you?" Leo asked.

"Rawls," the guy said, and grimaced. "Tobias Rawls."

"So you drove here," I said. "From where? How did you know the helicopter was coming?"

Gav took a few steps past Tobias toward the office. He stiffened. "Is that what you drove here in?"

Tobias jerked around, but Gav was already striding forward, to a vehicle parked just beyond the building. It looked like a cross between an SUV and a delivery truck, boxy and sharp-cornered. And it was covered in splotches of camouflage paint. My heart sank.

"You're a soldier," Gav said, spinning around to face Tobias. "You're one of them."

Tobias gave a laugh, short and bitter. "If you had any idea, you wouldn't say that."

"Then why don't you tell us what the hell happened?" I snapped.

Silence reigned until Tessa said, in a soft voice, "We just saw our home destroyed. You're not even going to tell us why?"

"You don't know what it's been like," Tobias said, looking away. He bit his lip. "We have a base a couple hours north of here."

"I didn't think there were any military bases in the province," Gav said. "Not anymore."

"It's not official," Tobias said. "It's supposedly been inactive for decades, but the government reinstalled a contingent there shortly after nine-eleven. At least that's what the commanders told us. There were eighteen of us, but a few got sick, the major got sick, and a bunch ran. Me and a couple other guys figured we were safer hiding out there until the virus situation was under control. Lots of rations, lots of fuel for the generator; we were pretty much set."

"Good for you," Gav said. Tobias winced, but he kept talking.

"We thought it was just going to be for a few weeks. But the news kept getting worse. The other guys got restless. We didn't want to go outside the compound because we were scared of getting sick, but they couldn't take staying inside all the time. They started going out and doing target practice through the fence: birds, deer, trees. Then, two days ago, this guy shows up—I don't know how he made it there—hollering about how we had to help him, how he just took off from the god-awful island where the whole thing started, and the virus got him, and someone there would have shot him if he'd stayed."

Tobias paused, looking at us, his expression vaguely accusing.

"We weren't shooting anyone," I said. "He must have

been—there was a group that started killing anyone they found who was infected. He must have been with them."

So stupid. If he'd just walked into the hospital, someone there would have done whatever they could for him. He must have thought we'd know he'd been part of the gang, that we'd turn him away.

"Well, running didn't do him any good," Tobias said. "He ended up shot anyway. He was coughing and sneezing as well as hollering, so there wasn't any way we were letting him in. Moore did him in with his rifle like it was a little more target practice. And then he and Donetelli got talking about your island, about the place where the virus got started being so close, and after a bit they'd worked themselves up into a real rage. Saying if people had stayed on the island, the rest of us would have been fine, and it'd be fair punishment for them to take the chopper over and unload a few missiles. Bigger target practice."

"There were kids," Gav said. "There were old people who couldn't have gotten out of their homes if they'd wanted to. We were just trying to hang on, like everyone else."

"I know," Tobias said, sounding miserable. "I wasn't up in the chopper, was I? After I heard them talking, I got one of the trucks and came down as fast as I could. I didn't think they'd do it right away. I was hoping maybe they'd simmer down and forget the whole thing. But they must have noticed I'd gone and decided they would beat me here. Which they did."

"You knew what they were planning and you left," Leo said. "You didn't even try to talk them out of it." There was no question in his voice.

"They wouldn't have listened to me," Tobias said. "They never did. They—I swear, you don't know what it was like."

"We know they blew up most of our town," I said. "You couldn't have said *something*?"

Tobias's shoulders hunched. "Look," he said. "I screwed myself over coming here. You think they're going to let me back on the base now? I did what I could."

Meredith squirmed beside me. "Kae," she said, "what are we going to do now? Are we going back to the island? What if the helicopter comes again?"

"Of course we're going back," Gav said before I could answer. "Whoever survived that, they'll need our help."

I glanced toward the strait, then down at the cold-storage box. Every muscle in me balked at the idea of bringing the vaccine back to the island. We'd had no idea any of this would happen. What else was coming that we couldn't see? Going back suddenly felt like a far bigger risk than leaving.

"You can," I said. "But I'm not. We could have lost the vaccine. I have to get it to someone who can use it, while I still have the chance."

"You want to just abandon them?" Gav said, gesturing toward the island.

My throat tightened. "Of course I want them to be okay," I said. "But I'm not a superhero, Gav. What can I do that they can't figure out on their own? Anyone who's okay knows where the food is, how to find shelter, and anyone who isn't, I couldn't help anyway."

"It's true," Tessa murmured. "We're not doctors."

"But I can do this," I went on, nudging the cold box. "I *have* to do this."

"We can't go anywhere without supplies—without a car," Gav protested.

"I know," I said. The SUV could have been blown up. Even if it hadn't, I didn't think I could set foot on the island, even for a few minutes. Once I saw the wreckage, I might not be able to leave again. "Maybe I can use the boat. The St. Lawrence would pretty much get me there."

"You'd freeze. What if there's a storm? Kae…" He stopped and studied my face. "You're not going to listen to anything I say, are you?"

I shook my head. "Not unless it has to do with getting these samples to Ottawa."

He exhaled in a rush, and his gaze settled on Tobias's truck. He turned abruptly.

"Give me your keys."

"What?" Tobias said.

"The keys to the truck. I want to take a look."

He held out his hand. Tobias blinked, and hesitantly handed over a single key on a ring. The rest of us watched as Gav strode over and opened up the back of the truck. He clambered inside, the metal floor ringing under his boots. The sound seemed to break Tobias's stupor.

"Hey!" he said, hurrying over. "That stuff's mine."

Gav poked his head out.

"You're pretty well equipped," he said. "Tent, sleeping bags, an awful lot of food."

49

"Like I said, there's no way I can go back to the base now. I've got to get by somehow."

"And that's another reason you weren't here earlier," Gav said. "Because you were stocking up your truck before you left."

Tobias's face reddened.

Gav jumped down and closed the back door.

"Tell you what," he said, his voice strained. "You make it up to us. You take me and Kaelyn to Ottawa, then drive us back when we're done there, and we call it even."

"You really have a vaccine?" Tobias said to me. "We could get rid of this virus for good?"

"I think so," I said. My spirits lifted. "If you'd help..."

He lowered his gaze from the five pairs of eyes trained on him. "Okay," he said after a few moments. "Yeah. It's not like I've got other plans."

"Am I coming too?" Meredith asked, squeezing my arm. My stomach twisted. I didn't want to bring her places where we couldn't be sure of being safe. But the island wasn't safe, either, not anymore. The guys in the helicopter could come back for another round. We'd been lucky to escape the first time.

"We should all come," Tessa said firmly. "It's dangerous for any of us to stay on the island, that's obvious. And I'm sure we can scavenge more food around here so there's enough for all of us. The most useful thing we can do is bring the vaccine to the right person. The more of us there are, the faster we'll be able to find someone who can help once we get to the city, right?"

After a couple seconds, Leo nodded. "I want to help!" Meredith said. Tobias shrugged as if it was all the same to him. I paused, unprepared for the sudden show of support, and Tessa gave me a small smile.

Gratitude washed over me. Yes. If we were all together, we could protect each other. Safety in numbers. I would never have asked them to risk it before, but now, with the situation on the island becoming even more precarious, it felt right.

We could get through this together, like we had so much else.

# SIX

Gav was the only one frowning.

"What about everyone else on the island?" he said. "We can't all leave without telling someone what happened so they can be prepared in case those psychos with the helicopter come by again."

"I'll go," Leo offered. He shrugged, his chin tucked inside the broad collar of his coat. "I've got the most experience navigating a boat, and the waves are getting a little nasty. I'll go to the hospital and fill them in, and then check on your car. If it's okay, I can bring it over on the ferry—if not, I'll at least bring any supplies that survived."

Gav's jaw tensed as if he was going to argue, but then he closed his eyes and inclined his head. "If the house is okay, it wouldn't hurt to grab some of the food there too. But I don't want to take more away from what's meant for the whole island."

His gaze slid to me. He didn't want to leave me, I realized, not even for a couple hours. That was why he was still coming with me, even though it was clearly killing him not to go back.

The words hurt coming out, but I had to say them. "Gav, I'll be okay. If you want to stay on the island and help, you should. We don't all have to go."

"No," he said. "I already decided, back when we first talked about it. We can leave tomorrow morning, just like we planned."

As Leo headed down to the dock, I pulled Gav to the side. "Are you really okay with this?" I said, my voice low. "You can tell me the truth, you know."

He ran a hand through his hair. "Of course it bothers me, leaving the island when it's practically destroyed. But leaving you would be even worse. From the first day I asked for your help, when you refueled the cars for the food run, you've been totally behind every idea I've had. Now it's my turn. I want to do this for you. You need me, I'm here—I want you to know that."

"Gav..." I said. I couldn't find the words to express what I was feeling. The passion and determination I'd watched Gav put into keeping the island going—to have all of it offered just to me seemed incredible, impossible. Gripping the front of his coat, I tugged him to me and tipped my face up to meet his lips, trying to put every particle of my gratitude into that kiss. He wrapped his arms around me, holding me tight.

"I know," I said softly when I eased back, and he smiled and kissed me again.

"If there's six of us, we're going to need more supplies," he said. "Let's see what we can find here."

So as the sky started to darken with the coming evening, the group of us raided the harbor office. The concession stand near the ticket booth now held only a few crumpled wrappers, but Tobias broke open the locked storage room in the back with a tool from his truck. Soon we'd added skids of bottled water and boxes of recently expired chocolate bars and honey-roasted peanuts to his stores of food. Tobias started shifting the truck's contents around to make more floor space. "We'll be better off sleeping in here," he said. "Smaller space to trap the heat." While he worked, Gav,

Tessa, Meredith, and I headed down the mainland town's major street, checking the storefronts.

Drew might have come through here, I thought, all those weeks ago after he took off. If he'd made it across the strait alive. Back then, some of these stores might still have been occupied. Now, everyone was long gone. Most of the doors hung open, swinging in the wind.

Gav pointed out a knitted-goods shop, and Tessa picked out extra sweaters and thick woolen hats for each of us. I started grabbing blankets while Gav dug a few plastic bags out from behind the register to hold our loot.

In the convenience store farther down the street, the last newspaper on the rack was dated November 5. I guessed that was when the owner had fled. Or gotten sick. The front-page headline read, *Friendly flu overwhelms hospitals*, the article below describing how medical centers across the country were running out of room. The grainy photo of patients crowding the hallway of a hospital in Halifax gave me a jolt back through time. A couple months ago, our hospital had looked like that.

All those people staring anxiously at the camera—they were dead now.

I made myself turn away. The shelves that would have held food were bare. I picked up a handful of lighters from the box on the counter, and a few magazines for kindling. Meredith squealed and rushed over to present me with a can of baked beans that previous scavengers had missed.

Nothing made a sound as we continued down the street except a small flock of twittering sparrows clinging to the useless telephone wires overhead. I didn't see a single human footprint other than our own. No smoke rose from the chimneys of the houses ahead of us. The place felt as if no one had lived there in years.

It made sense. Why would anyone have wanted to stay just a couple miles away from our quarantined island and its deadly disease? Maybe some of the townspeople had died, but most of them had probably just gone somewhere else.

Until the virus had caught up with them and they'd died after all.

"Do you think we should check some of the houses too?" Tessa asked as we came to a stop at the end of the road, where it branched off into two residential streets. "We might find some food."

"There's only so much room in the truck," I said. And Leo was bringing back more. But maybe we shouldn't pass up the chance when we were already here.

As I wavered, a sound drifted down the street toward us, faint but distinctive. My body went rigid.

In one of those houses, someone was coughing.

Tessa and Gav pulled their scarves tighter around their faces. But the scarves were intended to keep out only the cold, not killer microbes. My heart thumped. "Let's go back to the harbor," I said.

Gav paused, and then nodded. "As long as Leo brings food back from the island, I think we're okay."

I flinched when the sparrows leapt from the telephone wires and darted off, but we didn't see a soul. Still, when we reached the truck, I set my bags down and went straight to the cold box, which I'd left inside the harbor office.

It looked exactly the same as before. I crouched down beside it and rested my head in my mittened hands.

Meredith and I should be okay, with our post-illness immunity.

But what about Gav and Tessa and Leo? Maybe we could make it all the way to Ottawa without running into anyone who was sick, if we stuck to the small towns when we needed more gas, but in the city—in the city, there could be more people still alive than had ever lived on the island in the first place. We couldn't assume none of them would be infected or that we'd easily be able to avoid anyone who was.

Of course, the only other option was staying here and maybe getting blown up.

I lowered my hands onto the cold box. Maybe there was another option. We had five samples of the vaccine. Surely a scientist wouldn't need all of them to make more? It wouldn't be so selfish to give a few to my friends, would it, when they were the ones helping me get the vaccine where it needed to go?

An engine growled down by the water, and footsteps rushed past the door. Leo was back.

Outside, everyone else was already on the docks except Tobias, who hung back by the truck looking uncertain. Evening was falling fast, the light draining out of the smoke-tinged sky. A few solar lamps had blinked on throughout the harbor.

Leo had brought the speedboat back, so I guessed our SUV hadn't survived. But along with bags of food, he was handing out the jugs of gasoline Gav and I had filled.

"How bad was it?" Gav asked as we hauled Leo's plunder to the truck.

"The hospital's still standing," Leo said, and I let out the breath I'd been holding. "Your house too. But a lot of other buildings aren't. There must have been a blast near the harbor. Your SUV was tipped over, like it'd been thrown a little, and the windshield was shattered. It's lucky everything inside survived."

"Did you talk to Nell?" I said.

He nodded. "All the shaking made the generator conk out. She was trying to figure out whether they could fix it or if they'd have to start moving patients."

"What about Mowat and Fossey?" Meredith said. "Are we just leaving them?"

"They came racing to see me when I came in," Leo said. "Seemed pretty happy having the run of the place. I put the bags of food on the floor so they can eat as much as they need to."

"Thanks," I said, with a second wave of relief, and he shot me a half smile. The memory of our kiss flashed through my mind. My face flushed, and I dragged my eyes away.

"Nell didn't seem too upset when I told her what we were going to do," Leo went on, showing no sign that he'd noticed my reaction. "She said . . ." He hesitated and glanced at Meredith, who was scratching at the pavement with the toe of her boot.

"Meredith," Tessa said, "could you check the boat and make sure we got all the supplies?"

She frowned, and then seemed to shake herself. "Of course!" she said, and jogged toward the docks. Leo lowered his voice.

"She said it's probably good for us to get out of there for a while—the town's in such bad shape she might end up having everyone move across the strait anyway. And she said she really hopes we find the people we need."

All the heat washed out of me. No one had been interested in leaving the island when we'd realized the strait was now unguarded, because it hardly seemed worth giving up a place that was familiar for some unknown across the water. Nell must be desperate to be considering evacuating.

"Nothing left in the boat!" Meredith called as she came running back.

"Thank you for checking," I said, giving her a squeeze. "I guess we should eat, and then call it a night. We'll want to head out first thing."

"I've got a kerosene camping stove in the truck," Tobias said. "A hot dinner sounds pretty appealing right now."

"I saw spaghetti in the bags," Meredith said. "Can we have that?"

"Sure," I said. "Go on and get out a few cans."

"We heard someone coughing when we went further into town," Gav said to Leo as Meredith scrambled into the back of the truck after Tobias. "There are people still here. We'll have to keep an eye out."

A weariness passed over Leo's face. For all that I was trying not to focus on him, I felt a pang of concern. He'd only just come home a few weeks ago, and now we were dragging him away again. If he didn't think he could take it, he'd say so, wouldn't he?

"We'll want to alternate watches while we're sleeping, then," he said. "We can't be too careful."

He was right. And maybe I could take away one of the fears that must be haunting him, that was going to haunt me as long as he and Gav and Tessa were unprotected.

"I think the three of you should take the vaccine," I said.

Gav, who'd been about to speak, stopped with his mouth half open. Tessa blinked at me.

"There are five samples," I continued. "So we'd still have two. We're obviously going to run into people who are infected—we almost did today. I don't want one of you to catch it."

"We will run into people," Leo said cautiously. "I'd be surprised if we don't. But are you sure you don't want to hold on to them, Kae?"

"We don't even know if the vaccine works," Gav added.

"If it does, then it'll be a good thing you took it," I said. "And if it doesn't, then it won't matter that you did. Either way, it can't hurt. We don't have any other way of protecting ourselves while we're on the road. And I can't see why anyone would need more than one sample to understand what Dad did, when we have all his notebooks too."

"They make vaccines using parts of the virus, don't they?" Tessa said. "Is there any chance we could get sick from *it*?"

I hesitated. "I guess. My dad tried it on himself and he was fine for almost three weeks. He wouldn't have used it if he wasn't sure he'd gotten it right."

"If anyone *was* going to get it right, I'd say it's your dad," Leo agreed.

"Okay," Tessa said. "I'd rather take a chance on the vaccine than see what happens if we're exposed without it."

Leo wavered a moment longer and then said, "All right. Let's do this."

"Then we'll have three samples left," Gav said. "Because I don't want it."

"Gav," I started, but he motioned for me to wait.

"Give us a moment?" he said to the others.

He took my hands as Tessa and Leo drifted away to help Tobias set up the stove. "Kae," he said. "I can see why you want to do this. It just doesn't feel right to me. If I get some false sense of security from a vaccine that turns out not to be effective, maybe I'll make a mistake I wouldn't have otherwise. I don't want to have that idea in my head, that I'm safe."

"So just take it and assume it does nothing," I said. "We have no idea how bad it'll be in the city, Gav."

"I know," he said, and swallowed. "But I still—you know, my mom was one of the first to catch it? When we started hearing the news, all she'd say was, 'Someone'll come up with a cure in a few days, it'll all be fine, it always is.' She was so convinced that the doctors and the scientists could solve all our problems that she didn't take precautions, she didn't worry. And now she's lying somewhere in the quarry with all the other thousands of people the virus has killed."

"You'd never be like that," I protested.

"No," he said. "But taking the vaccine is going to change how I think. No one has that much control over their mind. You know that."

I did. I also knew how much it would hurt him if I said I wasn't letting him on the truck unless he took the vaccine, that I'd rather he stayed on the island. It wasn't fair of me, was it, to force something on him that he felt so strongly about, so that *I* didn't have to worry as much? It was his decision. He was already doing so much for me.

"You have to be *incredibly* careful," I said. "No playing the hero."

"No hero business," he agreed. "We're both coming back here safe, Kae. I promise."

The resolve in his eyes made everything else around me fade away. The cold. The long road ahead. The other boy who might be watching us right now. I slid my hand around his neck and kissed him. Gav kissed me back, his gloved fingers cupping my cheek. And for the space of that moment, at least, I believed what he'd said too.

# SEVEN

Our first day on the road, we passed homes and warehouses and off-ramps leading into towns, but we only stopped twice, by stretches of vacant land, to pour all our extra gasoline into the tank and to switch drivers. Now and then I caught a glimpse of what looked like chimney smoke in the distance, but that was the only sign of anyone still living. The truck's tires hissed endlessly over the snow-covered freeway.

For the first time, the gravity of what Leo had told us about the mainland completely sank in. The rest of the country hadn't been callously ignoring our island's plight. They'd been so overwhelmed they couldn't even save themselves.

In the middle of the second morning, Tobias wiggled a finger toward the dashboard and said, "We should stop at the next town with a clear enough exit ramp. Gas is getting low."

He'd been sounding more confident since taking the wheel the day before. Guilt pinched me. I'd snuck Tessa and Leo into the harbor office before giving them their doses of the vaccine, to avoid any argument. I wasn't going to offer something so precious to someone I hardly knew, who was only helping us out of obligation. Who might run like he did from the army base if things got tough. But it was harder to think that way with Tobias sitting next to me, drumming on the wheel with his fingers in time to a tune he was humming.

I shifted Meredith on my lap and peered at the map book. We'd passed the signs announcing that we were entering New Brunswick just a few hours before we'd stopped last night. It looked like we could make it to Ottawa in three days, as long as the snow didn't get much deeper.

As long as we could find gas.

"That exit looks good," Gav said from the backseat. He pointed to a lane where the wind had left the snow shallow, and Tobias nodded.

"Do you think there's any chance some places still have electricity, Leo?" I asked.

His coat rasped against Tessa's as he shifted behind me. "There were a few power stations still running, the last I heard," he said. "But most of them had broken down. And that was more than a month ago."

"If we can find a station that has power, Kaelyn and I should be able to get the pumps running," Gav said, squeezing my shoulder. "We've had some practice."

My stomach twinged as we passed a frost-encrusted McDonald's sign at the edge of the town. I didn't even like burgers that much, but I'd have all but killed for one now. A little taste of our old, normal world.

"Here we go," Tobias said, turning the wheel.

He pulled up beside a row of pumps labeled as full service, though the shop across from them was dark. The hoses lay in a tangle beside the pumps. I eased Meredith off my lap and stepped out into the January chill, shaking the feeling back into my travel-numbed legs.

"What should I do?" Meredith asked, her eyes wide.

"Just wait here, okay?" I said. Gav hopped out, and we hurried to the station shop together.

The inside had been ransacked: shelves toppled, papers and boxes crushed underfoot. I picked up a newspaper to check the date. November 16. That was two weeks after we'd lost all contact with the mainland.

The paper felt strangely thin, and as I paged through it I realized it was missing most of the usual sections. No sports, no entertainment. I wondered if the government had canceled those events to prevent people from mingling in public places, or if the organizers had stopped out of their own fear. After a glance over the headlines—*US president pleads for calm in face of global pandemic. Utilities failure imminent*—I dropped it onto the counter. I knew those stories. I'd seen them for myself on the island; could see them now in the desolation of yet another town.

Gav flicked the light switch on and off, getting no response. We squeezed behind the counter and peered at the various controls. He sighed.

"Doesn't look good."

"I guess it would have been too easy if we could have filled up the usual way," I said. "We've got the siphon tube." Leo had brought it with the rest of our supplies from the SUV.

We scanned the area as we came out, but there were no vehicles in the station's lot or outside the big discount store on the other side of the street.

"No luck," Gav said to the others. "We'll have to go further into town and find cars to siphon from."

As Tobias reached to turn the key in the ignition, Leo grasped the back of his seat. "Wait," he said. He peered through the window toward the town. "If there are any people around, showing up in an army vehicle...it might startle them. Give them the wrong idea."

"You don't figure we're safer in this than walking around?" Tobias said.

"I wouldn't count on it," Leo said, his voice tight. "A lot of people are upset with the military right now. I've seen people jump a guy who wasn't even a soldier, just for wearing a camouflage jacket. Okay? If you've got weapons, let's carry them in case we need to defend ourselves, but I'd rather leave the truck."

"Sounds all right to me," Gav said. "Keep a low profile, get in, get out, maybe no one will even notice us."

He shot a dark look at Tobias, who lowered his gaze. At least, I noted, Tobias's parka was plain gray, with nothing clearly army about it. "Fine," he said. "But let's make it fast."

I grabbed the bucket and the now-empty jugs from the back of the truck, handing some off to Tessa and Meredith. When we came back around, Tobias was showing Leo a red gun that looked like it was made of plastic.

"A flare gun won't do major damage, but it'll at least scare a person," he was saying. "Makes a pretty loud noise, though, so don't use it unless you have to. Anyone who doesn't already know we're here, they will as soon as you fire it."

Tobias must have had a weapon on him too. Probably one that

fired actual bullets. I remembered the woman I'd seen gunned down by a gang member in the street—weeks ago but still vivid in my mind.

"We're not going to shoot anyone," I said. "Not unless it's that or get shot ourselves."

"I don't want to use it," Leo said, tucking the flare gun into his coat. His stance was tense.

Gav joined us, holding a branch he must have found, as thick as his arm and nearly as long. "Better to be prepared than not," he said, taking the last couple of jugs in his other hand.

Tobias circled the truck, making sure all the doors were secure.

"Our food's safe in there?" Tessa asked.

Tobias gave her a thin smile. "It's an army vehicle," he said, patting the side of the truck. "No one's getting in without a bazooka."

We tramped down the road, past the fast-food restaurants and a one-story motel, toward the more tightly clustered buildings in what looked to be the center of town. A layer of ice crusted the snow, and our boots crunched through it as we walked. The sound seemed horribly loud in the silence around us.

We passed a couple nicer restaurants, a liquor store, and a jewelry shop. All the windows were shadowy. Meredith had paused to look longingly at a few beads scattered in the jewelry-shop window when three dogs trotted onto the road in front of us.

We all froze. The largest dog, what looked like a German shepherd mix, woofed quietly and continued on. The others, a bull terrier and a brown-spotted mutt, followed without a backward glance. All three still wore collars. Their tags jingled long after they slipped out of sight.

"Must be an awful lot of ownerless dogs in the world now,"

Tobias murmured. "Maybe they'd be better off if the virus got them too."

"There could be more," Gav said. "You think a flare gun would work on wild dogs?"

"They're not really wild," I said. "And they didn't seem interested in us."

"We don't know what else is around, though. Or how hungry they might be."

"Well, we either keep walking or we go back for the truck and announce to the whole town we're here," Leo said mildly.

"I'm all for the truck," Tobias said.

"There were just three," Tessa said. "And we're already here."

"Exactly," I said, breaking from the group to stride on down the road. "Let's just get some gas and go."

A few blocks further up, there were some mounds of snow that looked vaguely car-shaped. I headed toward them, hearing the others catching up behind me. We were just a few storefronts away when I saw movement up ahead and my legs locked.

A couple of figures in heavy coats were sauntering out onto the street, just beyond the second car. We waited as they approached. From the corner of my eye, I saw Leo's hand slip into the pocket that held the flare gun. My pulse started skittering.

"Hey there," one of the figures said when they were about ten feet away. His pale eyes glowered at us. "What're you all doing?"

"We're not trying to make trouble," Gav said. He held the branch low at his side but clearly visible. "Just need some gas for our car."

"This is our town," the man said, but he didn't move any closer. I wondered if it was just the two of them—there was no way they could fight all six of us, if it came down to that. "We don't care for strangers coming in and taking what they want."

"But we need it!" Meredith said. I reached for her, but she shifted away from my grasp. "It's really important. We have to get to Ottawa, to give them the vaccine, so we can stop the virus."

The man raised his eyebrows. "Vaccine? There's never been no vaccine for the friendly flu."

I didn't see much point in lying about it now.

"We have a new prototype," I said. "My dad was a scientist—he made it. We're trying to get to the city to find someone who can make more. We just need a little help getting there."

The man studied us for a moment.

"Well," he said to his companion, "maybe we should just let them be for the moment, don't you think?"

Without another word to us, they turned and ambled back the way they'd come. A prickle crept up the back of my neck. I was glad they were leaving us alone, and he seemed to be saying we could take what we needed after all, but something about his manner felt threatening.

"They weren't so unreasonable," Tessa said after the two had disappeared from view. I tore my eyes away and hurried on to the nearest car.

The gas cap resisted my tugging fingers. Gav tried the door, grimaced, and raised the branch to smash in the driver's-side window. Leaning inside, he popped the cap. I unscrewed the seal and fed the tube down into the tank. Then I brought the other end to my mouth, bracing myself for the taste of gasoline I was going to get if I wasn't fast enough, and sucked in. Meredith hovered by the bucket.

All that came up was air. I wiggled the tube around, trying to push it deeper into the tank, and sucked again. Nothing.

"It's dry," I said.

"Let me see." Gav knelt down beside me, but he had no more success.

"Someone else probably had the same idea," Leo said.

The second car proved to be as empty as the first. We walked a little farther, trying a pickup truck that appeared to have stalled in the middle of the road and a van half a block down one of the side streets, but neither gave us so much as a drop.

"Someone's drained them all already," I said. The man who'd tried to warn us off? "Let's get back to the truck. We can drive to the other side of town. Maybe whoever got the gas here only bothered with the main road."

"No argument from me," Tobias said, and Gav nodded.

"Meredith," Leo said as we trudged toward the gas station, "from now on, you shouldn't talk about the vaccine with strangers. I know you were trying to help, but people are afraid of getting sick, and some of them might not care that we need the samples to make more. They'd just want to get some for themselves."

Meredith lowered her head. "Okay. I'm sorry."

"It's all right," I told her. "Just remember." Hopefully there wouldn't be a next time.

There was no sign of anyone nearby when we reached the station. If they had come and gone, their footprints were lost amid the ones we'd made when we arrived. The truck's windows were undamaged and the doors secure. I started to relax as Tobias unlocked them. He hopped into the driver's seat while we chucked the bucket and jugs in the back.

A shrill squealing split the air, so piercing that my hands leapt to my ears. Just as abruptly, it cut off. Tobias twisted the key in the ignition again, but the engine was silent.

"What in hell?" he muttered, pushing open the door. He marched over to the hood and yanked it up, just as I reached him. For a second, we both stared down, motionless.

Every lid that could have been twisted off was gone. Every tube was snapped, every wire cut.

Gav hurried around and stopped with a hiss of breath.

"Can we fix it?" I said, even though I was already pretty sure of the answer.

Tobias's shoulders slumped.

"Not unless you've got a magic wand," he said. "The truck's dead."

# EIGHT

We'd only been worrying about keeping our supplies safe—it hadn't occurred to us that someone might wreck the truck itself.

"The guys in town," Gav said. "You think they did this to get back at us?"

I hugged myself. "Or to take what we have. They couldn't overpower us all at once. And they couldn't get into the truck. So they've stopped us from leaving while they decide what to do next." Like they were predators and we were the prey. They'd wounded us, and they were just waiting for the best opportunity to strike a killing blow.

Tobias started to pace. "We shouldn't have left it," he said. "What the hell do I do now?"

"What do *we* do, you mean," Tessa said quietly.

"We walk," Leo said. He jerked his hand toward the truck. "There's a tent in there, we've got the camping stove and food and warm clothing. We'll manage. But I say we get out of here before whoever's after us comes back with help."

"We're going to walk all the way to *Ottawa*?" Meredith said, her mouth twisting as if she'd tasted something sour.

We were almost halfway there already. I swallowed. "It'd be

practically just as far trying to walk back to the island. And the vaccine won't do anyone any good if we head back. Let's figure how much we can carry, quickly, and get out of here."

"We can find another car on the road," Gav said without batting an eye. "We'll only have to walk until then."

I wished I could have been that confident now that our plan had just been turned on its head. His conviction steadied me. "We could bring more if we all had backpacks," I said. I'd spotted two canvas ones among Tobias's army supplies, but they would only hold so much.

Tessa pointed to the discount store across the street. "I think I see sleds in the window. Those would carry a lot."

"If we have time to get them." Leo scanned the buildings around us and jogged over to the gas-station shop. In a few smooth movements, he hoisted himself onto the dumpster by the side wall, leapt up to grasp the edge of the roof with his hands and elbows, and swung his knee up. After a brief scramble, he was standing.

Tobias stared up at him. "You some kind of rock-climbing expert?"

"Dancer," Leo said. He turned, surveying the town and the freeway beyond. "I don't see anyone right now. Grab the sleds. I'll shout if there's a problem."

"Hey, are you helping, or are you going to stand around and moan while we get going?" Gav said to Tobias. Tobias's jaw set. As he clambered after Gav to sort through the supplies, I turned to Meredith.

"Come on, Mere," I said, as brightly as I could manage. Her body stiffened, but she pressed her lips together and nodded. She, Tessa, and I hurried toward the discount store.

The lock on the door was broken, probably by someone looking for food, but they hadn't touched the sleds. We pulled down six of the biggest ones that had ropes to pull them by and ran back to the truck. The plastic bottoms rasped over the snow behind us.

Leo gave us the okay gesture from the roof. "So we have to take the tent," Gav was saying. He started handing boxes and bags out to us. "And those two sleeping bags, and all the blankets. The food—let's fill the packs with that. Some of the water. We can refill the bottles."

"I have some purification tablets," Tobias said. "Here, we'll want the first-aid kit, and the stove and the extra kerosene. And the radio, of course."

"I don't think there are any stations to listen to these days," Gav said.

"It's a transceiver," Tobias said. "A good one. Maybe we can get in touch with these scientists in Ottawa, if they're there; get them to meet us halfway."

Gav gave him a skeptical look. "We got room?" he asked me.

"I think so." I took the bag of blankets and fit it into the sled I was keeping light for Meredith. "There's space on that one," I said, pointing to the next sled over.

"We're bringing it," Tobias said. "I'll take that sled if it's a problem for someone else."

"You think there are any army bases on the way that could help us?" I asked him. "Lend us a new truck, at least?"

Tobias ducked his head. "No one came to check up on us for weeks," he said. "We weren't getting any broadcasts on the usual bandwidths, either. I think it was the same thing everywhere. People got sick, or ran away, or holed up just hoping to get by."

"There were soldiers at the border," Leo said. "As soon as a few of them got the virus, most of them deserted."

I wasn't surprised, after seeing how the soldiers who'd been supposed to enforce the quarantine had run off, but his words made me colder. We really were alone in this.

"Vaccine," Gav said, sliding the cold box to me. I placed it carefully in the middle of my sled and then went to the front of the truck to grab the map book.

"There are a bunch of little towns down the road, one every few miles," I said after I'd flipped to the area we'd stopped in. "Maybe we won't even need to camp outside."

"I won't argue with that," Gav said. He came over and slid his arm around my waist. "Ready?" he asked softly.

"Yeah," I said, despite the nervous thudding of my heart. He hugged me close, a silent reassurance: We can do this. We will make it. I leaned my head against his shoulder, allowing myself a second's comfort. Any lingering guilt I'd felt over Leo's kiss melted away. All that mattered was getting through this, and I was so, so thankful I had Gav with me while we did.

Leo slid down off the roof onto the dumpster, and then to the ground, rejoining us. "Whatever they're thinking of pulling on us, they're taking their time," he said. "Let's not give them any more."

We marched up the ramp to the freeway, hauling the sleds. It was a lot harder to pull one that was loaded down. My arm was already starting to ache when we reached the road. One side was heaped with snow, the other covered with windswept ice. We kept to the latter, the sleds scraping along behind us, leaving no trail.

After a few minutes, we left behind the last of the town's buildings. Pines and spruces sprang up along the freeway. Leo twisted his sled's rope one way and another, and finally stepped inside it to let his waist take the weight. Before long, the rest of us had followed suit. It took some time to get used to, but after a while I was pulling the sled along like I'd been doing it my whole life.

Meredith strode beside me, her lighter sled veering a little to the left to bump into mine, her chin tipped up and her face set in the most incredible expression of determination. As if she'd decided she was going to walk all the way to Ottawa in one go. The twin braids I'd twisted her hair into the night before swayed where they poked from beneath her tasseled hat.

Beyond the road, I couldn't make out a single building now. If not for the freeway and the occasional mile marker, we could have been explorers lost in some vast wilderness. The breeze licked under my scarf, and I shivered.

Before the epidemic, I used to imagine wandering off the beaten track with nothing but some camping gear and a few notebooks, to watch the wildlife away from human activity. But it had never felt this lonely in my imagination. Maybe because back then, I'd always have known there was a town with running water and electricity and people who'd actually be happy to see me no more than a few days' hike away.

If squirrels and raccoons could manage to survive weather like this every year, we could too, I told myself.

"You made it most of the way back to the island on foot, right?" Gav said to Leo, after we'd been on the road about an hour. Leo nodded.

"After the border," he said. "There was hardly any snow then, but it still wasn't a lot of fun. I didn't have camping gear or a good stash of food like we do, though."

Meredith peered at him with open curiosity. "How did you do it, then?" she asked.

"Mere," I said.

"It's okay," Leo said. He laughed awkwardly. "I guess it was luck. And all those hunting trips my dad dragged me on—I knew how to make a fire, catch things to eat. And just not giving up."

"Look," Tessa said, breaking in. "I think there's a car."

There was: a gray minivan stranded in a drift of snow by the shoulder of the freeway, the glint of its side-view mirror catching the sunlight. Gav reached it first. The driver's-side door opened when he tried it, and he leaned inside. When he reemerged, he was frowning.

"The owners must have taken the key with them," he said. "I guess they figured they'd be coming back for it later."

"The cars along here are probably all a lost cause," Tobias said. "They'd only be left on the freeway if they were out of gas or broke down, right? We'd have a better chance in a town. If there's one parked in a driveway, the keys might still be in the house somewhere."

"And maybe the people it belongs to, too," I said. Alive, or dead.

Tobias looked away. "I'd say it's worth trying. There'll be people who just died at home, didn't want to bother with a hospital—they don't need a car anymore. I know my stepdad would have said screw you if anyone told him to stay squashed in some room with a bunch of other infected people."

"Guess it's a good thing you were off at an army base, then," Gav remarked.

"Believe me," Tobias muttered, "I didn't want to be there, either."

We tramped on, crossing a bridge over a frozen river. The rope cut into my middle as we climbed the low arch, but after we crested the top, gravity pulled the sleds so that they chased us down the opposite side. We all ran, laughing breathlessly by the time we reached the bottom.

"I wish the road went down the whole way," Meredith said, setting off another round of tired laugher.

It was only a few minutes later that Leo halted in midstride and motioned for us to stop too.

"You hear that?" he asked.

We hesitated. For a second, I could hear only the breeze ruffling the treetops. Then the faint rumble of an engine reached my ears, getting gradually louder.

"Car coming," Gav said. "Think we should ask them to give us a ride, if we can all squeeze in?"

"I wouldn't assume they're friendly," Leo said. "I'm not sure we even want them to see we're here."

"How are we going to know if we don't give them a chance?" Tessa asked.

I thought about how easily the guy in the last town had pretended to make peace, and then doubled back to destroy our truck. "I'm okay with not knowing," I said.

"Let's go, then," Tobias said. "Off the road, into the trees."

"Quickly," Leo added. "They're almost here."

The sound of the engine had grown loud enough that I could hear it even when we were talking. My pulse started to thump in my ears. Gav helped me heft my sled over the ditch, and we scrambled with it through the trees. We slid down a short slope, setting the sled down at the bottom. As he hurried back for his,

I went to help Meredith. She tripped coming down the slope and plunged forward amid the snow. Her sled dropped with a thump, but nothing fell out.

"You okay?" I whispered. She nodded, her face turned away.

As the others crouched beside us, the engine noise rose from a rumble to a roar. Tires thumped coming off the bridge. I froze, peering over the top of the slope through the trees.

A pale green van growled down the freeway. A woman with long flax-blond hair beneath a red hat sat in the driver's seat. She had one hand on the wheel and the other balancing a thin object that poked out through the open window. The tip of a rifle.

I caught a glimpse of at least one other figure in the van, and then it slipped out of sight farther down the road. We waited, silently, as the roar faded back into a grumble. I was just about to speak when it suddenly cut out.

We couldn't see them, but the breeze carried every sound. The squeak of the door as it opened, the thud as it closed. The clomp of boots on the icy asphalt. A crackle of static. And a hard voice that resonated through the trees, distinctly annoyed.

"You said they were heading for Ottawa?" the woman said. My skin went clammy. They weren't just dangerous—they were looking for *us*. They'd talked to the guy in town. Maybe this was the help Leo guessed he'd been waiting for.

The static crackled again, around a voice too distorted for me to make out. "Two-way radios," Tobias murmured. "Smart."

Whatever the voice on the other end said, the woman didn't like it. "Well, I can see ten miles of freeway from where I'm standing, and they're not on it," she said. "They must have taken some other route, unless you think they grew wings and flew."

More crackling.

"You're the one who didn't hold them up well enough. You're the one Michael's going to be pissed at."

Crackle.

"Yeah, and up yours," the woman replied. The van door whined open again, and the engine sputtered to life. Tires screeched on the ice. Half a minute later, the van sped past us in the opposite direction, heading back toward the town.

I sank down on the snow, my breath rushing out, and rubbed the cool surface of my gloves against my face. When I opened my eyes again, I noticed that Meredith had hunched against the trunk of one of the trees. A wet shine glinted on her cheeks.

"Hey, Mere," I said, "it's okay now. They're gone."

She answered with a whimper and stretched out her hand. My heart stopped.

The palm of her mitten was soaked through with blood.

# NINE

"I was trying to be quiet," Meredith said shakily. "I knew we didn't want those people to find us."

I peeled off her mitten as gently as I could, fighting to keep my own voice calm. "What happened? When did it happen?"

Meredith winced. Her small palm was slashed with a ragged cut, more blood already welling along its length.

"I think it was when I fell, when we were getting off the road," she said. "There was something sharp in the snow. It really hurt. But I squeezed and squeezed my hand, and that made it hurt less. I was being strong like you, Kaelyn." She gave me a pained smile.

Strong like me. I didn't feel all that strong right now.

"Here," Tobias said, offering me a roll of gauze, and I flinched. I hadn't heard him approach. "I think there's a couple antiseptic wipes in here too," he continued, pawing through the first-aid kit he'd popped open. I ripped open the thin packet he handed me and dabbed the cut.

"That was really brave, Meredith," Leo said. "You did good. You helped keep us safe."

She shifted her smile to him, and bit her lip as I started wrapping gauze around her palm. I'd done a pretty awful job of keeping *her* safe. I hadn't even noticed she was hurt. Tobias said he had a couple of those wipes—were we going to be able to keep the cut clean until it healed? What if it got infected?

I didn't even have a new mitten to give her. Her old one was too damp to keep her hand warm now. Why hadn't we picked up extras when we'd gotten the blankets and hats?

"Sounds like that bunch was called in by those guys in town," Tobias said. "They really want what we have."

"At least they gave up on this route," Tessa said.

"For now," Leo said. "There aren't that many roads. If they want to find us badly enough, they'll come back."

Gav kicked at the snow. "Maybe we should go back and settle this now. Convince them we're not worth messing with."

I remembered the muzzle of the rifle poking through the van window. "We're not going anywhere near those people!" I said, more sharply than I meant to. I pulled off one of my gloves, tugged it over Meredith's hand, kissed her forehead, and stood up. "I'm going to look at the map."

I grabbed the map book from the front of my sled and stalked off through the trees. After about twenty feet, I stopped and leaned against the flaking bark of a birch tree's trunk. My legs felt like jelly. For a moment, the firm surface of the tree behind me was the only thing holding me up.

Meredith's okay, I reminded myself. It was a bad scratch, but ultimately only a scratch. We had supplies, we had the vaccine, we had a map. Nothing had changed.

Except that at least a couple people with a gun were after us, and we didn't know how long or how far they'd chase us, and any one of us could get hurt worse at any time. By our pursuers, through another accident like Meredith's, from the cold. We hadn't even spent one night without heat yet. How many of those nights would there be between here and Ottawa? We had hundreds of miles to go.

Was I strong enough to get all of us through this?

Did I have any choice? If I suggested we turn back toward the island, everyone else would probably agree, but that journey wouldn't be any less dangerous. And it would mean passing the town where we'd lost Tobias's truck.

I dragged the crisp winter air into my lungs, hoping it would settle my thoughts, but they whirled on. I opened the map book. If we kept going toward Ottawa, we couldn't stay on the freeway. As the woman in the red hat had suggested, there were stretches where they'd be able to spot us from miles away.

The ground amid the trees was more uneven than the road, and covered with snow instead of ice, but I didn't think the going would be much slower. The sleds might slide easier. We could follow alongside the freeway through the forest until we found a new car and could put some real distance between us and the people in the van.

The others' voices rose and fell behind me, muffled by the trees. As I straightened up, footsteps crunched through the snow. I turned, expecting Gav. But it was Leo who was walking toward me.

"You all right, Kae?" he said.

The concern in his eyes and the way he said my name made my heart skip the way it had that day in the garage. A wave of frustration rolled over me, tensing my shoulders and closing my throat. I didn't need this too. Not now. Not ever.

"Just wanted a minute to think," I said.

"What happened to Meredith wasn't your fault," he said, even though he had to know just as well as I did that it was.

"It's my fault all of us are here," I said. "You told me it'd be bad. You knew people would be this crazy. But I decided to go anyway."

He didn't answer, only shrugged, lowering his gaze. I could see him pulling back into that distant place inside his head, and all at once I was twice as angry. I wanted the real Leo. The Leo who could smile through every snide comment our fifth grade teacher made about "foreigners." The Leo who practiced a spin a hundred times, stumbling, and just laughed and said he had to keep trying. The Leo who'd pulled off his favorite T-shirt to use as a bandage the time I fell out of a tree and cut the back of my head open, who ran to the nearest house to call for help and then sat with me and held my hand and told me jokes all the way to the hospital.

This boy standing in front of me, looking beaten—this boy who'd kissed me with his girlfriend just a building away and then pretended it didn't matter—this wasn't my best friend. And I had no idea how to get the boy who he had been back.

"You're doing what you have to do," Leo said finally. "Because of the vaccine. We all get that."

I wasn't sure that was true, but I didn't want to talk anymore. So all I said was, "Yeah." I moved to walk past him, and he caught me with a hand on my arm.

"Are *we* all right, Kae?" he asked.

There were four layers of cloth between his skin and mine, but I could still feel a faint warmth where he touched me. I pulled my arm away.

"Sure," I said, but the word came out so harsh even I wouldn't have believed it.

"I'm sorry," he said, his voice low. "What happened in the garage . . . it was a stupid thing to do. But I meant what I said. I'm not going to try—it's not going to happen again."

"You shouldn't have done it in the first place," I snapped.

Too many emotions to count flickered across Leo's face, but there was one I couldn't mistake. Hurt. "I'm sorry," he said again, stiffly. "I didn't know it was that awful."

My fingers curled into my palms. "I didn't say that. It's so much more complicated, Leo. Tessa's my friend. *You're* supposed to be my friend. I can't—"

I couldn't keep discussing this, not when Gav was turning toward us where he stood with the group by the road. "Kae?" he called, peering through the forest.

Leo was looking at me almost curiously. A cold spot formed in the pit of my stomach.

"Forget it," I said. "We've got to get going. It doesn't matter now anyway."

I stepped around him and headed back to the things that did.

We made it six more miles before we stopped for the night in a tiny town that was barely more than a scattering of houses, a church, and a convenience store along a road branching off from the freeway. Someone had driven a pickup truck into the side of the store. The store's window was shattered, and what we could see of the truck's front end was smashed flat. I wondered if the driver had been sick, hallucinating, when the accident happened.

Even though there were no footprints or tire tracks on the street, we walked down the road slowly, pausing every now and then to listen. No sound reached us but the wind. My eyes ached from the cold, and my legs from the walking. Numbness was starting to dull the nerves in my feet despite my two layers of socks and my thick boots. Meredith's head was drooping. But we still had a little farther to go.

To my relief, we found an unlocked house on our second try. We went in, wiping our boots on the inner mat out of habit. No one was going to care about the state of the floors. Pictureless nails dotted the living room, and the closets and beds had been stripped bare. The people who'd lived here must have tried to run from the virus. The emptiness of the town seemed to echo through the walls.

Gav poked at the fireplace. "Looks like it's usable," he said. "There are even a couple logs here that are hardly charred."

"If the people in that van are still searching for us, won't the smoke give us away?" Tessa said.

"We'd be okay once it gets dark," Tobias said. "I—I'll go have a look at the trees around here. If we can get some spruce branches, or elder, they don't make as much smoke."

"Really?" Gav said. "Wood's wood, isn't it?"

Tobias shrugged, his head low. "We had a whole section on how to evade the enemy if you're stationed outdoors. I saw it with my own eyes."

Within an hour, we had flames dancing in the fireplace, wafting a thin heat and tangy spruce scent through the living room. We all huddled close, taking turns warming cans of soup at the edge of the hearth. The feeling slowly prickled back into my feet.

"We should be careful how much we're eating," Leo said. "Now that we're going to be on the road longer than we expected."

"We can't cut back too much if we're going to have energy for walking," I pointed out.

"Army rations are pretty filling," Tobias said. "That's what they're made for. I'd figure we're good for another ten days." He paused. "It's water you've got to worry about more. We could melt some snow here to fill up the empty bottles before we go."

After we'd eaten, he and Tessa and Leo went out with the three pots we'd found in the kitchen, and came back with heaps of snow. "Careful," Tobias said as he set his by the edge of the fire. "We've got to pour a little water in first. Otherwise—you'd never believe it—the damn stuff can burn the bottom of the pot."

"Are we just going to sleep here?" Meredith asked. "On the floor?"

"We could bring the mattresses down from the beds upstairs," Tessa said. "Make it more comfortable."

Tobias nodded. "We'll stay warmer that way too."

Tessa and Meredith kept an eye on the melting snow while the rest of us headed upstairs. Gav and Leo took the queen mattress out of the master bedroom and hauled it down while Tobias and I grabbed the double down the hall. I tried not to notice the knick-knacks on the shelves, the books on the bedside table.

By the time we'd pushed the mattress to the top of the stairs, sweat had broken out on my forehead. "Better take your coat off if you're getting hot," Tobias said. "When your clothes get damp, it's a lot harder to keep warm later on."

I dropped the coat over the railing to retrieve later. "You know a lot about surviving in the cold."

"I've been through training," he said. "In Canada. Wouldn't have lasted long if I hadn't picked up a few things."

I looked at him then—really looked at him, for the first time since he'd told us what was going on in the harbor, when all I'd been able to see was yet another soldier who should have been protecting us and had failed. He was only a few years older than I was. He had parents out there, maybe brothers or sisters, friends —people whom he didn't know whether they were alive or dead. He'd had to leave the one certain shelter he had. Training or not, some part of him must have been scared. And he was still here.

"Thanks," I said. "For helping us, with everything. I hate to think what a mess we'd be in without you."

His head jerked around with a start. Then his stance relaxed and he gave me a shy smile. "Just doing what I know how to do."

As the rest of us laid out the blankets, Tobias turned on the transceiver radio he'd insisted we bring and took it out onto the front steps. Ten minutes later, he came back in, sprinkled with snow and shaking his head. "I'm not picking up any signals tonight."

We slept the same way we had in the truck, each wrapped in a blanket of our own and then squeezed together under the unzipped sleeping bags. My body balked at the cramped positioning for just a few minutes before exhaustion took over, and I drifted off with Gav's breath by my ear. It hardly felt like any time at all before the early morning sun streaming through the window woke me.

The fire had dwindled to embers, but the room still held a little warmth. The muscles around my middle throbbed when I sat up, from pulling the sled yesterday. I squirmed out from between Gav and Meredith, who were starting to stir, and went to check on the vaccine.

The temperature in the cold-storage box looked fine, but the freezer packs were getting slushy. I took three of the four out and set them in my sled, hoping they'd refreeze while we walked that day, then broke a bunch of icicles off the house's windows to refill the box.

By then the others were up. We gulped down a couple tins of canned peaches between us and gnawed on granola bars while we packed the sleds. As we carried them back outside, Meredith gave an excited yelp. "I see a car!" She gestured to a shape buried in the snow several driveways down the road. "Do you think there are keys in the house?"

"Can't hurt to check," Gav said. We all marched over. While he and Tobias started digging out the car, Tessa and I climbed the front steps. The door opened easily.

"If you were a car key, where would you be?" I said.

Tessa scanned the hall. "No key rack. No hall table. Maybe a drawer in the kitchen?"

A pair of woolly mittens lay in a basket just beyond the shoe rack. I picked them up so I could replace Meredith's damaged pair. My heartbeat kicked up a notch as we crept further into the house. What I'd said to Tobias before was true—the fact that the car was still here meant the owners probably were too. The fact that they hadn't complained about us barging into their house meant, if they were, they were dead. But thankfully we came upon nothing except a dusty counter, a coffee machine with the pot still a quarter full but ringed with ice, and, in the third drawer Tessa checked, a car key.

"Got it!" she said, sounding so triumphant I couldn't help grinning as we hurried outside.

The car, an old maroon sedan, was pretty much unearthed. Tessa unlocked the door and climbed inside. Beside me, Gav shifted restlessly. The engine coughed, sputtered, and then stead-ied into a low rumble. Meredith let out a little cheer.

Tessa backed it up two feet, three, and then the wheels started spinning against the snow pushed up in their wake. My heart sank. She eased the car back and forth a few times, making only a few inches of progress, then cut the engine and got out to study the problem.

"The snow's too deep," Leo said, stating what we were all real-izing. "We'd have to shovel a path right down to the freeway."

And then we'd only be okay as long as part of the road was just ice or shallow snow. We could hardly count on that.

"So we're going to need something bigger," Tessa said. "Like the truck."

"It's not going to work?" Meredith said, a tremble in her voice.

"Looks like no." I rubbed her back. "Don't worry, Mere. We'll just have to wait until we find one that's better equipped for the weather."

As if we hadn't been lucky just to find this car and its key. I glanced to the west, the way we were headed, and Ottawa seemed to shrink far away into the distance.

"Then we've got some more walking to do," Gav said, reaching for his sled. "Better get started."

# TEN

We walked for two days, stopping briefly in the few towns we passed and coming up with nothing we could drive. My stomach, hips, and legs perpetually ached. Conversation dwindled, and then stopped almost completely.

On the second afternoon we achieved a minor victory, finding a shelf of canned food in a garage, as well as a spool of steel wire. As we walked on, Leo used it to demonstrate the snare-making techniques he'd learned from his dad. "I hated the hunting trips he planned more than anything," he said, twisting the wire, "but they did pretty much save my life getting back to the island. If we're lucky, we can catch a few rabbits."

When we stopped for the night at a lone farmhouse a short distance off the freeway, Leo, Gav, and I set the six snares around the closest field. I woke the next morning to Gav sliding out from under the sleeping bag beside me. Only a faint glow of dawn light lit the room.

"Up already?" I murmured.

"I want to check the snares before everyone's awake," he said. "So they don't hold us up heading out."

My eyelids still felt a little heavy, but I suspected I wouldn't be able to get back to sleep. I slipped away from Meredith to join him.

The sun was just starting to rise beyond the trees, but I could already feel there'd been a shift in the temperature. The snow felt mushy under my boots as we circled the house. Somewhere to the left, I heard a faint trickle of meltwater.

It wouldn't last. January melts never did. As soon as the temperatures fell again overnight, the ground would be slick with ice formed over half-melted snow. We'd have to walk even more cautiously tomorrow. Drew had broken his wrist on one of those types of days—eight years ago, but I could still remember the crack of bone when his feet had slipped out from under him on the front walk.

Drew, of course, had turned it into an opportunity. He couldn't write properly with the cast, so he'd talked Dad into "lending" him the old work laptop that mostly sat in Dad's study gathering dust. When the cast was removed, Drew had headed off any request for the laptop's return with the open audacity he'd possessed even at ten years old. "Wasn't it nice not having me and Kaelyn fighting over the living room computer anymore?" he'd said, and Dad had let him keep it.

My chest tightened up at the memory. Drew was so smart. So determined. It wasn't totally crazy for me to think he might still be alive, was it?

"Nothing here," Gav said, bending to tug an empty loop of wire from beside the wooden fence that ran along the field. "Well, we might as well hold on to them."

He eyed the snare for a second longer before hooking it over the sleeve of his coat.

"You okay?" I asked as we tramped toward the next.

"Yeah," he said. "Just...a little impatient, I guess. I miss the truck." He laughed, but it sounded strained.

"Me too. At least we haven't run into that woman in the green van again."

"No kidding." He pulled up the second empty snare and looped it over his arm with the first. "It's funny," he said after a moment. "I keep thinking about how much I wanted to get off the island before. Have some long road trip with Warren, see the whole country and all the things I was missing. Figure out where I fit in. But then, this virus comes, and...it's all the same now. Everything's screwed up, everywhere."

A lump rose in my throat. "Gav," I said, quietly.

"And it turned out the one place I could make a little difference was right there on the island," he went on. "Who would have thought?"

"You've been amazing," I said. Could he really not know that? "And it's not going to stay like this. If the vaccine works, if people can stop getting sick, we can start fixing everything."

"Yeah," he said. He wrapped his gloved hand around mine and held it as we continued our circuit of the field.

The next three snares were undisturbed too. "I was hoping we'd get *something*," Gav said.

"When Leo was traveling back, it was still fall," I pointed out. "Most of the animals are hibernating now."

"Right." He paused as we headed toward the last snare. "You and him...You weren't ever anything more than friends, were you?"

"What?" I said, my face getting hot, grateful for the scarf that hid my cheeks. Had he seen something, overheard something? But what had there been to see or hear, really? The fact was, I could say with complete honesty, "No. We've always been just friends."

Gav stopped, sliding his arms around me. "I'm sorry," he said, his head bent beside mine. "I don't know why I was thinking about it."

"It's okay," I said. As if I could prove it, I nudged down our scarves and kissed him. His lips were dry but warm. He held me close for another few seconds, and I wished we were anywhere but in the middle of an empty field, hundreds of miles from anything familiar. Somewhere we could be our normal selves, if only for a moment.

When Gav drew back, the longing in his expression suggested he was thinking the same thing. A tingle shivered over my skin. But he just cocked his head and gave me a grin that was a little less strained and said, "We'd better finish up before the others send a search party."

As we came upon the last snare, I spotted a furry shape beneath the bush where we'd set it.

"Hey!" Gav said, hurrying forward. I followed, slowing when I made out a long slender tail.

"That's not a rabbit," I said. I forced myself to take the last few steps to Gav's side.

It was a cat, a brown tabby, its scrawny body rigid, head twisted where it'd struggled to free itself from the snare. I closed my eyes. From the looks of it, the cat might have died soon anyway, thanks to starvation or the cold. We might even have done it a kindness. What made my stomach lurch was the thought of what we might do with it now.

"Doesn't look like it has that much meat on it," Gav said

uncertainly. I could feel him watching me. And suddenly I wanted to hit something. This was all because of the virus. The virus had stranded us here with no heat or food or people to help. The virus had put us in the position where we had to consider eating what had once been someone's pet. I hated it. I hated it so much.

There was no way I was letting it beat us, no matter what I had to do.

I made myself shrug, exhaling my anger. "A little bit of meat could be the difference between making it one more day and... not making it, right?"

"True." He crouched down by the bush. "I think it's mostly frozen. We could pack it with snow so it stays that way, not use it unless we have to."

I nodded. "Let's get a bag. I don't want Meredith seeing it."

We didn't speak walking back to the house, but just outside the door, Gav turned and touched my face. Tears sprang into my eyes. I blinked, willing them away.

"I'm okay," I said. "I'm fine. I just want to get out of here."

"That makes two of us," Gav said with a crooked smile.

He went back with a bag for the cat and stashed it in the middle of his sled. We didn't mention it again.


The six of us didn't reach the next town until the sun had arced across the sky and started slipping back down toward the trees. Tobias spotted it first, pointing to a ripple of snow-patched rooftops in the distance. Clouds were bunching along the horizon above them.

Without speaking, we all picked up our pace to cross the last few fields. The warmth had let us open our jackets and loosen our scarves as we walked, but the soggy snow dragged at the sleds. Every muscle between my feet and my waist burned.

The town looked about the same size as the one where we'd lost the truck. I reached for Meredith's hand as we marched down the first street we came to, our sleds bumping sides. The emptiness was almost comforting. I'd rather we were the only ones here.

We didn't stop, but slowed to scan the laneways and side streets. On the first few blocks, we passed a couple cars, but both of them were obviously too small. Then I noticed a black pickup truck at the back of a driveway, its bed full of half-melted snow.

"You think that'd do it?" I asked.

"We might as well try," Gav said, brightening. "Let's take a look."

We tramped down the driveway together. Tobias tried the driver's-side door. It opened, but he shook his head.

"Looks like someone already tried to hotwire it and didn't know what they were doing," he said. Frayed wires dangled beneath the steering wheel. "I don't suppose any of you know how to fix that? 'Cause I don't."

Gav shook his head and kicked one of the tires.

"So, we keep looking," Tessa said calmly. "Sooner or later—"

She was interrupted by a low voice from the other end of the driveway. "Hey! It's been a long time since I've seen anyone over here!"

We spun around as footsteps thumped over the snow. A young man, tall and broad-shouldered, was lumbering toward us, sniffling and scratching a spot on his hip. His eyes flicked from us to the open door of the truck and narrowed. "What are you doing to Mr. Mitchard's truck? You shouldn't be messing with that!"

He rushed at us, his round face flushed, and I instinctively shrank back, grabbing Meredith's shoulder. Tobias froze, going white. Leo shifted to Tessa's side.

Only Gav went forward.

He charged between our sleds a second before the guy reached them, throwing out his arms. "Hold—" he managed. The guy looked like he might have stopped, but he slipped on the slushy ground and crashed into Gav.

They both tumbled over, a pained breath escaping Gav as the guy's shoulder smacked his chest. I shoved Meredith behind me and ran to help, not entirely sure what I intended to do. The guy who'd come after us rolled to one side, wheezing and then coughing. Gav scrambled up and backward, staying between him and us. He waved me back as I caught up with him. I ignored the gesture.

"He's sick," I hissed. "Your scarf!"

Gav's hand leapt up. He tugged his scarf back over his lower face. Leo and Tessa came up behind us. Tobias hovered by the truck, staring at our attacker as if transfixed.

It wasn't the guy he was afraid of, it occurred to me. Of course not. It was the virus. The enemy all his army training couldn't prepare him to fight.

"Man," the guy said, pushing himself up onto his knees. His jeans were soaked through from the melting snow, but he didn't seem to notice. "Whoa, I'm dizzy now. Why'd you do that? I just wanted to see what you were doing."

"Matt?" a voice called. A second figure appeared at the end of the driveway: a young woman, slender and delicate-looking in her puffy coat. She blanched when she caught sight of us and hurried over, covering a sneeze with her gloved hand.

"He ran at us," Gav said as she took the guy's arm to help him up. "We're just passing through—we don't want to hurt anyone. Just don't want anyone hurting us, either."

"I wouldn't have *hurt* you," the guy protested. "But you shouldn't be getting into other people's trucks. That's just not right."

"We were wondering if we could . . . fix it up for him," I offered, wincing inwardly at the weak lie.

The woman looked at us, tight-lipped. "I'm sorry," she said. "I understand. Matt, you freaked me out, wandering off like that! You don't even have a coat on. Let's get back to the house."

"But there's people," Matt said. "We haven't seen people in ages! I want to talk to them. Gets kind of boring only having you around, you know."

Even as he talked, I could see the cold seeping through his fever. He shuddered. "Maybe you all could come back to our place and hang out a bit? We're lucky—got a generator—it's nice and warm. There's that bottle of whiskey Jill's been making me save."

The woman, who I guessed was Jill, pulled at his arm. "We can go back and get you some dry clothes, and then these kind people will stop by in a few minutes. Right?" She smiled at us, her sad eyes saying the opposite.

"Sure!" I said, a little too brightly.

"We'd be happy to," Gav added, and then, softly, "You take care."

She nodded to us thankfully, and Matt sighed and turned to follow her. "Don't forget!" he called as they reached the street. "We've got lots to talk about. I don't even know your names yet!"

When we heard their door shut, I let out my breath. Tobias jerked forward, grabbing the rope of his sled.

"Let's get the hell out of here before that guy decides we've taken too long and comes back."

We didn't bother checking for more cars. We just walked through town and on into the stand of pine trees beyond the last few houses. The clouds loomed over us now, stretching across half the sky and dimming the sun. The breeze had risen. I zipped up the collar of my coat and pulled my hat down over my ears. My heart was still thumping.

I peeked sideways at Gav. He was striding along beside me as if nothing was different, as if he hadn't just thrown himself into what could have been a wrestling match with a guy half a foot taller and at least fifty pounds heavier. A guy who was sick.

I watched the trail appearing from under Tessa's sled in the snow ahead of me, feeling the minutes slip past, unable to speak. My emotions were so churned up I didn't know how much I was angry or afraid or just plain upset. Maybe we shouldn't go into the towns at all anymore. But we were never going to make it the whole way to Ottawa on foot, were we?

The wind whistled through the twigs of the trees. Snowflakes drifted down. One landed on my nose and melted there.

"You shouldn't have done that," I said finally. "You ran right up to him—"

"We didn't know what he was going to do," Gav said, an edge in his voice. "He could have wrecked the sleds, grabbed our food— broken the vaccine samples! Isn't that the most important thing?"

I wanted to say no. It wasn't more important than Gav's life. But I'd been letting him risk his life for the vaccine just by agreeing to have him come out here with me, hadn't I?

"I'm not saying it was smart," he went on. "It's not like I had time to think it through. It happened in a second—I reacted."

"I know," I said. "I just wish your natural reaction was safer."

He laughed, a little shortly. "Hey," he said, "at least I did something useful. More than I've done since we left the island, anyway."

"That's not true," I said, but maybe it was. On the island he'd had the food runs, the volunteers he kept organized, the amateur firefighters he joined in with when the gang tried to burn down another building. Now there was only one thing we needed: to get to Ottawa. And so far there hadn't been a single thing Gav could do to make that trip quicker or less unpleasant.

He hadn't even wanted to be here, not really. He'd wanted to be back there, helping the island recover from the helicopter's attack.

"Thank you," I said. "Maybe I'd rather you didn't do that again, but I'm still glad all our stuff is safe, and us too."

I took his hand, and the side of his mouth curled up, just slightly. As the trees thinned around us, the sky came into view. The clouds were choking it now, thick and gray. I blinked away the snowflakes that had started plummeting down even faster.

"I think we should get inside soon," Leo said. "It feels like a real blizzard's on its way. How far to the next town?"

The map was all but burned into my brain now. "At least a couple miles," I said, looking around. "There should be farmhouses along the way, though."

"I think I see a building over there," Tessa said, pointing. I followed her gaze. When I squinted, I could make out the faint angles of a structure in the distance, over the fields. It looked strangely translucent, as if it weren't totally real.

"I don't know if we should go that far from the road," I said. "What if we can't find our way back?"

Her eyes had lit up. "It's a greenhouse," she said. "It'll be warmer inside. I don't think it's that far."

"I'll take warm," Tobias said, hunched inside his coat. I looked at Gav and he shrugged, his expression resigned.

"Let's hurry, then," I said. The falling snow already felt heavier than it had a moment ago.

The next time I looked up, I couldn't make out the greenhouse at all. Cold prickled over the skin around my eyes. The freeze was setting in. With each step, my boots either cracked through the forming ice or skidded on it. My sled bumped and jarred. Meredith slid along beside me, pushing out as if she were on skates. Gav had pulled ahead of us.

The snow kept whirling down. It pattered against my face, coating my eyelashes. I wrapped my scarf tighter.

Then I blinked, and Tobias and Gav all but disappeared in front of me. Snowflakes clotted the air. It was like swimming through a blank page, nothing but white all around. My breath came heavy through the wool scarf. For a second I felt as if I were drowning.

Behind me, Tessa yelped. I spun around. Leo stopped by her side as she groped along the ground. "I tripped," she said, a frantic note in her voice. "I lost the rope. Where's the sled?"

I scanned the ground, but all I could see was snow.

"It doesn't matter," Leo said after a few seconds. "We'll come back for it. If we stop to look, we'll lose our direction."

Meredith was already slipping out of my view. "Mere!" I shouted. Leo and Tessa pushed forward with me. The frigid air pierced through my scarf, stinging down my throat. The rope of my sled dug into my waist, and in that moment I wished I could throw mine away and just run.

Then three figures wavered into sight just ahead. The others had stopped to wait for us.

As we caught up with them, a fourth figure shifted out of the white. It raised an arm, the business end of a revolver pointed straight at Gav's chest.

"Hello," a nasal voice said. "Going somewhere?"

# ELEVEN

We probably could have overpowered him—with six of us against one, the odds were in our favor despite the gun—but the stranger's next words were "Come on, let's get out of this crap," and the idea that he might have somewhere for us to go *to* overrode every other impulse. Without him, we were still lost in the blizzard.

It was only a few steps before he was opening a door ahead of us. Light streamed through the falling snow.

"In you go," he said, motioning with the hand that held the gun. "Leave your sleds outside; there's no room. We're not the kind of people who'll take what's yours."

I turned and gripped the handle of the cold box before I followed the others through the doorway. I wasn't letting that out of my sight.

We shuffled out of the blizzard and into a narrow wood-paneled room, hardly big enough for the seven of us to stand comfortably. A platform on one side held a bare double mattress, and a plastic crate stood in one corner. Otherwise, the room was empty. A light fixture shone dimly overhead. Whoever these people were, they had electricity.

The stranger shut the door with a bang. "Sit down," he said. "It looks like we'll be here awhile."

Melted snow was already puddling under my boots, the frost on my eyelashes dripping away like tears. The room was heated too.

Meredith plopped down on the edge of the mattress, so I joined her, tucking the cold box between my feet. Tessa sank down beside me. The guys stayed standing, Gav crossing his arms in front of him. To my relief, he was keeping a healthy distance between himself and the revolver.

"What the hell's going on?" he demanded. "Who are you?"

"I'm supposed to be asking you that," the stranger said. "You're the ones that came barging onto our turf."

He hunkered down on the crate and pulled back his hood. I registered his face, and looked again in surprise.

He was just a kid. At least a couple years younger than me, I guessed, his face soft and boyish and his forehead dotted with zits. Beneath his orange hat, which was stitched with a hockey team logo, his dark hair was pulled back in a limp ponytail that curled at the base of his neck. When we all stayed silent, he tapped the gun against his leg and narrowed his eyes.

"I saw you coming as soon as you were out of the woods, you know," he said. "I could have shot you."

"You even know how to fire that thing?" Tobias asked.

"I'm a good shot," the boy said. "You'd better believe it. Practiced on the firing range with my dad every month after I turned thirteen. You'd have been dead if you'd looked like some of those asshole raiders. Good for you that you didn't. So, where are you coming from?"

"South of Halifax," I said.

His eyebrows rose. "You walked all the way from the coast?"

"We had a truck," Gav said. "It broke. We've been walking the last few days."

"Where do you think you're going with all that stuff?" the boy asked, motioning to the door.

"Why do you need to know?" Leo said quietly. "Are you planning on letting us leave when the storm's over?"

"We only came this way to find shelter," Tessa said. "We didn't mean to disturb anyone."

"I don't know what's going to happen," the boy said. "I don't get to decide that on my own. I was just keeping watch."

"So who does decide?" I said. "You're saying 'we,' and 'our'— where is everybody?"

He looked at me as if I'd asked the most stupid question he could imagine. "In the other cabins," he said. "You won't see most of 'em for a while even if you stick around. This is the quarantine cabin. New people don't go any farther until we know they're not sick. We all had to do it." He stopped, some of the color washing from his face. "Oh, shit, I forgot." He fumbled with his coat with his free hand, digging out a crumpled face mask and jerking it over his head.

"You don't have to worry," I said. "None of us are sick."

"I'd rather not take the chance," he replied. His gaze dropped to the cold box at my feet. "How come you didn't leave that with the rest of your stuff? What've you got in there?"

I slid my legs in front of it instinctively. "You don't need to worry about that, either," Gav said, a threat plain in his voice.

The boy stood up. "Look," he said. "I told you we don't steal here. But I've got to check. You could have guns in there or something."

While it was hardly normal room temperature in the cabin, it felt well above freezing. I didn't want him poking around in the box, letting the cool air out. Who knew when I'd be able to repack it with ice? But as he stepped forward, Gav moved in front of him, and I could see that neither of them intended to back down. So I did the only thing I could think of that might stop the situation from getting worse, if the boy was being honest about the people we were dealing with.

"It's vaccine samples," I said quickly. "But they've got to stay cold—every time I open the box there's a chance they'll start spoiling."

The boy cocked his head, but he didn't come any closer. "I heard the vaccine was a dud."

"This is a new one," I said. "We're trying to find someone who can replicate it, to make enough for everyone. That's why we were walking by here—that's why we'll leave as soon as the storm's over. If you'll let us." I paused. "Unless you've got doctors here who might be able to do it." From what I'd seen of the area, it hadn't looked developed, but I hadn't expected electricity or heating, either.

The boy didn't give an indication one way or the other. "You could be lying," he said.

"So could you," Leo answered.

"We've have to be some special kind of idiots to keep our guns sealed away in a box instead of on us where we could actually reach them, don't you think?" Tobias said.

The boy rolled his eyes. "Yeah, yeah," he said. "All right, calm down. But don't think you're going anywhere soon. Like I said, that's not my decision." He sank back down onto his crate. "You should probably get comfortable. From the looks of outside, I think you're here until morning."

The sunlight beaming through the cabin's open door woke me. My neck pinched when I raised my head. Sometime during the night, four of us had slumped across the mattress at odd angles: Meredith huddled in a ball against my shoulder, Gav at my other side with his arm bent around his head, Tessa squished into the corner. Leo had come over beside her, dozing against the bed's platform. Even in sleep, his face looked tense. Tobias still sat by the wall, his skinny legs drawn up in front of him, his eyes alert and wary as he watched the woman in the doorway.

She stepped inside, studying us through dark-framed glasses that rested at the top of her face mask. Her hair, chestnut brown laced with gray, brushed the tops of her broad shoulders. The boy with the revolver hovered behind her.

They looked alike, I realized. The hair, the shoulders, the way they stood. Mother and son, if I was going to guess.

I pushed myself upright, my feet bumping the cold box at the edge of the bed. The woman's gaze fell to it, then lifted to meet my eyes. Gav stirred, yawning.

"Justin told me you have a vaccine," the woman said briskly, and Gav flinched upward at the unfamiliar voice.

"That's right," I said.

"A working vaccine?"

"It hasn't been thoroughly tested," I said. "But my dad was confident enough that he tried the vaccine on himself. He never got sick."

The woman scrutinized us. "May I see it?" she asked.

I didn't like it, but we couldn't expect them to take everything at our word. At least this woman seemed like someone who could make decisions. "Quickly," I said. "We have to keep the samples cold."

She nodded, crossing the room. Meredith shifted beside me, blinking awake. I popped open the lid and pulled up the top of the plastic container that held the vials.

"All right," the woman said after only a second, and I closed the box. "I suppose, if that really is a vaccine, you know enough about it to tell me what it does?"

It was a test, I suspected, but one I could easily pass. I'd read more about vaccines in the last couple weeks than I'd ever wanted to know.

"The vaccine contains an inactive form of the virus," I said. "One that can't make you sick, but still provokes the immune system to produce antibodies to fight it. Which means if you're exposed to the actual virus later on, your body can recognize it right away and make the antibodies fight it off fast enough to kill it before it gets a real hold."

"What if we have someone here who's infected," she asked, "and we'd offer you supplies in exchange for one of those samples? Presumably you don't need all three."

I thought of our dwindling stash of food, but it didn't matter. I wasn't going to lie.

"It wouldn't do them any good," I said. "Like I said, the vaccine prepares the immune system in case you get infected later. If a person's already infected, it's too late—it can't help. I'm sorry."

The corners of her eyes crinkled with a smile before I'd even finished speaking, and I realized that had been part of the test too.

If we'd been lying in the first place, we wouldn't have hesitated to trade some of our fake vaccine for whatever else we needed to survive. There probably wasn't anyone sick here.

"Wonderful," the woman said. "I thought by now—" She shook her head, as if recalling herself. "I wish I could offer you more while you're here, but most of our facilities—the dining area, the showers—are shared, and I'm afraid it's our policy that any newcomers have to stay in the quarantine cabin for two weeks before joining the rest of us. We can bring you a hot breakfast to eat here, though. I take it you don't intend to stay long?"

"No," I said. At the mention of showers, I could suddenly feel every inch of oil and dried sweat that must have been clinging to my skin and hair. And to be able to wash Meredith's hand properly... "We're safe," I continued, getting up. I gestured to Leo and Tessa. "About as safe as anyone can get. Tessa and Leo have taken the vaccine, and Meredith and I are immune. We both had the virus weeks ago, and recovered."

At the mention of their names, Tessa sat up, wincing, and Leo opened his eyes.

"Both of you?" the woman said, her eyebrows arching.

"Kaelyn was lucky," Meredith said. "And the doctors used her blood to help me."

"We'd be so grateful if you'd let us just get cleaned up before we go," I said. "My cousin cut her hand—I haven't been able to really take care of it."

Her eyes softened. "And you two?" she asked, glancing at Gav and then Tobias.

"No vaccine, haven't been sick," Gav answered for both of them. "But we're fine. You see us coughing or sneezing?"

"Well, I'm afraid I can't justify bending the rules that far," the woman said. "We can bring a few buckets of warm water and some soap out here, if that would help, as well as the food. For the other four of you, though, I think we can rescind the quarantine, as a special case."

"What if they wear masks?" I said. "We can't just go off and leave them stuck in here."

The woman's jaw tightened, but before she could speak, Gav nudged my arm. "It's okay, Kaelyn," he said evenly. "I get it. It's not like we'll be sticking around." Then, to the woman, "We'll be happy just to get some food and water. Thank you."

In his corner, Tobias shrugged.

Meredith sprang to her feet. "We can take a *real* shower?" she said. "Where?"

"I'll show you," the woman replied, her voice amused, and stepped back to the door.

Gav shooed me away. "Just come back quick," he said, and tapped the cold box with his heel. "I'll keep watch over these for you."

Meredith was already scampering out the door. "Okay," I said. "We'll be right back."

"Step carefully," the woman said as we came out of the cabin. "It's all ice. We spray down the yard regularly to keep it that way —no footprints. It's one of our precautionary measures. We've only had a few unfriendly intruders wander out this way, but we can't be too careful."

I found my balance on the slick ground. We were standing in a clearing surrounded by forest on three sides. A semicircle of cabins like the one we'd just left curved around a larger wooden building.

The tall greenhouse Tessa had spotted yesterday stood behind it, glinting in the early morning sun.

The woman motioned to the forest at our left. "We moved your sleds into the trees where the spraying wouldn't reach them. But you should find they're as you left them."

"No offense," Leo said, shading his eyes against the glare off the ice, "but who *are* you, and where are we?"

"Oh!" she said, sounding honestly surprised. "My apologies. My name's Hilary Cloutier. And you've met Justin." She patted her son's shoulder, and he scowled.

"This was once an artists' colony," Hilary explained as we started toward the larger building. "A place off the grid for painters and writers and composers to spend a month or two focusing on their craft. There's quite a large generator under the gathering house. For the most part, we rely on natural light, but we have heat and enough power to run the stove."

"That's convenient," I said.

"We didn't end up here by chance," Hilary said. "I'm a sculptor—I worked here for a month every year. When services started failing and people were panicking in our town, this was the first place I thought of, somewhere we might be safe. Everyone here came for the same reason."

A sculptor? "So how do you know I wasn't just making things up about the vaccine?" I asked.

She laughed. "Oh, my sister was a nurse. I'm naturally curious. I badgered her with so many questions when we first heard about this mysterious virus. Before, well . . ."

Her laugh had been a little stiff, and the "was" didn't escape me. "I'm sorry," I said.

"Have you gotten any crops growing in the greenhouse?" Tessa asked.

Hilary nodded. "Oh, yes. We have precautions there too, of course. In case someone comes through who'd try to run us out and take over if they knew the colony was functioning. We keep the vegetable plants spread out and let the weeds grow around them so it looks as if it was abandoned. But we've produced some carrots and beans and peas and tomatoes, and the pear tree is just starting to bear fruit."

We stopped outside a door in the side of the gathering house. "Where are you planning on taking the vaccine?" Hilary said.

I hesitated automatically, but Meredith had obviously decided these people were trustworthy.

"Ottawa!" she announced. "We're going to find scientists and doctors so they can make more vaccine for everyone."

"Ottawa." Hilary's eyes went distant. "We have a couple from Ottawa with us. Maybe you should talk with them." She opened the door. "Well, this is our bathing area. The water won't get too hot—we have all our heat settings turned down so as not to strain the generator—but there's plenty of it. There should be soap inside, and extra towels on the shelf. Come around to the front when you're finished. Everyone's having breakfast."

On the other side of the door we found a rack with towels that were drying, and a shelf holding folded towels and bottles of liquid soap. Two hallways branched off from that small room, marked with signs for men and women.

"Pretty amazing what they've got set up here," I said.

"They could probably be totally self-sufficient with just the greenhouse," Tessa said. "Grow fruits and vegetables and grains for bread . . . though the space restrictions would be a problem, depending on the number of people. With lentils for protein and spinach for iron, they wouldn't even need meat. I'd like to take a look at what they've got."

"I bet she'll give you a tour if you ask," I said as we parted ways with Leo.

At the other end of the hall, we stepped into a changing room lined with open shower stalls. I might have felt awkward showering with company, but seeing Tessa strip off her clothes like it was nothing, I figured if it didn't matter to her, it wouldn't matter to me.

The first blast of lukewarm water from the showerhead jolted a breathless giggle out of me. Grinning, I rubbed the grapefruit-scented soap over my body from head to toe. I hadn't showered in weeks, not since the water filtration broke down on the island. I'd forgotten what a glorious feeling it was: the drumming of the spray on my skin, the slippery froth of soap under my fingers, the lightness of hair that's squeaky clean.

When I'd washed myself thoroughly, I joined Meredith and helped her rinse the lather out of her thicker hair. Then I examined her injured palm. The cut had scabbed over, the edges already starting to flake away over healed skin. No infection redness.

"You took good care of it," I told her. She tipped her face into the spray, smiling.

"Do we really have to go right away?" she asked as we were toweling off. "Maybe Tobias can call someone on his radio from here, and they'll come get the vaccine from us."

Something in my chest twisted. I could hardly blame her for hoping. "I wish he could, Mere, believe me," I said. "But I don't know if anyone's still trying to reach out on the radios. Our best bet is to keep going." My nose wrinkled involuntarily as I pulled on my travel-worn clothes. At Tobias's advice, we'd been using a little melted snow to wipe ourselves down and rinse our underthings each night on the road, so they weren't gross, but they weren't exactly clean either.

"Okay," Meredith said, shooting one last longing look at the showers before we headed out. *She* didn't have to go, I realized abruptly. If we asked Hilary to take her in . . .

And left her with strangers? Hilary might have seemed nice, but I'd hardly known her half an hour.

Leo was waiting for us in the towel room. "Ready to go?" he asked, his shoulders hunched inside his coat. I wondered whether he thought we could completely trust the people here.

"We should take our breakfast over to the quarantine cabin and eat with Gav and Tobias," I said as we stepped outside, "so they know we haven't forgotten them."

We half walked, half skated along the icy ground to the other side of the building and almost slid into Justin as we came around the corner. I caught my balance by gripping the wall.

"Hey," Justin said, his voice low. "Are you really going to take off again today, to keep looking for someone to clone that vaccine of yours?"

"That's the idea," I said.

He opened his mouth as if he was going to continue, but then Hilary leaned out of the doorway behind him. "There you are," she said. "Come in. You must be starving. Justin brought a tray to your friends."

"I was just talking to them," Justin said.

"You can talk inside where it's warm, can't you?"

He sighed, but followed us in without comment.

We stepped into a huge room with wood-paneled walls that matched those in the quarantine cabin. Several rough picnic tables stood in rows across the tiled floor. Two older couples were gathered around one of the tables, murmuring to each other. The clatter of dish-washing echoed from a doorway at the other side of the room, which I guessed led to the kitchen. A rich doughy smell filled the air. My mouth started to water.

Leo had gone still beside me. I followed his gaze to a small black shape sitting on a ledge near the kitchen door. A speaker, I recognized, as a faint melody reached my ears beneath the voices and the clinking of dishes. It had a small MP3 player mounted in it. The song was one I vaguely remembered as being on the radio a lot a few years ago, a dance-pop one-hit wonder.

"One of our younger members brought the player," Hilary said. "The speaker was already here. I can't say the music is to my taste, but it's all we have. We decided it was enough of a morale boost to outweigh the electricity usage. Would you like to sit near it?"

"No," Leo said, shaking himself as if coming out of a daze. "That—that's okay." But as we walked across the room, I caught him swaying slightly with the beat.

He used to live on music. It must have been weeks, maybe months, since he'd heard any. I had the urge to grab his hand and squeeze it.

Then Tessa did exactly that. My throat tightened and I looked away.

Hilary stopped at a table where a woman who looked to be in

her thirties was sitting. "I thought you would like to speak with Lauren," she said, nodding to me and then to the woman. "She and her husband, Kenneth, are the couple from Ottawa I told you about. Justin and I will get your oatmeal while you talk. You were there until December, isn't that right, Lauren?"

The woman nodded, pushing her hair back behind her ears. Her face was drawn, her eyes deep-set, giving her an almost skeletal appearance. "For all the good it did us," she said.

Excitement sparked inside me, overriding my discomfort. If we got the details from someone who'd actually been living there, maybe we could make up for some of the time we'd lost. "I guess Hilary told you we're heading that way," I said as we sat down. "Where was the government operating from when you left? Should we just go to the parliament buildings to find someone in charge?"

Lauren laughed. "Government? Operating?"

"Well, it's the capital," I said. "There's *someone* still there, isn't there?"

"There were riots at Parliament Hill a couple of weeks before Ken and I left, when the epidemic was getting severe," she said. "Violent riots. People were being turned away from the hospitals, you know—having to camp out in tents in the parking lots and on the sidewalks—people were dying on the street...." She cringed. "The rioters, they broke right in. MPs and senators were shot. The buildings were damaged. After that, all the government officials still left cleared out. I don't know where they went. Maybe Toronto? Maybe they all had their own little hideaways like we do. Even the soldiers who'd been protecting the place vanished."

My heart plummeted. "But..."

She looked around the table at us, her eyes darkening. "I can see you had your hopes up, and I'm sorry. But Ken used to work near Parliament Hill, and he saw them packing up out front and driving off. I can tell you for sure, there's no one trying to help the rest of us in Ottawa—not anymore."

# TWELVE

Lauren's words sent me into a tailspin. No one with authority left in Ottawa? Even the highest level of government had fled?

Then we'd come all this way for nothing.

I was so hungry my stomach was practically gnawing on itself, but even so, I had to force down the porridge Hilary brought. As soon as I'd finished, I went to the quarantine cabin to tell Gav and Tobias what we'd learned. Gav nodded as I repeated Lauren's account, as if he wasn't at all surprised. Which maybe he wasn't. One of the first things he had ever said to me was that we couldn't trust the people in power to look out for us, that they were always going to look out for themselves first.

"Come here," he said when I was done, holding out his hand, and Tobias turned the other way, looking awkward. I sank down into Gav's lap and let him wrap his arms around me. Tears welled up in my eyes. I blinked them back as well as I could. I was the one who'd dragged us out here. I couldn't break down now.

"I'm so sorry, Kae," Gav said, hugging me close. "At least we know now, before we went any farther."

"Yeah," I murmured. And we'd found out in a place with power and heat and food, and space enough for us to stay as long as we needed to. Hilary had suggested as much over breakfast. But none of that took away the ache in my chest.

When I'd pulled myself together, I found Tessa and Meredith in the greenhouse with Hilary. It was hard to tell they were actually growing any plants on purpose, with all the boards lying around and the weeds sprouting between the actual crops. "We're not harvesting as much as we could otherwise," Hilary said, "but it's safer to leave it looking as uncultivated as possible."

We walked from board to board to keep from leaving footprints. Meredith swayed, arms out, as if they were a series of balance beams, while Tessa ambled between the plots, asking questions like "Have you tried spacing onions between the carrots?" and "What do you have for fertilizer?" Hilary just about jumped for joy when Tessa said they could get lettuce seeds to sprout if they just put them in a spot with more shade.

When we went back to the gathering house for lunch, Leo was still there, sitting with his eyes closed as the music washed over him, looking more relaxed than I'd seen him since we'd left the island.

The decision should have been easy. If there was no point in going to Ottawa, of course we'd stay in the colony, at least until the weather warmed up and we had a better chance of making it back to the island alive. But when I lay down next to Meredith in the empty cabin Hilary had offered us for the night, the ache inside me had only gotten bigger.

The greenhouse was wonderful, but it wasn't completely supporting the twenty or so people living in the colony. The oatmeal, the crackers with our soup, the pasta at dinner—those had been scavenged. What were they going to do when all the houses in the area were bare? When the oil for their generator ran out?

Hilary acted like they were going to get by like this forever—like they could live here in a bubble, untouched by the rest of the world. But life didn't work that way. Every group of living things was part of an ecosystem. Every group had to deal with predators and competitors, with the demands of the environment. Maybe the colony could keep this up for another few months. Maybe another year. But sooner or later, no matter how many precautions they took, the rest of the world was going to come crashing in. Like a helicopter dropping missiles on an unsuspecting island.

Were they really okay living like this, as if a few months ago they hadn't had real houses and jobs and *lives*?

Dad and Nell and the volunteers at the hospital had kept working even when the halls were overflowing and we had no support from the mainland at all. Surely there were other people out here who hadn't given up? What if the only thing standing between fixing the world and its staying like this was my continuing to carry the vaccine until I found those people?

But as I closed my eyes, another question followed me into sleep.

What if I kept going and we didn't make it, and everyone who'd come with me died because of the choices I made?

The next morning, we all gathered in the quarantine cabin. Leo sat on the mattress, Tessa beside him. Tobias was standing by the small window, and Gav leaned against the wall, his elbow propped on the cold-storage box. I sank down next to him while Meredith hopped onto the bed.

"I think it's pretty clear there's no point in going to Ottawa," I said. "If the situation was as bad as Lauren says it was more than a month ago, it'll only have gotten worse. So we need to decide what we *are* going to do."

Tessa nodded. "I think Hilary and the others would like to know where we stand. Whether we want to stay."

"So." I looked at my hands, and then around at the others, trying to gauge their reactions. "That's one option. Staying, at least until the weather's better for traveling. They have room. And we could keep trying to contact someone through the radio."

Tobias stepped away from the window. "So we just throw in the towel?" he said.

"I—" I said, caught off guard by the vehemence in his voice. He didn't let me continue.

"The chances we're going to catch the right person on that radio at the time they happen to be on, this far in the middle of nowhere, are pretty much none," he went on. "People need that vaccine *now*, don't they? That's why you left your island in the first place. Just because one city is a no-go doesn't mean they all are."

"What's it to you?" Gav said. "A week ago you didn't even know there was a vaccine. All you wanted to do was hide on your little army base and wait for the rest of the world to pick up the pieces for you."

Tobias flushed. "Okay, that's true," he said. "And I sure didn't plan on joining up with a bunch of teenagers. But for once in my life I know I'm doing something important. I want to keep doing that—don't you?"

He sounded so determined that I felt ashamed for considering giving up. But he was here on his own, and I had my friends and Meredith to consider too.

Of course, if he wanted to keep going, maybe I didn't need to drag all of them along. Maybe I could do what I needed to without risking their lives in the process.

"You didn't let me finish," I said, sitting up straighter. "I said that was one option. The other is to keep going. I've been thinking. . . . Lauren said the government might have moved to Toronto. It's the biggest city in the country. That means the most hospitals, the most doctors—the most police to keep the peace. And if we can find a car, it's only about five hours farther than Ottawa."

There was a pause, and then Leo said, "Sounds worth a shot."

"Toronto," Gav said, with a weariness in his voice that spoke of the hundreds of miles we had left to travel. Before I could say anything, Tessa broke in.

"I'm not going."

Leo's gaze jerked toward her. "What?"

"I'm staying here," she said steadily. "If I keep going with all of you, I'm just another mouth to find food for. Here, I can help. The colony needs someone who knows about farming, if they're going to make it."

"Why didn't you say something before?" he said.

"I decided right before we all came over here," she said. "It doesn't really change anything for the rest of you, does it?"

Hurt flashed across Leo's face. "Can we talk for a minute?" he said, standing. "Just you and me?"

"I know the vaccine's more important to you than what the colony's doing," Tessa said. "That's fine."

"Can we just—" He gestured toward the door. Tessa hesitated, then got up and followed him out. Meredith frowned.

"I don't think we should be fighting," she said. "We're the good guys."

Just a second ago, I'd been thinking about leaving everyone behind. But now that the possibility was real, it made my stomach churn. I should have seen Tessa's decision coming. From the second she'd spotted the greenhouse in the distance, I should have known.

Gav shrugged. "It's her choice whether she comes or stays, isn't it?"

I looked at him, hard.

"You don't really want to come, either."

He opened his mouth and then closed it again. "I don't want to stay *here*," he said, and then tapped the top of the cold box. "And I know how important these are. But I get how Tessa feels. This whole trip, I've pretty much been extra baggage. I don't know where to find a car. I don't know how to get us to Toronto or anywhere else. That doesn't matter, though. Whatever the plan is, I'm part of it. You're not doing it on your own."

"Gav," I said, "I wouldn't be—"

He touched my cheek before I could finish. "I told you before, and I'll keep telling you: I'm not leaving you," he said softly, and kissed me. His fingers grazed my skin, and his lips were warm and steady against mine. Then Tobias cleared his throat and Meredith giggled. I eased back, blushing.

"You should probably go see if those two have worked out who's staying and who's not," Gav said with a smile. "Then come back and tell us when we're leaving."

"We can make it there," I said as I stood up. "We're going to find a way."

"Of course we are," Gav said.

Meredith trailed after me out of the cabin. Leo was standing by the nearest cluster of trees, his face tucked into his scarf and his arms tight at his sides. Alone.

"Mere," I said, "can you go back to the cabin and see if we left anything—hats or mittens or whatever?"

"But I want to know what happened with Tessa," she said.

I raised my eyebrows at her. "Mere. We'll talk about it later, okay?"

She let out a huff of breath, cloudy in the cold air, and skidded off across the icy clearing.

I walked over to Leo, stopping a few feet from where he stood. He didn't look up, but he had to know I was there.

After a minute, he raised his head enough to uncover his mouth.

"She didn't think it mattered," he said. "I think she was honestly surprised I was upset. She said of course it didn't make sense for us to stay together if we need to do different things. She said hardly anyone does stay together when they're sixteen, anyway. Why would we expect it to be forever?" He laughed, haltingly. "I wasn't expecting forever. I was expecting maybe she'd at least talk to me before making a decision like this."

"I don't think Tessa's very good at that," I said. "Giving people a chance to disagree, when she's already decided what she's going to do."

"Yeah," he said. His mouth twisted. "I know you might think this isn't true, but I care about her. A lot. If that's more than she cares about me, well . . . Oh, well. She's got to do what's right for her."

"Still hurts, though," I said, and saying it I realized I was hurt too. I'd seen Tessa as a friend. We'd been through an awful lot together the last few months. But she hadn't said anything to me either, even though she'd probably been considering staying since she first asked Hilary about the greenhouse.

I wasn't sure I would have tried to sway her decision. Probably not. Which was probably why she hadn't bothered bringing it up. Life always looked so straightforward to her. It must have been nice.

"You know," I said, "you could stay with her. The vaccine—it's my thing, I know that. I don't want you to come if you'd rather be here."

He paused, his brown eyes so dark they looked almost black.

"You don't want me to come if I'd rather be here," he said, "or you don't want me to come, period?"

My throat tightened. "Leo . . ." I started, but I didn't know what to say.

"I don't want our lives to stay like this," he said. "I don't know if this vaccine is going to make a difference, but it could. It's the best chance we've got. I want to fight for that. But if I've messed everything up so badly that you don't feel right even having me around, then I'll hang back, out of your way. You just have to tell me."

There was a certainty in his voice that I hadn't realized I needed to hear. He didn't sound beaten or scared. He sounded like himself. And that was enough for a little light to open up inside me, like hope.

"Everything's weird with us now," I said. "But I don't want it to be. Maybe it sounds stupid, but I just want to have my best friend again."

The corner of his mouth tipped up. "Okay," he said. "Watch." He smoothed his fingertips over my forehead, so swiftly I hardly had time to feel them, and did the same to himself. Then he flung out his hand toward the trees, as if throwing something away as far as he could.

"There," he said. "All the weirdness, gone. Nothing left but plain old friends, like we're supposed to be."

It had only been a gesture, but right then, I felt released. As if he'd scooped out all the awkward and unpleasant feelings with that sweep of his hand and tossed them away. I grinned.

"Work that magic to find us a car, and we'll really be getting somewhere," I said.

I was about to ask him if he wanted more time, maybe to talk to Tessa again, when Justin came running through the open end of the clearing. He stopped when he saw us, panting.

"Take shelter!" he said. "Van stopped about a half a mile down the road from here, three people got out and headed this way. They don't look friendly. One of 'em had a rifle."

I stiffened. "What color was it? The van."

Justin looked at me as if I'd asked whether the gun was pretty. "It's green. Go! Under the beds in the cabins—you can pull out the siding and hide underneath. I've got to tell them to shut off the generator."

A green van. As Justin scrambled toward the gathering house, I went cold from the inside out.

"Meredith," I said, and ran across the field as fast as the ice allowed.

# THIRTEEN

I burst into the cabin, the rush of the door fluttering the sheet on the bed. Meredith wasn't there. "Mere—" I called, and caught myself. What if the people from the van were close enough to hear?

Something was scraping over the ice outside. I hurried out, swaying as I dashed around the side of the cabin.

Meredith was pushing herself back and forth on the ice behind it. She squealed as she slid into me, and I folded my arms around her, the relief that washed over me almost as cold as my panic.

"We didn't leave anything," she said. "Is Leo okay?"

"He's fine," I said. "Come here, fast."

I dragged her back into the cabin. Bending down, I pressed my hands against the side of the bed, feeling until my fingers caught onto a notch I could grip. The wooden panel popped out. The space underneath couldn't have been more than two feet high, but there was enough room for both of us to squeeze in even with our coats on.

"Get in," I said to Meredith. "We have to hide. Someone's coming."

It was almost sad how quickly her attitude changed from playfulness to obedience—she crouched by the bed without stopping to ask who was coming or why. I pulled the blanket and sheets off the mattress. If the idea was to make the place look uninhabited, it'd be better to hide those too. Then I squirmed under the bed after Meredith. The panel slid back into place with a tug.

Less than a minute later, footsteps pounded by outside. The door swung open. I tensed. The people from the van couldn't have crossed half a mile already, could they? A chill slipped around the cracks in the bedframe, and I understood. Someone was letting the air out of the cabins so no one would be able to tell they'd been heated. So the whole colony would look deserted.

All that bravado Justin had given us the other day, about how he'd have shot us if we'd looked dangerous, that had been for show, I realized. Of course they wouldn't go around killing intruders on sight. If nothing else, the sound of their gunshots would have told people for miles around someone was here.

Meredith wrapped her arms around me, her breath sounding ragged in the narrow space. I hugged her close. I didn't know if Tessa and Leo and everyone else had made it into hiding in time. Would someone have thought to go to the quarantine cabin and tell Gav and Tobias what to do? Gav would remember to hide the cold box, wouldn't he? Would that be enough to protect us?

Hilary had suggested they'd managed to make raiders dismiss the colony in the past, but these people were looking for more than just food. They were still after us, the woman with the red hat and whoever was with her. Maybe someone had seen us in the town where that sick couple had approached us, and passed word on. Maybe they were just checking every group of buildings between that first town and Ottawa.

Either way, they clearly had no intention of stopping before they found us.

I started to sweat inside my layers of clothing, but I didn't dare move. Meredith curled her fingers into my coat. Outside, there was only silence.

Then a voice rang out in the yard.

"What's with all the goddamned ice?"

"Who knows?" a woman replied. "Check the buildings, look for signs that someone's camped here. You find anyone, haul them out. We can hurt 'em, just don't kill anyone yet."

*Yet.* The word echoed in my ears. I bit my lip as the cabin door squeaked. Feet clomped inside. Meredith clutched at me, and I squeezed her back.

The thin beams of sunlight around the edges of the panel shifted as the intruder walked from one end of the cabin to the other. The desk drawer rasped open and shut. The chair toppled over with a clatter that made Meredith flinch. The footsteps approached the bed, and I cringed at the sudden thump over our heads. Checking under the mattress, I thought, my eyelids tightly shut. That was all.

The intruder shifted, and kicked at the side of the bed. My eyes popped open in time to see the panel tilt, just slightly, the sliver of light widening. My heart stopped. *Don't notice,* I prayed. *Don't notice. Don't notice.*

There was a moment of silence, and then the intruder stomped out again. I exhaled in a rush, my lungs burning, and hugged Meredith tighter. She whimpered into my coat.

More doors creaked outside. There was a scritching sound, a smack, and a groan, and I suspected someone had just fallen on the ice. Despite myself, I smiled.

"The place is dead," someone said.

"Let's get going before we waste any more time, then," the woman's voice replied.

The footsteps faded away. I counted to a hundred, then a hundred again, and there wasn't another sound.

"Are they gone?" Meredith whispered in my ear. I nodded against her, but inside I felt sick.

They were gone for now, not for good. And I didn't want to find out what they'd do if they finally caught us.

After Hilary called in to us that it was safe again and we crawled out from under the bed, I sat Meredith down on the mattress. She stared up at me with still-frightened eyes. Of all the choices I'd had to make since the epidemic started, this was one of the easiest, but that didn't make seeing it through less hard. I swallowed and said, "What would you think if I said you could stay here?"

"What about the vaccine?" Meredith said. "If we stay, no one will get to use it."

"Not *we*," I said. "Just you. And Tessa. I'll have to talk to her, but I think she'll be okay with keeping an eye on you while I'm gone. It's pretty safe here, right? You'll have lots of food and somewhere warm to sleep. And when I find someone who can work with the vaccine, I'll come right back and get you. Okay?"

Her chin wobbled. "You don't want me to come?"

"Mere." I knelt down in front of her. "I don't like leaving you. But the people who came today are going to keep looking for us. You remember how mean the gang on the island was? Leo says these people could be even worse."

"What if they hurt you?"

"We'll be careful," I said. "Tobias is a soldier, remember? He knows how to protect people. But it's easier when there aren't so many of us to protect."

"I could look after myself!" she said. "I'm a lot more brave now than I used to be." And then she burst into tears.

"Mere," I said, pulling her into my arms. For a second, I doubted my decision. "Hey, hey, it'll be okay."

"I'm trying to be brave," she said between gulps, "and strong, so I can help, but I'm scared, Kaelyn. I'm scared something bad will happen to you."

A lump rose in my throat, and my own eyes prickled with tears. "You are brave, and strong," I said. "Even strong, brave people get scared. It'll be easier for me to look after myself if I know you're somewhere safe, I promise. Waiting for me and doing your best not to worry means being brave too. Do you think you can do that?"

She choked back a sob, and then nodded. "I like it here," she said. "But you'll come back soon, right?"

"Fast as I can," I said.


Tessa didn't even hesitate when I asked her about Meredith. "Of course," she said. "I'll get her to help me in here, keep her busy."

She beamed at me as she crouched over a bed of seedlings in the greenhouse. Her knees and fingers were smudged with soil, and she looked totally at home. I couldn't be angry at her for wanting that, but I felt like I had to say something.

"Seems strange," I said. "Going off without you. We've stuck it out together for so long."

"You're not leaving me here," Tessa pointed out. "I'm choosing to stay behind. Like I would have stayed on the island with Meredith, if it wasn't for the bombing."

I'd almost forgotten the original plan. It had started to feel so normal for all of us to be traveling together. But this wasn't quite the same. She was planning on staying here as long as they needed her, I could tell. And when I came back, I'd only stop in long enough to pick up Meredith. We were parting ways permanently.

The weight of all the things she didn't know sank into my gut: my jealousy toward her when I'd still been pining over Leo, the kiss in the garage, the tension between him and me that we'd only just resolved.

"I want you to know I never thought you were just an extra mouth, okay?" I said. "I was glad to have you there."

"I'm glad I was there too," she said. "Deciding to stay here—it's really only about me, Kaelyn. Since we lost the greenhouse on the island, and then my parents didn't make it back when Leo did, I've felt . . . lost, I guess. I hardly wanted to move. And then we got here, and it's the first time I've really had the urge to dive in, to get to work, in so long. I can't let that go. I know you understand—it's like the vaccine for you."

It felt so strange, being choked up and wanting to smile at the same time. But I did smile. "Yeah," I said. "I get that."

We didn't hug, because we never did, but I reached out, and she took my hand and gripped it just for a moment.

With the people from the van possibly still in the area, it didn't seem safe to leave right away. So when Hilary invited us to stay until the next morning, I thanked her. But I hardly slept.

I'd told Meredith I'd be back soon, but that might not be true. This night could be the last time I spent with her, if the woman in the red hat caught up with us, if a blizzard took us unawares too far from shelter, if we ran out of food before we found a working car.

So many ifs. So many of them awful.

But if I was leaving for all the people who needed the vaccine, then I was leaving for Meredith too. Without a way to fight the virus, the world would stay like this forever. Probably it would get even worse. How could we rebuild if every time people came together they had to worry about getting infected? By going, I was trying to protect her not just now, but for her whole life. As scared as I was, I wanted to be that strong, brave person she saw when she looked at me. So I would be that person, for as long as I needed to be.

That thought settled over me like a sort of calm, and I finally drifted off.

We ate an early breakfast of stale Cheerios and powdered milk— Leo, Tessa, Meredith, and I—alone in the dining room. I hugged Meredith and kissed her on the cheek. After we said our good-byes, Hilary walked with me and Leo to the quarantine cabin, carrying a tray with cereal for Gav and Tobias. No one else had come to see us off—not even Justin. I wondered if he was on watch again.

Gav was sitting on the bed, coat zipped and hood up, like he was ready to head off that very second. But he pulled off his gloves to accept the bowl. I knew him well enough to recognize the tension in his shoulders, the slight stiffness in his expression that betrayed his apprehension. Guilt curdled in my stomach. It was my fault he was starting to feel trapped, useless. He'd come all this way for me, and I didn't know how to make the journey easier for him. All I knew how to do was keep going.

Tobias was fiddling with the radio transceiver on the floor. He'd asked me to bring it in from the sled for him yesterday so he could give it another shot.

"Anything?" I asked him.

He shook his head. "Just a lot of static."

Hilary hovered while they gulped down the cereal, then collected the dishes. She paused in the doorway.

"I wish we could offer you some food for the road," she said. "I'm afraid we're just not at the point where we can safely spare any. But you'll always be welcome back. Just, please, don't mention to anyone that we're here. And take care!"

Gav stood up, stretching, after the door closed behind her. "I have the feeling they're just glad to get rid of us," he said.

Leo shrugged. "They didn't have to help us at all."

I swapped the ice packs in the cold box for the ones I'd left outside overnight to refreeze. Tobias wrapped the radio in its plastic casing, and we stepped into the forest where our sleds had been stashed.

"There's only five," Tobias said.

"The blizzard," I said. "Tessa fell and lost hers between here and the freeway. What did she have?"

He studied our supplies. "The second box of rations, the one that was full," he said. "Nothing else important that I can tell."

"We might as well look for it while we're heading that way," Gav said. "But I don't think we should hang around too long."

We shifted our supplies so we could fit the blankets and empty gasoline jugs from Meredith's sled onto the other four. Then we set off toward the freeway. As we pulled out into the field we'd crossed in the blizzard, I scanned the drifts for any sign of Tessa's sled. A lot of snow had come down that night. It was fluffy, puffing out as I pushed through it, but it would have buried anything on the ground.

When we came to the thin stretch of trees that bordered the

freeway, I hesitated. I could see the deep tracks the van's wheels had cut through the snowy road. We could spend all day searching the field and maybe still find nothing, or we could spend it putting more distance between us and the people with the rifle.

"I'm not sure exactly where we are," I said, checking the map book. "But as long as we're near the freeway, I can figure it out as soon as we get to another town."

"Let's keep moving, then," Gav said.

We marched along in silence, the sky brightening as the sun rose over the tops of the hills to our right. The sleds whispered over the loose snow. Every now and then one of us would hold up a hand and we'd all stop, listening. But we didn't hear a single engine. A flock of chickadees chattered at us from the branches of a juniper tree. Occasionally, the wind rose enough to rattle the bare twigs. Otherwise, the only noise was our feet.

Gav and Leo started discussing the possibility of using the snares when we stopped for the night, and Tobias asked me a few questions about Dad's work. The memories didn't sting quite as much as they used to. We paused at the crest of a slope, the rooftops of a small town visible up ahead, and pushed the sleds down before following.

I went first. About halfway down, my feet caught on a slick patch beneath the snow and whipped out from under me. I fell on my butt, sliding the rest of the way to the bottom.

"You okay?" Gav called. An instant later, he yelped and whooshed down beside me. As I got up, wincing and brushing the snow off my jeans, Leo skidded down sideways as if on an invisible snowboard.

"Dancer's reflexes," I said, pointing at him. "That's cheating."

A mischievous glint I hadn't seen in ages lit up in his eyes. "No," he said, "it'd be cheating if I did this." He scooped up a handful of snow, gave it a quick squeeze, and tossed the hasty snowball my way. It hit me square in the chest.

"All right," Gav said, scrambling to his feet. "This is war."

"Come on, Tobias," I said. He was still standing at the top of the slope, glancing back the way we'd come. "We need the soldier on our side."

"Three against one?" Leo protested, and Gav and I both pelted him with snow.

"You started it!" I said.

Tobias didn't move. His forehead had knit. As Leo balled up another handful of snow, I wavered. "Tobias?"

He turned and said evenly, "There's someone following us."

# FOURTEEN

We all went still the second Tobias spoke. "The van?" I said.

Tobias shook his head. "No. One person, on foot."

He unsnapped a couple of the buttons partway down his coat, sliding his hand inside as he watched. I braced my foot against a solid chunk of snow and craned my neck, trying to see over the top of the slope. Then Tobias relaxed.

"It's the kid," he said.

We scrambled back up. A figure in a black coat was trudging along the path we'd trampled, his face turned toward us, dragging behind him the sled that had been Meredith's. His orange hat was a blaze of color amid the snow.

"Justin," I said. "What's he doing?"

When he saw us all staring, Justin waved and trudged faster. He ran the last short distance to the edge of the slope, his breath coming in huffs.

"You walk faster than I thought you would," he said.

"Is something wrong?" I said. Meredith, or Tessa—

"Everything's good," Justin said. "I'm coming with you. Wherever you're going now."

For a second we all just eyed one another.

"You didn't think your mom would let you come," Leo said,

breaking the silence. "So you snuck off instead of talking to us about it up front. Yeah?"

Justin flushed. "She doesn't get it," he said. "I'm tired of . . . of hiding all the time while pricks like those guys in the van walk in, looking to take our stuff, to mess with us. It's stupid. I don't want to sit around and pick beans and cook oatmeal and pretend it's okay. It isn't. It sucks. I want to *do* something, like you."

"But your mom must be freaking out," I said.

"She'll know where I am," Justin said obstinately. "I left a note."

Which might have helped a little more if *we* knew where we were going to be, between here and Toronto. Or if we were even going to get there.

"How old are you, anyway?" Tobias asked.

"Fifteen," Justin said, and paused. "Next month."

I winced, but Gav was studying him. "That's not *that* much younger than us," he said.

"There's a pretty big difference between sixteen or seventeen and fourteen," Leo said. "And that's not the point. The point is he didn't talk to anyone, he just took off." He glanced at Justin. "If you'd talked to us first, I might feel okay about it. But not like this. Do you have any idea what this is going to do to your mom, how much she's going to worry about you?"

"You don't think he should get a few points for determination?" Gav said. "He's here now. It's not like we can make him go home, unless you want to haul him all the way back. We might as well keep going and give him a chance."

"You want to be responsible for him?" Tobias put in.

"I can take care of myself," Justin protested. "Who's in charge here? Just tell me what I've got to do to prove it, and I will."

Leo and Tobias both looked at me, as if it was my decision. Why should it be up to me? There were four of us.

"We all have to agree," I said. "It involves all of us."

"So what do you think, Kae?" Gav said.

I hesitated. Hilary had trusted us enough to take us in, feed us, and shelter us. She'd accepted Tessa and Meredith into the colony. I didn't like the idea of repaying her by helping her son run away. Fourteen . . . fourteen was young. Three years ago, I couldn't have imagined going on a road trip without my parents, let alone walking across the country in the middle of winter.

But then, I couldn't have imagined that walk six months ago, either. The virus had changed all of our lives. Maybe, these days, fourteen wasn't so young after all.

"Are you really okay with what you're putting your mom through?" I asked. "We don't know how long it'll be before we can come back. We don't know if we'll be able to make it back at all."

For a second, Justin looked like a scared kid, even younger than the almost-fifteen he claimed to be. Then his mouth tightened. "Yeah," he said. "I got it. Anything happens to me, it's on my shoulders, not yours. It's my life."

It wasn't, though. What he did affected all of us, as long as he was with us. But Gav was right. We didn't have any way of stopping him from following, not unless we gave up a whole day of traveling to take him back. And even then, who was to say he wouldn't come running after us again?

"Fine," I said.

Tobias shrugged. "As long as he carries his own weight."

Leo was frowning. I caught myself hoping he was going to come up with some reasoning so perfect it would convince Justin this wasn't a good idea. But he just sighed and said, "All right. I don't like it, but I can live with it if you can."

We moved some of the supplies back onto the fifth sled and set off across the snow. As Justin hurried to join Gav in the lead, an uneasy feeling welled up inside me.

One more person's life was on the line because of me and Dad's unproven vaccine.


My uneasiness over Justin's arrival faded a bit when he pulled five pears out of the bag he'd brought with him. "Right off the tree," he said, handing them out as we walked.

I raised the pear to my face and smelled it. Saliva filled my mouth. When was the last time I'd eaten fruit that wasn't from a can or a jar? I couldn't even remember.

I allowed myself one big bite, unable to hold in a hum of pleasure as the tart juice slid down my throat, and ate the rest in nibbles so it lasted.

The taste lingered in my mouth long after I'd finished, as we passed through another town that didn't offer any viable cars. Tobias spotted a transport truck on the freeway in the late afternoon, so we veered over to take a look, but there was no sign of the keys. As evening fell, we found ourselves in a particularly long stretch of forest. I was starting to worry that we'd be camping outside that night when we came across a mobile home in a wide clearing.

The aluminum door was swinging open, whining softly in the breeze, but the owners had built a deck out front with an awning that had kept the snow from getting inside. Squeezing onto the benches in the cramped dining room, we warmed canned stew and peas over the camping stove. With the door closed, the thin heat that rose off the burning kerosene took the edge off the chilly air. After we'd gulped down our meal, Tobias got out the radio.

"You ever hear anyone on that?" Justin asked.

Tobias shook his head. "It can't hurt to try, though," he said. "It's not like I've got much else to do. I'd better take it outside—don't think it'll like the metal walls."

He slipped out, and I heard him set the transceiver down on the deck's patio table. A moment later, his voice filtered through the door, using the name of the freeway to identify us. "This is Route 2 New Brunswick. Can anyone hear me? Over."

There was no reply. Tobias paused and then repeated his message. Gav poured a little water into a pot full of snow, and Leo set it over the stove. I padded down the narrow hall to check the bedroom. It held a double bed with a twin bunk on top. We'd manage. At least we had walls around us.

I was just heading for the door to get the sleeping bags when a sharp female voice crackled on the other side.

"We hear you, Route 2 New Brunswick. Over."

I started, hitting my elbow against a cabinet, and Gav stood up. As one, the four of us inside rushed onto the deck.

Tobias was staring at the radio. Justin shuffled around him. "So say something!" he hissed, and then reached for the mic. Tobias jerked it away from him.

"This is Route 2," he said, his hand shaking. "Who is this? Over."

"Group of concerned citizens, trying to look out for each other," the voice replied. It was tinny and laced with a low buzz of static, but clear enough that I could make out every word. "Where are you calling from? Do you need help? Over."

"Ask them what kind of people they have in their group," I said, dropping into the chair beside Tobias. He repeated my question into the mic.

"All sorts," came the response. "We make no judgments. There are a few doctors here, if you're needing medical intervention. Over."

The right kind of doctor would know how to formulate more of the vaccine. "How close do you think they are?" I asked Tobias, my heart thudding.

"I don't know," Tobias said. "This is the best radio we had on the base—on a clear day we could get signals from overseas. Depends on how good their transmitter is."

Gav rested his hands on my shoulders. "Who cares how close they are? They're *there*."

"If we can trust them," Leo said. "We don't know anything about them. The people in the van—they had radios, didn't they?"

"Two-ways," Tobias said. "With those things you're lucky if you get a couple miles of reception. There's not much chance they'd be close enough and happen to be listening right when I broadcasted."

"It doesn't sound like the woman who was in the van," I added. Her voice—*Don't kill anyone yet*—echoed in my head, low and flat, without any of the nasal sharpness of the woman on the radio. "But we don't know if they can help us yet."

Even if they didn't have anyone with them who'd know how to replicate the vaccine, could we hope they might know where to find someone who could? Or lend us a vehicle so we could keep looking?

Static fizzled, and a man's voice cut in. "Still there, Route 2? Over."

"We're here. Over," Tobias said.

"What is it you're looking for?" the voice asked calmly. "If there's something you need, we may be able to help. Over."

He sounded so reassuring that I started to relax. Maybe the walking and the worries about the cold and food and the people in the van could be over now. Maybe I'd get to go back for Meredith as soon as tomorrow.

"Tell him we're looking for a scientist or doctor who's working on . . . a cure for the virus," I said. "I don't want to say exactly what we have until we've gotten a chance to talk with them face-to-face."

Tobias relayed the message.

"I can't say we have the friendly flu licked yet," the voice replied. "But we have people here trying. Where are you located? We can give you directions to us, or we may be able to send someone to pick you up. Over."

I looked around at the others. "What do you think?"

"I don't see any reason to think they're lying," Gav said. "This is what we've been looking for, isn't it? Why wouldn't we go check them out?"

"We still don't know who they actually are," Leo said. "Even if they're not the ones who've been following us . . ."

Justin scratched his head. "They sound all right to me."

"They don't even know we have anything useful," I said. "They probably figure we're asking about doctors because someone here's sick, and they're still offering to let us come to them. Why would they bother unless they really want to help?"

"I don't know," Leo said. "Why are they randomly scanning the radio in the first place?"

"What's the point in being out here if we're not going to trust anyone we manage to get in contact with?" Gav said, throwing up his hands. "Hell, if we're not going to believe anyone, we should have stayed on the island and tried to manufacture the vaccine ourselves!"

There was a moment of silence, and Leo lowered his head. "You're right," he said. "I'm being paranoid. But I still think we should go cautiously."

"We will," I said, and turned to Tobias. "Tell them the name of that town we passed—that was, what, about four miles back? If they can come to us, that'll be easier."

"We should be able to manage that," the voice said after Tobias gave the directions. "Give us an hour or so. You hang tight. Over and out."

Tobias set down the mic, but when he reached to turn off the radio, I said, "Let's leave it on for now. What if they need more information?"

I glanced over at the sleds we'd pulled out of view behind the trailer. We weren't going to be able to take all our supplies with us—I doubted they would fit in whatever vehicle they sent. Maybe we'd be able to come back for them later?

A shiver of excitement raced through me. "We did it," I said aloud, needing to hear the words to make it completely real. "We found someone."

"*You* did it," Gav said. He wrapped his arms around me, kissing a spot behind my ear.

"It was Tobias who actually made contact," I pointed out.

"I wouldn't have had any reason to contact them if it wasn't for those," Tobias said, tipping his head toward the cold box.

I set my hands on it. "Maybe we should hide them until we're totally sure these people are legit," I said. "We'll meet their doctors, I'll ask them some questions, then we'll decide what to do."

Nothing about this was certain, after all. Even if these people were friendly, it could be another dead end. But at the very least, they seemed willing to try to help. Maybe I could finally hand off this responsibility to someone who actually knew what to do with it.

"If that's what you think we've got to do," Gav said.

"Yeah," I said, picking up the box, but I couldn't help grinning.

"I guess after this you're all going home," Justin said, sounding dejected.

Leo gave his shoulder a light shove. "If you'd been through everything we have, you'd be happy about it."

"For all we know, we might still—" I started, and a voice leapt from the radio speaker.

"Hello?"

I spun around as Tobias snatched up the mic. "Route 2 still here. Over."

"Good. Good." A rushed breath hissed through the speaker. "I need to ask you something that might sound kind of strange. Do you have a vaccine?"

It wasn't either of the people we'd spoken to earlier, the woman or the man. The voice sounded like a younger man's, or an older boy's. His words hit me like a slap, but I stepped forward, feeling there was something important in them that I was missing.

"What vaccine?" Tobias said, raising his eyebrows at me. "Over."

"Look," the new voice said, "whether you do or not, they think you're the ones who have it. The people they sent to pick you up, it's the vaccine they'll want. I don't know if they'll believe you if you say you don't have it. They're going to expect you to just hand it over. And they're going to hurt you if you don't."

My heart thumped, painfully hard. "Who *is* this?" Tobias asked.

"It doesn't matter," the voice said. "It is you, isn't it? Look, these aren't people you want having the vaccine. The best I can tell you is to head east. There's an island down by the south end of Nova Scotia—people there were still working on the virus—my dad—"

With those words, recognition clicked in me. Before I even knew I was going to move, I'd yanked the mic from Tobias's hand.

"Drew?" I said

There was a pause. "How do you know my name?"

I laughed, tears springing to my eyes. "Drew, it's Kaelyn. The vaccine, it's Dad's. But he—there wasn't anyone left who could make more, that's why we brought it out here. Where are you?"

"Kaelyn? But you—you were sick. I thought you must have— shit. She's coming back. Kae, get out of there. Wherever you told them to find you, leave. Please. I'll try—I'll try to get back on another day, around this time. Please just—crap."

The static fizzled and faded away into a faint hum that said nothing at all.

# FIFTEEN

For a few seconds, we stood there frozen, but Drew's voice didn't return.

"You know him?" Tobias asked me.

"He's my brother," I said. "He left the island a few months ago. I didn't even know if he was alive."

And he'd thought I was dead. But we were both alive and I'd found him. He could be so close. If only I'd been able to talk to him longer—Leo's voice, low and urgent, broke through my shock. "He said we have to leave. Whoever's coming, they could be halfway here by now. Where can we go?"

"I don't get it," I said. "How would Drew even know about the vaccine? Who *are* these people?"

Gav had gone to the side of the deck. On the other side of the clearing, about a hundred feet away, the open ground gave way to pine forest.

"I'd sooner trust a guy from the island than a bunch of people we never talked to before tonight," he said. "The forest looks pretty thick—we could take off through there."

I peered over the railing, and my stomach dropped. "The snow," I said. "Look at the mess we've already made around the trailer. If we take off for the trees—for anywhere—our footprints are going to be like a neon sign pointing our way."

"There's snow everywhere!" Justin said.

Tobias walked down the steps and around the home, surveying the landscape.

"There's the fence here," he said. "It looks old, but I'd bet it'll hold a person's weight. We could climb along it as far as the forest—won't leave any tracks that way."

"What about our supplies?" I said. "We can't carry the sleds like that."

"We can push them under the home," Leo said, following Tobias. "There's a gap between the cinder blocks. We'll hide them and come back for them later. That's probably the best we can do. Just... bring the vaccine. They'll take that for sure if they find it. If they don't, if they just find the place looking abandoned, maybe they'll think it's the wrong one."

He sounded doubtful, but he was right. It was the best we could do. I hurried inside to grab the cold box and the bag with Dad's notebooks. Tobias shoved his radio into one of the kitchen cupboards. Then we tramped around the home and studied the fence.

The line of weathered wood ran from near the freeway to some point beyond the trees on the other side of the clearing. It didn't look very sturdy. I turned my head, straining my ears. I hadn't heard a motor yet, and the man on the radio had said they'd be here in an hour. But maybe he'd lied.

"Let's do it one at a time," I said. "So we don't put too much weight on it."

"You should go first, with the vaccine," Leo said.

"You sure you don't want me to carry it, Kae?" Gav asked, offering a hand.

The thought of letting go of the cold box made my chest tighten. "No, I can manage. Can you take the bag?"

He accepted it from me, and I turned to the fence. It shouldn't be that hard. How many branches had I clambered across as a kid, searching for birds' nests and squirrel hollows?

I placed the cold box on the top railing and gripped the wood with my other hand. Bracing one foot against the lower railing, I swung my leg over. I teetered for a second, then steadied myself against the post behind me. So far so good.

Testing my balance, I found I could let go with both hands and hold myself in place with my legs pressed tightly against the sides of the fence. I lifted the cold box, set it down a foot farther along, and shuffled after it. One step at a time.

The first post I came to proved difficult. The cold box started to tip as I hoisted myself over, and my breath rushed out in a gasp. I groped after it, clutching at the fence with all the strength in my legs. For a second, I tipped too.

My leg twisted around the post, shin slamming into the wood, catching me. The cold box jerked to a stop, dangling by its handle from my fingers, just a few inches above the snow. The sudden jolt made my shoulder throb. Gritting my teeth, I yanked the box back onto the fence and scooted forward another foot.

"Kae?" Gav called.

"I'm good," I said. "Getting the hang of it."

My shoulder kept aching as I climbed onward, but I was more careful at the posts now, and the box stayed in place. I scrambled past the first few trees, then hopped off into the snow, swallowing, my throat raw with the cold. Back by the mobile home, Gav was already stepping onto the fence.

The guys came less tentatively, having less to carry and having seen how I'd managed. When Gav was halfway to the trees, Justin followed. The boards creaked but held. As soon as Gav jumped down beside me and hollered back, Leo climbed on. He shuffled along quickly, hardly brushing the top rail with his hands.

Gav handed the bag back to me, and we crouched down amid the underbrush, where we could still make out the mobile home across the clearing. Night had fallen, the snow graying as the stars glinted into sight overhead. Justin paced back and forth behind us.

After he'd done it a few times, I said, "Stay still. You can't be moving around when they show up, or they might hear you."

He made a sound of annoyance, but after a couple seconds he hunched down beside us.

Leo reached us a moment later. "I feel like I'm in a James Bond movie," he said. "It's not as much fun as it looks on the screen." The tension in his voice drained the joke of all humor.

When Tobias had joined us, Justin tugged his hood lower.

"So what do we do now?"

"What do you think?" I asked Tobias. He was the only one here with training in avoiding an enemy. "Should we go farther in?"

He eyed the trees. "I'd figure now that it's dark out, if we just stay still, they won't be able to see us without coming right into the forest. And there's no reason for them to do that, since we didn't leave tracks. I'd rather stay where I can keep an eye on them."

We huddled there, silent, as the indigo of the sky deepened into black. A few wisps of snow drifted down from the branches overhead. Gav folded his hand around mine and squeezed it. And somewhere in the distance, an engine rumbled faintly. In a moment, I heard it again, getting louder.

Tobias reached into his coat and drew out a large black pistol.

Justin whistled softly through his teeth, and Gav elbowed him. Tobias rested the gun on the tops of his knees, the muzzle pointed away from us. I found myself staring at it.

"I'm not going to use it unless I have to," he murmured. "But if I have to..." He glanced at Leo. "You still got the flare gun?"

Leo nodded, his jaw clenched.

We waited. The engine's growl crept steadily nearer. Lights flickered by the freeway. The growl ebbed, and cut out. Car doors slammed.

"Hello?" a woman's voice called out. "We're here about a call on the radio. Picking you up, as promised."

The hinge of the mobile home's door rasped as it opened.

"No one," a man said a moment later. "Maybe this is the wrong place."

"It's a mobile home, a little more than four miles outside town, just like they said it'd be," the woman replied. "And look at the footprints. Someone was here."

They came around the side of the home, the glow of the flashlights on the snow splashing back at them, and my breath caught in my throat. The woman in the lead straightened her red hat over her blond hair, tucked her rifle under her arm, and nudged one of the cinder blocks with the toe of her boot. Two men ambled along beside her.

It was the woman I'd seen in the van.

Of course it was. Drew had said they just wanted the vaccine. How could the people we'd talked to on the radio have known there was a vaccine if they hadn't already heard? These people and the ones we'd talked to, they must all be connected, more organized than I'd ever have guessed. How many of them were there, working together?

And what was Drew doing with them?

"They're around," the woman said. "Must have gotten spooked." She raised her voice. "Hello? Route 2? We're here responding to your radio call."

The flashlights skimmed the clearing. The woman shifted her rifle, and one of the men took out a pistol.

"They going to be armed?" the other asked, so quietly I barely made out the words.

"Paterson didn't think so," the woman said. "But who knows? You remember how to handle this."

*We can hurt 'em, just don't kill anyone yet.*

"But once we've got it?" the first man murmured.

"Yeah," the woman said. I guessed that was the "yet." My fingers clutched the handle of the cold box.

"Hello?" the woman called again. They started into the clearing. She walked straight down the middle, the man with the pistol following the fence and the other edging along the far side of the field. They were all heading our way. I held as still as I could, tucking my chin into my coat collar, my heart pounding. They hadn't stopped to think about footprints. They just knew we'd been here, and there were only so many places we could have gone.

If I hadn't been sure I'd done the right thing, leaving Meredith at the colony, I was now. The woman was halfway across the clearing. In a minute the beam of her flashlight would be grazing the trees.

Then she stopped. She looked up at the forest, then at her companions, scanning the entire area. She was going to turn around,

I thought. She was going to go back, stake out the mobile home, check along the road, I didn't care, as long as they turned and walked away. Please.

"We can't help you if you won't talk with us," she said. Keeping up the charade. They didn't know we'd seen them before, I realized. That we would recognize them as the enemy.

She took one casual step toward the trees, not even looking our way anymore, and Justin broke from our huddle.

"Give me the gun," he said to Tobias, so low and fierce Tobias seemed to respond automatically, his hand twitching upward. He blinked, catching himself, not quickly enough. Justin yanked the pistol from his grasp.

"Justin!" I hissed, throwing out my arm to try to grab him, but he dodged me.

"There's only three of them," he said. "Three. We can take them. *I* can take them."

The woman was walking toward us faster now, gesturing to her companions. She'd heard him.

"If someone's there," she said, raising the rifle, "come out. We can have a nice, calm conversation."

Tobias lunged at Justin, and Justin ran. The rest of us scrambled to our feet as he raced toward the edge of the trees. The flashlight beam wavered over him, and the woman strode forward, her mouth twisting into a fake smile.

"Hey, kid—" she said as Justin jarred to a halt at the edge of the clearing. I saw in her expression the moment she registered the gun. She yanked up her rifle. In the space of a heartbeat, Justin squared his shoulders, aimed the pistol with both hands, and fired.

The sound of the shot rattled my eardrums, and my pulse

hiccupped. The woman fell, blood streaking down her face. She'd only been ten feet away, and he'd hit her right between the eyes.

Justin inhaled shakily. The two men were running toward us now, and he didn't move, just stared. "Justin!" Gav shouted. As the four of us reached the field, Justin lifted his arm and pointed the pistol, single-handed, at the guy with the gun. In the time it took Tobias to grab his shoulder, he fired once, twice, three times.

The first two shots went wild, but the third hit the man in the thigh. He doubled over, groaning, but he was still holding his gun. As he raised it, Tobias ripped the pistol from Justin's trembling hand, sighted, and shot the guy in the head. The man slumped.

"The other one! The other one!" Justin started babbling, waving his arm toward the third figure, who had spun around and was charging back toward the road. Toward their van. "He's seen us! We can't let any of them go, right? He'll come back with more, and—"

"Shut up!" Tobias snapped. He took two steps forward, stopped, and fired at the second man. I didn't see where the bullet hit, but the guy's body flinched and toppled over. I brought my hands to my ears.

Gav slid his arm around me. Tobias exhaled, dropping his gun hand to his side. The weight of the silence settled over us, as we stood there, alone in the clearing where three corpses marked the snow.

# SIXTEEN

Three people dead, because of us. Because we'd killed them.

As the realization sank in, my legs wobbled. I dropped to the ground, hugging my knees. Gav crouched with me, the gentle pressure of his arm around me feeling terribly distant. An acid taste rose in the back of my throat. In that moment, it was all I could do to keep my dinner down.

"Wow," Justin said to Tobias. "That was some shooting."

Tobias whirled on him. "What the hell were you doing?" he said. "That was a fucking mess, and it's *your* mess. I could have missed that last shot. I could have gotten to you too late to stop the other guy from shooting you!"

"They were going to find us," Justin protested. "Now we're safe. I *saved* us. None of you had the balls to do anything."

"We didn't need to do anything yet," Leo said quietly. "They were looking like they might turn back. And if we were going to do something, there are better plans than running out into plain sight and then freezing up."

Justin flushed. "I got her," he said, pointing to the woman's body. "That one I did perfect. I didn't know—I've never shot anyone before. It shook me up a little. Next time that won't happen."

"Next time?" I said, raising my head. "How many people are

you planning on shooting? We came all this way so we could stop people from dying. We're not supposed to be killing anyone!"

Gav dragged in a breath, straightening up. "Well, it's done now, right? It was done stupidly, but it's done. It sounded like they'd have been happy to kill *us*, once they got the vaccine."

"They might have just given up," I said, knowing that was more a wish than a possibility.

"I don't think they'd have moved on too quickly," Tobias said. "They knew we were here. But that doesn't mean we couldn't have handled it better."

"Look, I'm sorry, okay?" Justin snapped. "Next time I'll let all of you get shot instead, if that'll make you happy."

I pressed the heels of my hands against my eyes. My thoughts were so scattered I couldn't seem to catch hold of any of them. The space around me felt strangely empty.

The cold-storage box. I'd left the vaccine samples in the forest.

I got up, a little shakily, and walked back through the trees to pick up the box and my bag. The others were standing in the same semicircle when I returned.

"If there's anyone within a few miles of this place, they probably heard the gunshots," Leo said. "Someone might come to see what's going on. And whoever sent those people, when they don't report back, another group might head here to check things out. We can't stay."

He was right. I hugged the bag. "Where are we going to go?"

Gav looked toward the road. "The van," he said. His face had gone hard. "One of them must have the keys. We might as well use what we have."

"We know it can handle the snow," Tobias said, nodding.

Every bone in my body resisted the thought. The thought of getting into the van where the woman had sat with her rifle—the woman who was lying there dead—made me shudder.

"Won't it draw attention to us?" I said. "Anyone who sees us going by might recognize it. This group seems to have people all over the place. How can we stay out of sight if we're using a van they'll know?"

"We could only drive when people wouldn't see it easily," Leo said. "Travel at night, rest during the day."

"I don't want to stay in a house with that van outside like a signpost," I said. "That's crazy. It's the one thing they'll be looking for."

"So we take it just for tonight," Gav said. "We could get pretty far before the sun comes up."

"What the heck else can we do?" Justin demanded.

I bit my lip. The answer was: nothing.

"Okay," I said. "We get as far as we can and ditch it before it starts getting light. Right?"

Everyone nodded. Tobias turned to Justin. "You're the reason these people are dead," he said. "You should be the one looking for the keys. See up close what killing someone really means."

Justin's face looked a little pinched, but he pressed his mouth into a flat line and trudged over to the woman's body. Not wanting to watch, I hurried toward the mobile home. There was a thump as he rolled her over, and I cringed. The body of the second man was a dark blot amid the snow. I walked past it without letting my gaze stray from the place where we'd hidden the sleds, my hands curled tight in my pockets.

The others caught up with me at the home. We hauled the sleds out from underneath it one by one. I set the cold box in mine and pulled it over to the road. The green van was waiting there, parked on the gravel shoulder of the freeway. I hesitated, and then tried the door.

They hadn't even locked it. Not that we could have driven it anywhere without the keys. A two-way radio lay on the dashboard. As I went around to open the back doors, it crackled.

"Brunswick Third Division, an update?" a woman's voice said. The same nasal voice that had spoken to us on the transceiver. The one who'd offered us help. Leaving the sled by the back of the van, I pulled myself into the passenger seat and picked up the two-way. When it started to crackle again, I switched it off.

The seat was more comfortable than the one in Tobias's truck. I guessed the woman in the red hat's "division" had been able to be pickier.

Brunswick Third Division. That suggested there were at least two other groups on patrol, didn't it?

We'd gone from huddled in the dark while three predators stalked us, to better off than we'd been since we left the island. Even if Justin hadn't gone about it the best way, I had to admit that what he'd done had helped us. Was there something wrong with me that I still wished it hadn't happened? Maybe I was too soft for this survival stuff. Too stuck in the morality of the life I'd left behind to do what I needed to keep the lives we had.

I didn't want to be soft. But I didn't want to be like the people who'd hunted us down, either.

"Let's leave that two-way here," Tobias said, coming over with two of the other sleds. "At this point, I'd believe they've got some way of tracking those things."

I realized I was still clutching it in my mittened hand. I stepped out of the van and hurled the radio over the fence. It plopped into the snow. Tobias watched it fall, his eyes distant and his jaw tight beneath the shadow of his hood.

"Is that the first time you've..." I started, and trailed off, uncomfortable with the question.

"Killed someone?" Tobias filled in. "Yes. I managed never to get shipped out, and there aren't a whole lot of enemy soldiers to engage around here." He tossed some of the empty gas jugs into the back.

"Justin was right, you're good with the gun," I said. "I'm sorry you had to use it."

"That's what the training's for," he said. "I just got as good as I could at everything so the sergeants wouldn't have as much to harass me for. To tell you the truth, I only signed up for the armed forces because it was the one way I could put some distance between me and my stepdad. It turned out I hated it almost as much as I hated him." He stepped back to meet my gaze. "But I don't hate that I'm here," he added. "You just do what you've got to do to get by."

"Yeah," I said, my throat dry. And from the other side of the clearing, Justin's voice rose, strained but triumphant.

"Found the keys!"

I woke up in the dark, my cheek cold from pressing against the window. I blinked, searching for some sense of equilibrium.

We were in the van. Gav was driving, Leo looking at the map book—the map book I'd given him last night after I'd traded seats with him. Justin was drooped against Tobias, eyes closed and lips parted, a faint snore escaping them. Tobias had balled his scarf into a pillow to sleep, but he was stirring now.

Outside, the glow of the headlights streaked across the road. The sky was dull and overcast, only a smudge of moonlight showing through the clouds. The glimpses I caught of the trees lining the road didn't look all that different from what I'd seen shortly before I fell asleep. For a second I had the uneasy sense that we'd been driving in place, going on and on and getting nowhere.

Gav must have noticed me lift my head. "If the clock's right, it's almost five," he said. "We just turned off onto a local highway so we can look for a place to drop the van. The tank's almost empty, anyway."

"How far did we get?" I asked.

"We crossed into Quebec around two," Leo said. "Just one more province to go!"

One more to go. We were so much closer than we'd been even a day ago. For a moment I contemplated keeping the van. We could make it to Toronto in just a few more days. . . .

But the people on the other end of the radio would be looking for it soon, if they weren't already. There wasn't exactly a whole lot of traffic to blend in with. And to leave it sitting in some town while we searched for gas, like a signal flag—we'd be asking to get caught.

"There's a mailbox," Leo said, pointing to a shadowy shape. The van slowed as Gav eased up on the brake. We rolled up to the mailbox and carefully turned down the driveway beside it. The van lurched, and Justin sputtered awake.

The headlights slid over the edge of a porch. The door stood ajar, only darkness beyond it. No one home.

"I'll bring the van around back so nobody can see it from the road," Gav said. When he'd parked, we all climbed out, Tobias carrying the rifle he'd taken from the dead woman. A frigid breeze cut across my cheeks. I tugged my scarf up. The heat from inside the van was already seeping out of my bones.

Gav and Leo turned on their flashlights, and I tried not to think about the last people who'd been holding them. But Gav's light must have caught my face, because he stopped while the others went around to unload our supplies. He lowered the flashlight and touched my arm with his other hand.

"Hey," he said softly. "How're you doing?" The drive seemed to have done him good. He looked more at ease than I remembered seeing him the last few days.

"I'm okay," I said. "Just, you know, nervous." A yawn stretched my jaw. "And tired."

"We could crash here for a few hours."

I shook my head. "I'm not going to be able to rest until we're away from that van. Let's put a couple miles between us and it, at least."

"I think we can manage that." He leaned forward to kiss me and then pulled me into a hug. I hugged him back, my eyes squeezing shut against sudden tears. I hadn't known how much I needed someone else to hold a little of my weight, just for a moment.

"You think there's any gas left in the tank?" Tobias asked as we stepped apart. He held up the empty jugs.

"We might be able to fill one or two," Gav said. "It'd be good to have a little on us."

As he unscrewed the gas cap, I turned toward the looming presence of the house. Maybe it wasn't totally empty.

"While you're doing that, I'll take a look inside," I said. "See if there's any food."

"Good idea," Gav said.

"I'll come too, Kae," Leo said. "I don't think we should be going anywhere alone these days."

Gav didn't speak, just looked at Leo and then turned back to the van. I followed the beam of Leo's flashlight onto the porch. As the light swept the front hall, it caught a series of grimy boot prints tracked across the hardwood floor.

"Looks like someone's already been through here," I said.

We searched the kitchen quickly, finding nothing but a few dishes in the cupboards. The stairs creaked as we headed to the second floor.

It looked as if someone had stripped the blankets off the beds, but the queen in the master and the two singles in the second bedroom were still wrapped tightly in their sheets. The cloth gleamed white when Leo ran the beam of the flashlight over them. I paused, thinking of our dark coats as we walked across the snow.

"We should take these," I said, fingering the cloth. "We can wrap them over our coats so we blend in better. We'll be harder to spot from far away."

"Like arctic foxes," Leo said. When my eyebrows rose, he held up a hand. "Hey, you pounded just about every fact about them there is into my head that month when you were obsessed with having one as a pet! I remember things."

I cracked a grin, and his mouth curved with a hint of a smile. Right then, he looked like his old self again. A twinge of warmth fluttered in my chest: a pull toward him, a memory of his lips brushing mine.

I hadn't forgotten the kiss, or how it had made me feel. Well, maybe I never would. But the air seemed clearer between us after our talk at the colony, like we both knew where we stood. So it was easier to breathe in and nudge the feeling aside.

"I really thought it was going to work," I said, untucking the sheet. "How old were we, seven? But Drew had to overhear and crush my dream. 'They arrest people for taking endangered species, you know.'"

"So that's why you gave it up."

"Yeah." My amusement dampened. Thinking about Drew and where he was now. Who he was with.

I should have been happy he was alive. I was happy. It was just that the happiness was kind of numbed by the worry and fear that had come with it.

"What do you think he's doing with these people, Leo?" I said.

Leo's expression turned serious. "We don't even know exactly who they are," he said.

"We know they'd rather get the vaccine for themselves than let us find someone who can make enough for everyone. And they're willing to lie to people, to hurt them, to get what they want."

Leo shrugged and looked toward the window. His face was wan in the reflected glow of the flashlight. "You probably just described almost every person still alive right now, Kae. Maybe he had to join up with them to survive."

"But this is *Drew*," I said. "You know him. He was like a freaking crusader, posting all over the internet, challenging injustice. It was kind of annoying sometimes, but that's how he is. How can he help people who go around stealing and killing?"

"People change," Leo said. "When the world's going to hell like this, sometimes you do things you wouldn't have ever thought you'd do, because you don't see any other choice."

"You mean like Justin?" I crossed my arms over my chest. "He *wanted* to shoot those people. It wasn't just about surviving."

"Maybe," Leo said, his voice strained. "But I can't judge him. I've done worse."

The words hung in the air for a moment. Then I scoffed. "I don't believe that. You would never—"

"You don't know, Kae," he interrupted. "You have no idea...." He sat down on the edge of the bed, his head drooping. "I know you think I haven't wanted to talk about how I got back to the island because of everything I saw. But it's not that. It's because of what I did."

My heart stuttered.

"So what did you do?" I said.

For a few seconds I thought he was going to clam up again. He sucked in a ragged breath. And then he started talking with a hollowness that was almost as hard to hear as his words.

"I had to get home, back to the island," he said. "But I hardly had any money at school. I stole all the cash out of my roommate's wallet so I could pay for a bus most of the way to the border. I thought I was going to have to walk the rest, but a woman who was heading there too, she saw me and offered me a ride. She was sick. She was wearing one of those masks, but she kept coughing. I was terrified I was going to catch it from her. So I took off. At a rest stop. I jumped in the car and just left her there. I told myself she was going to die anyway, so it didn't really matter."

He stopped, swallowed, and went on. "And then there was the quarantine camp at the border. It was supposed to be just for a week, but the soldiers changed their minds every other day—it was two weeks, and then three—it started looking like they were never going to let us cross over, and the place was getting crowded, and supplies were running out, and they kept hauling people away who started showing symptoms. . . . I grabbed a guy's coat, the only one he had, and a bunch of food that was supposed to be for everyone, so I could make a run for it."

"Leo," I said, and he shook his head.

"I had this idea I was a good person, you know? Like you said about Drew. That was just who I was. I would never have believed I could be that selfish. But I was. All I could think about was getting home, getting there alive. I don't even know if I would take it back if I could, because I don't think I would have made it otherwise." He laughed. "I was so scared to see my parents—like they'd know what I'd done—to see how they'd look at me. Some little part of me was relieved that they were dead, so I didn't have to find out. How awful is that?"

He kept staring at the floor, as if he was afraid to see my expression. Imagining Leo stealing, abandoning someone who'd helped him, made my stomach ache. But I couldn't say I'd rather he'd died than made it home. Like Tobias had said last night, *You just do what you've got to do to get by.*

"You were trying to get back so you could help your parents, Tessa—everyone," I said. "That part's not awful."

"I don't know," he said. "It seems like I screwed things up even more after I got back. I want to be the person I'm supposed to be.

Tessa's boyfriend. Your best friend. I feel almost normal, now and then. But then I think of what's happened and the horribleness just rises up and I can't pull myself out."

I thought of how angry I'd been at him for not being himself, and my eyes prickled. He'd been carrying all this, every minute of every day. "You can't help how you feel," I said. "You've been through a lot. I was upset, yeah, and it wasn't totally fair. I should have tried harder to talk to you."

"I didn't want to tell you," he said. "Anyway, maybe I'm not the person I used to be anymore. Maybe this is who I am now. A thief and a cheat and practically a murderer and not really a good person at all."

"You're not—" I said, but he went on without letting me continue.

"Maybe when life gets tough enough, we all turn into bad people. I used to think most people want to do right, when they can, but now..."

I sat down beside him. "What if you're wrong? What if it just takes a while for people to stop being scared and start thinking straight again? You remember you told me to think of people like animals?"

"Well, they're acting like it, aren't they?" he said.

"Yeah. And you don't say an animal is 'bad' if it fights with another animal over the same food or a place where they both want to live. It's survival. People panic; instincts take over." I paused. "Like Justin, I guess. But if there wasn't any more reason to panic, people could start acting like people again. That's why we're bringing the vaccine all this way, isn't it? So life can get back to normal."

He finally looked at me. "You really believe that? That everything could go back to how it used to be?"

"Yeah," I said. "I do."

"I hope you're right," he said. "Because most days I don't feel like I could go back to the old me, the good one. Not ever."

# SEVENTEEN

Justin eyed the sheets skeptically as I explained how we could use them, but he didn't argue when I handed him one. We cut up the queen-size ones with Tobias's army knife, covering each of the sleds with a white cloth and knotting the rest around the collars of our coats. They rippled with the rising wind.

The brownish glow of the coming dawn tinged the clouds along the eastern horizon as we backtracked to the freeway. My heart skipped a beat. "Let's keep our distance from the road, like before," I said. "And only talk if we have to. We need to be listening so we can hear anyone who's coming before they see us."

We set off across the fields. Scattered snowflakes drifted down, brushing my face with tiny nips of cold. The air above the chimneys of the few distant country houses was still and clear, and no tracks marked the snow except the ones we made.

We'd crossed into a new province, but everything was just as dead.

Even people who hadn't gotten sick had probably ended up heading to the hospitals in the towns and cities, I told myself. Bringing family members who were ill, and staying in the hopes they'd be able to take them home again. Or getting stranded when gas ran out. Not everyone who'd lived here was dead. But I thought of what I'd said to Leo just a few minutes before, about the world going back to the way it used to be, and the certainty I'd felt then wavered.

What did I know about the world anymore? I hadn't expected to come across a group like the colony, or this network of marauders, or to find out that the government had abandoned Ottawa. The truth was, I had no idea what we'd find in Toronto. I had no idea whether there was enough left of our world for anyone to pick up the pieces.

We passed the last field and wove through a mile of spruce forest. As we tramped out the other side, the wind whipped over us, spitting a gust of snowflakes into our faces. There weren't many coming down, but they were whirling faster now, mingling with puffs of snow the wind whisked off the ground. I wiped my face and adjusted my scarf.

"It's getting a little nasty," I said, even though my gut knotted at the thought of stopping so soon. I remembered how quickly the first blizzard had overwhelmed us. If it got that bad, our pursuers would have to stop too. "Maybe we should find a place to hole up until the wind dies down."

Justin squared his shoulders and pulled in front of me. "This is nothing," he said. "How'd you make it all the way from the coast if you can't take a little wind?"

*If it stays this way I'll be fine,* I thought. *If it gets worse...*

"The clouds don't look that dark," Gav said, trudging on. "I think we'll be okay for a little longer."

The clouds *were* lighter than those the other day. Still, I started scanning the landscape as we walked. Maybe half a mile away, a group of houses clustered around a laneway off the main road. Beyond them, a farmhouse stood alone except for the barn squatting behind it. It was closer to the freeway and farther from us than the others, but something about it made me look again. I squinted against the wind. By the side of the house, a lumpy brown heap leaned against the yellow siding.

Firewood.

I glanced at the chimney, but there wasn't even a trickle of smoke. Abandoned like the others, I guessed. But it must have a working fireplace.

The wind blasted a stinging wave of snow at me. I shook it off. The flakes in the air seemed denser now. When I looked at the house again, I couldn't make out the woodpile anymore.

Justin kept striding along ahead of us. If the storm held off a little longer, we'd be fine.

I'd taken maybe a dozen more steps when the wind shifted, shrieking past my ears, pelting me with snow from all sides. Tears leaked from the corners of my eyes and froze on my skin. The houses had vanished from view. Even Justin hesitated, looking back at us. The chill cut down my throat and into my lungs. I lowered my head.

We could stand here and hope the storm died down as quickly as it had come, but every second we wasted, we were getting colder and more tired. The image of the yellow house lingered in my mind. It wasn't that far. If we could find it when we couldn't even see it.

I closed my eyes, picturing the house. Birds could migrate across hundreds of miles and always return to the same spot. Cats and dogs could cross vast distances of unknown territory to find their homes. Whatever innate sense of direction they had, maybe I had it too, somewhere deep in my brain.

My chest tightened as the wind buffeted me, but I made myself move. One step, and then another. Picking my way through the snow. I waved to the others, pulling the white sheet around in front of me so they could see my coat more easily. Numbness crept up my legs where they pressed against my jeans, but I ignored it. *Just walk to the house. Don't think, just walk.*

It felt as though I'd been walking for hours when the toe of my boot snagged and I stumbled. A hand caught my arm, steadying me. I didn't even look back to see who it was, I was too afraid of losing my sense of space. My teeth had clenched to keep from chattering. But the house was out there—a house with wood and a fireplace and walls to keep out the wind.

I pressed onward as fast as I could manage. I had to get there before I lost it.

The wind twisted, pummeling me from behind, and I staggered forward. My hands hit a solid surface. I stared down at them, at the surface beneath them, for a moment before I realized what I was seeing. A wall covered with pale yellow siding.

When we'd talked about book-burning in school, I'd cringed at the thought. But I felt no remorse as I pulled books off the shelves in the living room of the yellow house. We were cold. There was a cast-iron stove behind us, and a couple of logs in the firewood holder, but nothing smaller. And paper made easy kindling.

I ripped several pages out of a dog-eared copy of *Gone with the Wind* and stuffed them into the stove. Gav lit the closest one. We closed the stove door. The flames flickered against the clouded glass.

"You think the logs will catch?" I asked.

"If they don't, we can help 'em along with some of the camping-stove kerosene," Tobias said behind me. He shivered and shuffled closer.

Snow was whipping past the window in a wild fury. "At least no one's going to see the smoke through that," I said. But I didn't think we could risk sending anyone out to find the woodpile either. I'd heard stories of people getting lost in a blizzard just a few feet from their houses.

The big snowfall when we'd stumbled on the colony had only lasted one night. Maybe we wouldn't need more wood.

When the flames started to dim, we shoved in more pages. After a few rounds, the fire started seeping into the logs. It crackled, heat emanating through the room.

"I don't see any vents or radiators," Leo said. "I think they heated the whole house with the stove."

"I bet we could cook on it too," Gav said, tapping the flat top with the poker.

We stood around it, soaking up the warmth, a tingling spreading through my legs and face as the skin that had numbed came back to life. After a while I shrugged off my coat and laid it on the marigold-print sofa.

"It looks like we're here at least until tomorrow," I said. "Let's check the place out."

"Someone should keep an eye on the fire so it doesn't die," Tobias said, and Gav handed him the poker.

"Thanks for volunteering," he said with a crooked grin.

"I'll fill up the pots with snow to melt," Justin said. "My water bottle's empty."

"Just don't go off the porch," Leo said, and Justin made a face.

"I'm not stupid."

There were no shoes or jackets by the front and back doors, but when Gav and I poked around the bedrooms upstairs, we found dressers full of clothes. The beds were neatly made. A family photo hung in the hallway: mother and father, older son, and two younger daughters, all with dark brown hair and freckles. Gav caught me studying it.

"You figure they ran?" he said.

"They'd have taken more of their things," I said. "Probably one or two of them got sick, and they all went to the hospital."

"And never came back."

"Yeah." Because they'd been stranded, or because the virus had leapt from one to another until it had killed all of them.

We met Leo in the kitchen. "I found a bag of potatoes and a couple turnips in the basement," he said, setting them on the counter. "Most of the potatoes are soft, but there might be a few we can use."

"Potatoes and turnips for dinner," Gav said, flexing his hands. "I can make an actual meal out of that. We've got some canned turkey, don't we? Did they leave us any spices?"

"I only saw salt and pepper shakers in the cupboard," Leo said.

Gav grimaced. "I guess that'll have to do."

The heat of the stove was drifting into the kitchen. "I should put more snow in the cold box," I said. "Maybe I'll keep it on the porch to make sure it stays cool enough."

We'd left the sleds in the front hall and at one end of the living room. Mine was just outside the kitchen. I lifted the sheet covering it, and stiffened with a hitch of breath.

"Something wrong?" Leo asked.

"The cold box," I said. "It's not here."

"What?" Gav said, his head snapping around.

I stood up, my mind spinning. I couldn't have lost it in the storm, could I? I would have felt the load lighten . . . or maybe not, with the wind blasting against me. But I'd wedged it in so tightly, and the rest of my cargo was there.

"Neither of you moved it?"

They shook their heads. I marched into the living room. Tobias was adjusting one of the logs with the poker. The pots Justin had filled sat in a ring around the stove, the heaps of snow already disintegrating.

"Have you seen the cold box?" I asked.

Tobias furrowed his brow. "It's on your sled, isn't it?"

"Not anymore." I swallowed, my mouth dry. Maybe I'd moved it without thinking. We'd come into the house in such a rush. I jogged to the front door, braced myself for the onslaught of wind, and checked the porch. Only snow. I strode back into the kitchen. Gav and Leo joined me, opening and closing the cupboards. Nothing.

It had to be here. I hurried to the small sunroom off the kitchen and jerked to a stop in the doorway.

Justin was sitting on a lawn chair by the wide glass windows, the cold storage box at his feet, the lid on a nearby table. The inner container was open too. He was holding one of the sample vials level with his eyes, squinting in the dim sunlight.

He started when he saw me. The vial slipped in his fingers, and for one heart-pounding second I thought it was going to fall and smash on the tiled floor. Then his hand closed around it more tightly and he lowered it to his lap.

"What are you doing?" I said, my pulse still racing. "You can't just walk off with those."

Justin's lip curled petulantly. "I was only *looking* at them. This vaccine doesn't look like much, does it? Not like something that'll save people's lives. You could almost think someone just peed in these." He wiggled the vial so the amber liquid rippled against the glass.

"Put it back," I said, stepping forward. I was so angry and panicked all at the same time that my voice shook. "You're letting all the cold air out—you're going to ruin them. No, you know what, let me."

I held out my hand. He sighed and gave me the vial.

The other two samples were secure in their tray. I slid the third in beside them and closed the plastic container.

"They'll be fine, Kaelyn," Gav said behind me. "It hasn't even started warming up back here."

I snapped the lid into place and straightened up. He was right. The cold from outside was radiating through the windows and into my sweater. When I exhaled, the air in front of my face misted.

"That doesn't make it all right," I said. "If he'd left the box open too long, they could have frozen."

"But I didn't," Justin said. "I was careful."

"How can you be careful when you don't know anything about them?" I said. "Just taking them out was careless!" I grabbed the handle of the cold box, glaring at him, and turned my gaze on Gav and Leo, who'd joined him in the doorway.

"From now on, nobody touches this box except me. Okay?"

"Kae," Gav said.

*"Okay?"* I repeated.

He shrugged. "Of course."

"Never would have in the first place," Leo said.

I glanced back at Justin. "Fine," he muttered.

It was enough. I hauled the cold box to the front hall and set it on the porch, hidden behind the railing. Then I stomped upstairs, pushing open the doors until I found the one room I was sure no one would follow me into. Sinking down onto the closed toilet seat, I dropped my head into my hands. Tears started to dribble through my fingers.

In the quiet, I could still hear yesterday's gunshots ringing in my ears. The thud of the woman in the red hat falling.

The roar of the wind outside reverberated into my bones.

It was too much.

I let out a long, shuddering breath. The tears slowed, and I wiped my eyes. Gradually, the wave of emotions rolled back, leaving a sort of calm in its place. I stood up and leaned over the sink, examining my reddened eyes in the mirror. Between them and my hat-flattened, wind-tangled hair, I looked like a mess. But I looked determined too.

I'd had a right to be angry at Justin, hadn't I? There was a lot I didn't know, I could admit to that, but I knew how to handle the vaccine better than anyone here. If there was one thing I should be able to call the shots on, it was that. And I had. He couldn't have taken the samples out for more than a minute; I'd caught him before they were damaged. I didn't think he'd do it again. They were safe now.

"That's what's important," I said to my reflection. We still had so much farther to go. So much longer I had to keep that vaccine safe. I wasn't going to let the reason we'd come all this way get screwed up, whatever I had to do.

Because if we lost that, we had nothing left to hope for.

# EIGHTEEN

I woke the next morning to the wind spitting snow against the window.

Only a dull light penetrated the storm still blustering outside. But the air against my face was faintly warm. Thanks to the stove, for once we hadn't needed to spend the night all squished together.

I rolled over cautiously. Gav's eyes were shut, his shaggy curls drifting over his forehead, one hand reached toward me. We'd taken the master bedroom last night without really talking about it, and I'd been so exhausted that I'd fallen asleep the moment my body hit the mattress. But now, even though we were both dressed and he was sleeping, my heart skipped a beat. I was lying in bed with my boyfriend. For the first time in weeks, we had a room to ourselves.

On the island, we'd never done more than make out. Being constantly worried about the virus didn't exactly make for the most romantic mood. And we'd only been dating, if you could call it that, for a couple of months. I wasn't sure I wanted more yet, and Gav had seemed happy to follow my lead. But I'd thought about going further. I was thinking about it now—about what could happen if he woke up and pulled me closer.

After a few minutes, Gav had shown no sign of stirring and

I was no closer to falling back asleep. Anxious thoughts started creeping into my head. Had the fire gone out overnight? How were we going to get to the woodpile for more logs?

I crawled out of bed, pulled on my sweater, and headed downstairs. To my relief, flames were flickering merrily in the window of the stove. Three fresh logs lay in the metal holder. Leo was sitting on the living room floor, one leg bent beside him and the other stretched out straight, his head tipped to his knee. He eased upright, swiveled to switch legs, and saw me.

"Hey," he said.

"You got more wood."

"I found some rope in the basement." He pointed his thumb toward a coil resting against the side of the log holder. "I tied one end around my waist and the other to the doorknob. That wind is wicked. I'm not sure how much it's bringing snow down and how much it's just whipping up what's already on the ground."

He leaned over his other leg. I slipped past him and sank onto the sofa, pulling my feet up beside me. Watching him stretch somehow felt totally normal and totally strange at the same time. But it heartened me.

"I haven't seen you warming up in a while," I said. Not since he'd gotten back to the island. Maybe our talk yesterday had made a difference—released him, in some small way, to return to the things he cared about.

"We had a pretty strict morning routine in New York," Leo said, twisting his torso around, pretzel-like, and shooting me a small smile. "I realized I miss it. I guess I'm just a sucker for punishment."

"Always were." He'd been pretty strict with himself before

anyone had talked about trying for a New York dance school. But back then there had been theaters and big-city performances to dream about. Who was he going to dance for now?

"Tessa said you really liked the school," I said.

"I loved it as soon as I walked in there for my audition. It was like a world where everyone slept and ate and breathed dance. I could mention techniques or choreographers, and everyone knew what I was talking about." He bent one arm behind his head and pressed down on the elbow with his other hand. "Not to knock Mrs. Wilce's teaching—she was pretty with it for someone who'd been out of the industry for a decade—but there's so much that I had no idea I didn't know."

And the virus had stolen that perfect world away from him after just a couple months. All those things he didn't know, he might never get the chance to learn. An ache formed behind my collarbone.

"What did you do for the audition?" I asked.

"A contemporary piece," he said, stretching his other arm. "Choreo-ed it myself, with some suggestions from Mrs. Wilce. I used a Perfect Mischief song—'Orbits'—you know that one?"

I knew it by heart. Leo had been obsessed with that song the last summer vacation we'd spent together on the island, when we were fourteen. Before we'd fought. He'd played it for me on his iPod, sharing his earphones with me, and even though that'd been a few days before my feelings had leapt from friendship to more, I'd listened to the song over and over when I got back to Toronto, remembering how close together we'd stood. I'd kept listening after our fight, even though the melody could bring tears to my eyes.

"We're on different orbits," the chorus went, "but in the end we always meet again. We always meet again."

And in the end, here we were, even if it was under pretty crappy circumstances. In spite of the awkwardness, the feelings spoken and unspoken, the way we'd both changed, I was happy for that. Looking at him, a rush of affection I didn't have to feel guilty about swept through me. He was still my best friend. I wasn't going to lose him again.

"It's a good song," I said. "I wish I could have been there to see it."

Leo paused and glanced around the room. "I could show you, you know," he said. "There's enough space if I push the armchair over to the wall."

"You don't have the music."

"I thought that too," he said. "Missed it more than anything. But then I figured out I still have it, up here." He tapped his head. "This is one excellent brain radio."

I couldn't help smiling. "Okay, let's have it, then."

He shoved the armchair to the side and peeled off his socks and sweater so he stood barefoot on the hardwood floor in his T-shirt and loose jeans. Then he crouched, his arms relaxed, his head bent forward. "Cue music," he said, and hummed the opening notes of the song. In my mind I heard the guitar swell to join the piano. And then Leo moved.

He unfolded his body and leapt and spun, the way the vocals spiraled out from the drumbeat, falling back to earth and seeming to topple but then twisting himself back onto his feet. Even if I hadn't known the song, I would have heard it, watching him.

The rhythm played out in the patter of his skin against the floor and the jerks of his breath, the melody in the flow of his limbs. At the place where the chorus would have begun, he whirled around six, seven times before catching himself and then tumbling over, reaching up into the empty space above his head. His hand fell. I knew without his speaking that this was where it ended.

He stood up, panting but grinning. There was a glow in his face and a light in his eyes I hadn't seen since years ago. Since, probably, the last time I'd seen him dance. I wished I could hold that joy there forever.

This was why we had to fix things. Because in a world where people were too scared of getting sick to even talk to each other, where there were no songs, no audiences, and no stages, the virus was killing Leo and everyone like him even if they never caught it.

I'd been so focused on him that I hadn't noticed the figure coming down the stairs. "Whoa," Justin said, clapping his hands. "How'd you even *do* that? That thing, where you jumped right into that roll—that was freaking awesome. You're like a secret ninja or something."

Leo laughed, and in that moment I forgave Justin for at least part of what he'd done.

I looked behind me, out the window, feeling like right now the view couldn't let me down. But beyond the glass, the air was still swirling with snow.

Sometime in the afternoon, Tobias found a pack of cards in a drawer, and he, Leo, and Justin sat down in the dining room to play poker for scraps of paper. I was walking over to join them when Gav grabbed my hand.

"C'mere," he said, looking at me like there wasn't anyone else in the whole world, and a warm tingling raced over my skin.

I followed him up to the bedroom we'd shared. As we stepped inside and Gav kicked the door shut, a funny feeling rose in my stomach, excitement and nervousness and uncertainty all fluttering together.

He kissed me, and the nervousness went away. I stepped back so my shoulders rested against the wall, pulling him with me, tangling my fingers in his hair. He kissed me again, on the mouth, and then on the cheek and the side of my jaw.

"You know," he murmured, "the one thing I was looking forward to about taking off across the country was it being just the two of us. I'm very disappointed with how that turned out."

"And what did you think we'd be doing if it was just the two of us?" I asked, raising my eyebrows.

Instead of answering, he leaned forward, his lips brushing mine. Which maybe was an answer. As the kiss deepened, his hands slid around my waist, tracing the skin beneath the edge of my sweater. A heat welled up inside me, from the places where our bodies touched up to the top of my head and down to the soles of my feet. The snow and the wind and our meager pile of food faded away. Part of me, a pretty big part, wanted to melt into him and stumble over to the bed and let the moment carry me far from here.

But when everything else slipped away, I could still feel the long road between me and wherever the vaccine needed to be, stretching into the distance in my head. Like a leash that kept tugging at me even when I couldn't move. It was a rigid little knot in the middle of my chest.

My arms tightened around Gav. I kissed him harder. His hands edged up my back, and I didn't want them to stop. But the knot wouldn't loosen. It only tugged tighter as I tried to ignore it.

I lowered my head and leaned into him, tucking my face against the crook of his neck. His heart was thumping even faster than mine.

"Kae?" he said, and then, "I didn't mean it like—I wasn't trying to push."

"I know," I said quickly. "There's just... There's too much in my head. Too many worries that won't shut up. Can I, like, get a rain check? Until after we're done, we've handed off the vaccine, and this is over?"

Gav laughed and hugged me. "Is that a promise?" he said into my ear. I smiled against his skin. Then I eased back just far enough that I could kiss him in my reply.

Beyond the bedroom window, the snow kept tumbling down.

Three days later, the blizzard was still raging. Every now and then the snow lightened up enough that we could make out the swaying trees by the road, but they soon disappeared again. And the wind never stopped howling.

"I didn't know a storm could last this long," I said, when we were sitting at the dining table eating lunch. Or what passed for lunch these days. Mine consisted of a can of tuna. It wasn't much, but if we'd been eating normally, we'd have run out of food already.

"I lived up north for a couple years when I was a kid," Tobias said. "This isn't too unusual."

The tuna stuck in my throat, but I forced it down. I was trying not to think about the small stack of jars and ration bars left in the kitchen. Leo's snares were useless in this weather. I found myself eyeing the paper wrapper on the can, wondering if there were any calories in that. Or in the frozen grass outside.

Stomachs could adapt. Koala bears managed to live completely on poisonous leaves. Of course, they'd had thousands of years to evolve, and we had less than a week.

"If it keeps up much longer, we can try to get to one of the other houses nearby, check for more food," Gav said, but none of us had caught so much as a glimpse of the neighboring buildings since the storm had started. The rope we used to get the firewood wasn't going to stretch that far.

"We'll see," I said, trying not to think about that either. Trying not to think about how aimless the rest of the day would be. To pass the time, we'd get out the cards or the board games Justin found: Risk and Battleship and Clue. Gav might play, or he might go upstairs to pace and stare outside, as if a supermarket was going to appear in the snow. After dinner, Tobias would get out the radio. The static was warped and whistling now, and he admitted that the storm was scrambling any signals heading our way. But we kept trying, kept hoping to hear Drew's voice come crackling out of the speaker.

I got up to throw away the can. And outside, the endless wind beat at the walls, and the endless snow rasped against the windows, on and on and on.

# NINETEEN

I'd lost count of the days by the morning I woke up to blue sky outside the bedroom window, like a surprise Christmas morning.

I leapt up and padded over to the glass, half afraid it was some sort of trick, a mirage. It wasn't. The fields stretched out crisp and white, reflecting the rising sun. Not a single cloud marred the perfect sky.

It was the best present I could ever remember getting.

I wavered a little on my feet, hunger-driven faintness catching up with me. All I'd eaten the day before was a can of corn and a small portion of the stew Gav had mixed up over the wood stove, after frying some meat I'd decided not to ask about. As I'd choked it down, I hadn't been able to stop picturing the cat frozen in the snare.

But none of that mattered now. I threw myself onto the bed beside Gav, as if it really was Christmas morning and I was ten years younger, and shoved his shoulder.

"Wake up!" I said as he winced. "The storm's over. We can leave!"

His eyes popped open and he shot up.

"Let's get out of here, then," he said as he scrambled out from under the blanket.

I pulled on my boots and hurried down the hall, banging on the bedroom doors. "Storm's stopped!" I called. "We're heading out!"

By the time Gav and I had carried our blankets from the bedroom down to the sleds, the others were up. We gathered in the kitchen, my gut twisting as I looked at the row of food left on the counter. Five ration bars. Two cans of peaches. Three cans of peas. That was it. But we'd be on the move again today. We'd find more. We had to.

"Save the ration bars," Tobias said. "We can break 'em up if we need to. But we'd better all eat before we get walking, or we won't make it far."

"Maybe we should check the barn before we go," Leo said as I peeled the lid off a tin of peaches. "There might be something useful in there."

I'd been so excited about leaving I'd forgotten there was part of the property we hadn't explored. "Good idea," I said, sipping syrup out of the can. My stomach clenched. I'd never realized that when you got this hungry, eating could hurt more than going without. When I wasn't eating, the hunger faded into a dull wooziness in the background. At the taste of food, it grew claws.

"Let's do it quickly," Gav said. "We're losing daylight."

We had to shove the front door a few times before we could push it through the snow that had been blown onto the porch. Slogging through the knee-high drifts, we crossed the yard to the barn. The wall that faced us had a wide, garagelike door on one side. Justin hurried over to a button on the frame and jabbed at it. The door creaked up, the gears whining. I sucked in a breath.

Just a few feet away, inside, stood a truck with a snowplow

mounted on its front. Tobias let out a low whistle, and Gav laughed. I just stared. This really was some kind of Christmas.

"Are there keys?" Justin said, bounding inside. The others guys followed him, peering through the truck's windows, examining the tires. I stepped into the shelter of the barn. A second car was parked deeper inside: a small two-door with patches of rust along the bumper.

The surge of excitement faded into an uncomfortable chill. There was only room for the two vehicles here, and I hadn't gotten the impression from the house that the family was wealthy enough to own three. Why would they have left on foot?

Maybe a friend had brought them to the hospital. Or maybe some of them had made it back, headed out on foot to search the neighbor's houses for food, and been lost in a storm like the one that had brought us here.

"Got it!" Gav shouted from the far corner. The key jingled against the ring as he lifted it off the hook. "Let's make sure this thing runs."

He hopped in and turned the key. The engine rumbled. "Still has a third of a tank," he said, leaning out. "We can get pretty far on that and what we siphoned from the van."

The smell of exhaust clouded the air as Gav pulled the truck out of the barn. He fiddled with the controls, raising and then lowering the plow. "That is sweet!" Justin said. He clambered into the passenger seat and peered over the back. "Room for all of us too."

Of course there was. The family would have gotten a truck that could hold all of them: Mom and Dad, brother and sisters. The photo in the upstairs hall swam up in my memory. I turned away from the sunlight.

The garage area took up only part of the barn. Now that my eyes had adjusted to the dim interior, I could see a door set in the side wall. I stood there for a minute, while the guys experimented with the plow. This was the last room on the property that we hadn't checked.

I balked for a second, without any real reason. Someone needed to look. It might as well be me. Forcing my legs to move, I walked over and pulled open the door.

On the other side, a short row of empty stable stalls led toward a broad, high-ceilinged room. Bales of hay were stacked against the far wall. The light from the high windows made them shine pale gold. I took a step forward, my body relaxing, and my gaze stuttered over a dark stain on the cement floor just beyond the stalls.

A dark stain, and, in the shadows, the curve of an upturned hand.

I strode past the first two stalls and jerked to a halt. I must have made a sound, but I didn't hear it, only felt myself clapping my fingers over my mouth, as if I could cram the shriek back in. As if that would make what I was seeing less real.

The hand on the floor belonged to a small figure with her head turned away from me, long dark hair fanned out around her bluish face. Three other bodies lay closer to the wall amid the shreds of hay that scattered the floor, reddish stains beneath them. Two had the hoods of their coats pulled up, obscuring their faces, but the other, the man, was sprawled as if holding his hand out to me, dried blood caked in his hair and around his head, the angular shape of a revolver just inches from his outstretched arm.

Feet pounded across the concrete in the room behind me. I stumbled backward, bracing myself against the frame of a stall.

"What happened, Kae?"

Gav's voice sounded as if it were coming from far away, much farther than the thudding of my pulse inside my head. I spun around.

"Hey," he said, his eyes widening when he saw my expression. I opened my mouth to tell him, and all that came out was a sob. He wrapped his arms around me, pulling me to him. "Hey, whatever it is, we're all okay."

*They aren't,* I thought as I shivered against him. We had eaten their food and burned their wood and slept in their beds, while they were lying out here in the cold and the blood. . . .

Someone brushed past us. The footsteps stopped with a sharp intake of breath.

"What is it?" Gav said.

"Four of them," Leo's voice replied. He swallowed audibly. "Four bodies. Looks like . . . looks like the whole family."

"There were five," I said, curling my fingers into Gav's coat. "In the photo there were five."

Gav squeezed me closer. "From the virus?" he asked Leo.

"Shot," Leo said. "I think by the dad, and then he shot himself."

"What?" Justin said, pushing past us. "What's going on?" I looked up as he barged past Leo. He flinched, backpedaling, when he saw the bodies.

"How could he do that?" I said. The scene was burned into my brain, too neat for me to blame it on some crazed hallucination. He'd brought them out here purposely, in order to kill them. His own kids. His wife?

"We don't know what happened, Kae," Gav said quietly. "Maybe they were all sick, and he thought this was better than making them go through the worst of it before they died."

"He had the plow," I said. "They could have at least tried to find help." Instead he'd just decided, for all of them, that it wasn't worth going on.

Maybe I should have understood. There was a time when I hadn't wanted to keep trying anymore. When I'd thought I was alone and there wasn't any point. But I'd been wrong. I hadn't been alone—I'd had Gav and Tessa and Meredith. If I hadn't kept trying, Meredith would probably have died, and the vaccine samples might have lingered in the research center's lab until there was no one left to find them.

And even at my lowest moment, I'd made the choice only for myself. I would never have brought anyone with me over that edge.

"Let's just go," Leo said. "We can't do anything for them."

That much was true. "Yeah," I said, turning my head away.

Justin had regained his usual enthusiasm by the time we'd walked out to the truck. "I'm the first driver!" he called, holding up the key he must have taken out of the ignition when Gav left it.

"You're fourteen," Tobias said. "There's no way you have your license."

"I've practiced," Justin said. "My dad used to take me out on Sunday mornings and we'd drive around the side roads. It's not like there's any cops around to pull us over and check."

"I'm going to bet you didn't practice on unplowed freeways," Leo said.

"Anyway," Gav said, "I found the key. I'll drive first. Let's get going."

He held out his hand, but Justin stepped back, folding the key into his fist. "Give me a chance," he said. "I thought you all wanted me to pull my own weight."

Tobias sighed. "I guess your dad did teach you how to shoot a gun, all right."

"I don't think this is the best time to find out if that goes for driving too," Leo said.

"Come on!" Gav said. "We're wasting time."

He snatched at Justin's hand, and Justin shoved him away. But Gav had been in plenty of skirmishes before. A sound of protest hadn't even left my mouth when he grabbed Justin's other arm and twisted it behind his back. As Justin thrashed out with his free elbow, the key slipped from his fingers. A silver glint arced through the air and dropped into the snow beyond the edge of the driveway, vanishing. My heart stopped.

Gav's grip loosened, and Justin yanked his arm away. "Now look!" he said. "What the hell was that? You made me lose it."

"If you hadn't been acting like a five-year-old in the first place," Gav snapped, scanning the snow. "I should have—"

"Stop it!" I shouted. My voice seemed to echo in the silence that followed. I pushed my hands back through my hair. If we kept squabbling like this, we were never going to make it to the city. The truck could be useless now.

My mind tripped back to the man in the barn, the decision he'd made for his family, and I pushed the image away. Putting my foot down about this didn't make me the slightest bit like him. I was keeping us alive.

"We have to get to Toronto," I said. "Nothing else is important. So the people who've passed their driving tests will drive, and the people who haven't won't, and we're not going to fight about it. We're not going to do anything at all unless it gets us closer to the city or stops us from starving to death. And anyone who doesn't like that can just stay here and do whatever they want to do instead. Okay?"

I must have sounded more fierce than I felt inside. "No argument here," Leo said meekly, and Gav said, "Sorry. I got carried away." Tobias nodded, his eyes downcast. After a moment, Justin's shoulders slumped and he mumbled, "Right. Got it."

We converged around the area where the key had fallen, sweeping our hands over the snow. I glanced up at the sky, inwardly pleading, *Don't let the day end like this.*

Leo gave a cry of victory and held up the key. I rocked back on my heels with a gasp of relief. Gav straightened up, accepting the key from Leo when he offered it. He reached out to squeeze my shoulder.

"Toronto, here we come."

# TWENTY

The last hours before we reached Toronto ticked away with the shrinking numbers next to the city's name on the freeway signs we passed. 156. 117. 78. 33.

As we rolled closer, buildings replaced the fields and forests that had lined the roads for most of our journey. The sun sank, darkness setting in, but none of us said a word about stopping. We'd hardly rested since we'd piled into the truck yesterday morning, just stopping once that afternoon in a small town to siphon gas and search the houses for food. Otherwise, we'd been trading off driving and navigating duties, with whoever ended up in the backseat doing their best to nap.

Tobias was driving now, finding his way by moonlight and the sweep of the truck's high beams. I peered out the windows from my seat in the middle of the back, only groggily awake, but too wound up to sleep. Here and there, lights flickered in the distance. Maybe lanterns, maybe fires. My hopes leapt with each glimpse.

Light meant people. We'd spent so much of the trip trying to avoid meeting anyone else, but now our mission depended on it. On finding the right people, here.

The sign at the city limits was so encrusted with snow I almost couldn't make out the words: WELCOME TO TORONTO. "We're here!" I said. "We made it!"

Justin pounded the dashboard up front, Tobias pumped his fist in the air, and Leo let out a weak "Woo-hoo!" Gav, who'd been dozing against my shoulder, shifted.

"My turn to drive?" he murmured.

"Go back to sleep," I said, leaning the side of my head against his. "The driving's almost done."

He straightened up instead, blinking.

"Where do you think we should turn off?" Tobias asked.

"I don't know," I said. I was the only one of us who'd lived in Toronto, but the size and busyness of the city had intimidated me so much I hadn't wandered much outside our west end neighborhood. I squinted through the glass, my head foggy. "There's no point in trying to look for people at night. I guess we should find a place to crash and get started in the morning."

Justin responded with a jaw-popping yawn. "Sleep sounds good."

"We don't want the truck to catch anyone's eye," Leo said. "It'd look like a pretty great prize."

"Let's take the next exit, then," I said. "It'll be harder to find someplace secluded downtown."

"Here we go," Tobias said. We fell silent as he eased the truck off the freeway and down the exit ramp.

We passed a set of dead streetlights and crawled along a wide road lined with strip malls. All of the windows were smashed, and trails of footprints looped through the snow in the vacant parking lots. Tobias clicked off the high beams, leaving only the dim glow of the truck's running lights and the moon overhead.

A faint but shrill sound pulsed somewhere in the distance. For a second I thought it might be a siren, that there might be actual police officers still there, but as we drew closer I recognized it as the harsh beeping of a car alarm. I wondered how long it'd been going with no one to turn it off. How long it would go before its power source ran out.

"Hey!" Justin said. I caught a flash of movement from the corner of my eye. As I turned my head, two figures darted past one of the stores up ahead. They vanished into the shadows so quickly I would have thought I'd imagined them, if Justin hadn't been staring after them too.

"They don't seem too friendly," Tobias said.

"Let's put some distance between us and them before we stop," Gav said grimly.

Beyond the windows, the buildings slipped by like ghosts. I hugged myself. Before, the city had felt big and busy, but also bright and energetic—*alive*, like all that action was the pulse of a living thing. I'd known it wasn't going to be the same now, but I hadn't expected it to feel so empty. So dead.

It had to be better when the sun was up. Darkness could make any place feel haunted.

We'd driven a few more blocks when a scream split the air somewhere behind us. "No, no, no, no, no!" the voice shrieked. "They can't, they can't do it!"

I cringed. Someone caught up in the violent hallucinations the virus brought at the end, I guessed.

"Jesus," Justin said. The shrieking broke off abruptly, as if someone had made it stop.

Leo's shoulder had tensed against mine, his mouth a pale line. I wondered how much the city reminded him of New York, of what he'd gone through there.

I found his hand, resting by his knee, and curled my fingers into his. He exhaled and squeezed back tightly.

The strip malls gave way to smaller stores and offices, the roofs of a residential neighborhood beyond them. "How about here?" I said, and Tobias nodded, turning down the next street. We passed two-story homes and bungalows as we wound around the corners, leaving the main road far behind. Finally, we picked a detached house with a wide driveway. Tobias pulled around and parked on the back lawn so the truck was hidden behind the house.

"Not much we can do to hide the trail from the plow," he said. "We should trade off watches in shifts like usual."

The knob on the back door had been bashed off, but we searched the house from basement to attic and found no sign anyone had stayed. After a hurried meal over the camp stove, Leo pulled a blanket around himself and went to sit on the radiator, where he could see the truck through the dining room window and the street through the living room.

"Wake me up in a couple hours and I'll switch off with you," Tobias said, and Leo just nodded.

With no fire, we set up the tent to hold our body heat closer and crawled in, cocooning in our blankets under the sleeping bags. I pulled my hood up and huddled against Gav. Even as my eyes drifted closed, my heart raced on, a frantic drumming in my chest.

We were here. We'd done it.

The excitement lingered, but I couldn't shake the feeling that was creeping through it. The feeling that we were a bunch of fish swimming into a crocodile's mouth, and all we could do was pray its jaws didn't snap shut.

\*   \*   \*

When I woke up, cold and stiff, and poked my head out of the tent, light filled the living room. I shook off the blankets and stepped out, going to the window. The scene outside looked like a normal winter day, serenely white. The sunlight flowed into me, warming the icy tendrils of fear that had sprung up the night before.

Gav was sitting by the doorway. He must have taken over the watch at some point in the early morning. He smiled at me, but his eyes looked tired. I wondered how much he'd slept.

"You should have woken me up for one of the shifts," I said.

"You needed the rest," he said, as if he didn't.

The blankets rustled inside the tent, and in a few minutes we were all up, passing around a box of stale crackers as we packed our things.

"What's the plan?" Tobias asked.

"I want to see if the hospitals are functioning," I said. "It'll be easier to figure out what to do once we know exactly what's going on here."

"The truck's going to be even more noticeable now that it's light out," Leo said.

I considered the map book. "There aren't any hospitals nearby. I think we have to do a little driving. Let's see what we find, and if we need to stay another night, we'll look for a good place that's central, so we'll be able to do more on foot."

We clambered into the truck, Gav at the wheel.

"It looks like there's a pretty big hospital a couple miles west down that main road," I said. "I'll let you know when to turn off."

The footprints outside the stores were even more visible in daylight, but the people who'd made them stayed out of sight. Smoke drifted up from the chimneys of a few houses off the main strip.

As we turned down the street toward the hospital, we passed a couple of figures bundled up in coats and scarves, trudging along the sidewalk in the same direction. They stared at the truck and its plow, nothing of their faces visible except for the glint of a pair of glasses. Then one bent over, gloved hand pressed to where his or her mouth must have been behind the scarf. Coughing.

Tire tracks marked the road in front of the hospital, but they looked old, half filled with fresh snow. The lot was clogged with snow-covered cars. We parked outside the front entrance.

Gav reached for the car door, and I grabbed his arm.

"No," I said. "We can already see there'll be sick people here. I'm immune. Leo's had the vaccine. The rest of you are vulnerable. So you should guard the truck, and we'll go in." I looked back at Leo. "If that's okay with you."

"Makes sense," he said. "I'm not going to sit here while you go alone."

"I'm happy to stay away from the sickos," Justin said, leaning back in his seat. Tobias didn't say anything, but remembering how he'd reacted when we'd met the infected couple in the other town, I was pretty sure he didn't mind.

"You don't know who you're going to run into in there," Gav said. "What if two of you aren't enough?"

"If it comes to that," Leo said quietly, "I have one of the guns."

Gav's shoulders were tensed, and his hand hadn't left the door. "All right," he said. "But I'm going to watch the clock. You take more than half an hour . . ."

"Fine," I said, raising my hands. "Just be careful. And if you see anyone go by who looks, I don't know, official, grab them and explain why we're here, okay?"

I left the cold box with our precious cargo locked in the truck's covered bed. The hospital doors, high and glassy, stood half open, propped by a couple of concrete blocks. A man slipped out as Leo and I approached, his arms clutching something I couldn't see. As he disappeared around the corner, he let out a sneeze.

For a second, my legs locked. Even after I'd recovered, I'd never gone into the island's hospital without protective gear, just in case the virus mutated. And Leo had even less security, only the protection of an unproven vaccine.

I pulled my scarf tightly around my face, and Leo did the same. "Let's go save the world," he said.

We eased past the front doors and into the reception area. A girl who didn't look any older than twelve was pawing through the drawers behind the admissions counter. She stopped to scratch the back of her head. Papers were scattered on the counter and the floor beneath it.

The halls beyond were dim, only occasional streaks of sunlight reaching them from windows within open rooms. Coughs and sneezes echoed from farther inside. We picked a direction and started walking.

Beneath the scarf, my breath felt thick against my face. Down one hallway, out of sight, someone was sniffling and banging what sounded like two metal objects against each other. Farther on, a man with a red nose and flushed cheeks hustled from one room to the next. Boxes and vials clattered. He jerked around when I peeked in, and snarled, "Back off! I was here first."

We hurried on.

A moment later, a yell bounced off the walls, and two women scrambled around the corner ahead of us.

"I saw it!" one was shouting. "It's mine!"

Leo reached for my arm, and we leapt back against the wall as they stumbled past us. The first woman skidded, and the second tackled her. When the second squirmed away, she was gripping an amber bottle.

"It's mine!" she spat, and ran for the front doors. The first woman pushed herself to her feet, her breath coming in little sobs, and wavered back the way she'd come. I leaned against the wall, my pulse thudding.

Leo was rigid. "I'm starting to think we're not going to find—"

He stopped, his eyes twitching toward something behind me. I turned.

A different woman had come up beside us. Tangled gray and black hair fell around her face, and a small, sad smile twisted her mouth.

"Looks like we got here too late," she said.

My shoulders sagged in relief. So we weren't the only sane people in the city.

"Where are the doctors and nurses?" I said. "What happened to this place?"

The woman shrugged. "What happened to all the hospitals, I suppose. I heard it, but I didn't know how bad it was. Soon as the medicine started running out, everyone wanted to take what they could while they could. . . . It wasn't safe for anyone working here. 'Course, they didn't seem to be helping much as it was. I don't suppose I can really blame them for leaving."

"So they're all gone?" Leo said.

She inclined her head. "If you wanted to find a doctor here, you should have come a couple months ago."

"Where did they go?" I asked.

"Beats me. Maybe they're just sticking close to their families like the rest of us who are still alive." She sighed. "I don't know why I'm even here. Wallace and I were fine for so long, you know, but the itch came on him yesterday, and then the cough, and I thought, I can't just watch. I have to go out and see if I can find anything. But it looks like I'm finding a lot of trouble and not much else."

Her dark eyes flickered toward the hall and back to us, and narrowed with deeper consideration. "You don't look sick, either of you."

"A friend," I said quickly. "We were hoping someone could help him. I guess we're out of luck."

As if to emphasize my words, three men charged around the far corner, hauling an electronic device the size of a bar fridge. What did they think that thing was going to do without electricity? I had the sinking feeling they were just taking whatever hadn't already been stolen, indiscriminately.

"Come on," I said. "Let's get out of here." And, to the woman, "Thanks. Good luck."

"It's just one place," Leo said as we hurried out the doors.

"I know," I said, and my foot bumped against a solid object in the snow.

The impact jolted some of the snow off the thing I'd hit. It protruded, a narrow brown shape, from the drift beside the trampled path leading to the doors. I'd been staring at it for a few seconds before recognition sank in.

A boot. The toe of a boot. In the rippling of the snow, I could almost see the outline of a leg, a chest—I looked away. There was snow everywhere. How many bodies lay beneath it? My stomach lurched.

"It's just one place," I repeated softly. I strode on toward the truck without glancing back.

Gav read my face as I climbed in. "No?"

I shook my head and picked up the map book. The lines and street names swam before my eyes. I blinked, trying to focus.

"Some of the hospitals could still be working," I said. "And there'd be government labs and corporate ones, right? Those would be more protected; the people working there wouldn't have had to leave."

Of course those labs didn't publicize their locations on city maps, which was what protected them in the first place.

Drew might have known where some were. He'd explored the city far more thoroughly than I'd ever wanted to. If he was still okay. If we could manage to reach him again.

I swallowed the lump rising in my throat. "We could try city hall next," I said, tapping the curved shape on the map down near the waterfront. "They won't have labs, I don't think, but there might be government people around who know where to go."

"If they haven't all left too," Gav said.

"You have a better idea?" I asked him.

He grimaced apologetically. "No. You're right, it makes sense to try there."

He pulled the truck back into the middle of the road. We wove through the streets toward city hall, following whichever were least clogged with snow and cars. Some were packed solid with vehicles in a permanent traffic jam, like a parade of ice sculptures.

"Freaky," Justin said as we backed out of one choked road we'd mistakenly turned down. "Where'd they all think they were going?"

It wouldn't have mattered, I thought. By the time people had gotten that scared, there wouldn't have been any truly safe place left.

We were only a few blocks from city hall when Leo stiffened. "Cut the engine," he said.

"What?" Gav said.

"Just cut it!"

Gav yanked the gear stick into park and twisted the key. The second our engine stilled, I heard another rumbling in the distance.

"Good ears," Tobias said.

Leo didn't answer. As we listened, the engine sound grew louder, then gradually faded away without crossing our path.

"Couldn't that have been some of the government guys we're trying to track down?" Justin asked.

"Anyone who's kept a car running in the city this long . . . they'll have had to fight to do it," Leo said. "Fought and won."

"Let's not run into them, then," I said.

The road that ran past the square outside city hall was deserted. Mounds of snow covered the courtyard where in other years a huge skating rink had been set up. My middle school had taken us there on field trips.

Tobias stayed with the truck, taking over the driver's seat with the rifle across his lap, and the rest of us picked our way toward the building through the shallowest drifts. I tried not to think about what might be lying under the snow.

I couldn't see beyond the line of windows and wooden doors. As we approached, I realized they were barricaded, cabinets and cubicle dividers pushed up against the glass, crisscrossed with boards where it had started to crack.

Someone had been in there. Someone who'd wanted to prevent anyone else from getting in. It looked like they'd been successful.

Which meant they could still be there.

Justin jogged to the nearest set of doors and tugged on the handles. They didn't budge. He smacked the wood with his gloved fist.

"Hey!" he shouted. "Open up!"

I hurried to the next door and pounded on it. "Please!" I said. "We have something that can help the city. We just need to talk to someone!"

Only silence answered us. I waited a minute, then banged on the door again.

"Look at the way they shut themselves off in there," Gav said. "They don't care about the city anymore."

"So we force our way in and make them help!" Justin said.

"No," I said, turning. "We'll give them time, and if no one—"

My voice failed and my breath caught in my throat.

Gav had taken off one of his gloves and pulled back the opposite sleeve of his coat. He frowned at the building—I wasn't sure he'd even noticed what his hand was doing.

He was scratching his inner forearm, so hard the pale skin was going pink.

# TWENTY-ONE

"It's okay," Gav said. "It's nothing, Kae."

His scratching fingers had stilled when he'd seen my expression, and he was giving me his usual confident smile. But even as the words came out of his mouth, his jaw twitched and his hand clenched. And I knew. The itch hadn't stopped.

"What the hell!" Justin said, backing away.

"It's *nothing*," Gav insisted. He yanked his glove back on and shoved his hands into his pockets. "But there's no point in staying here. We keep yelling, we're just going to draw attention."

Attention we had already probably drawn with the truck. I narrowed my thoughts to that one concern, blanking out the fear. "We have to find a place to stay," I said. "It looks like tracking someone down might take a few days."

Leo watched me cautiously, but he didn't argue. "An apartment or condo building would be good," he said. "More doors between us and the street."

"We need a fireplace," Gav pointed out.

"There are condos with fireplaces," I said. "Real ones, not just gas. We went to a friend of my dad's place a couple times when we lived here; he had one."

We all headed back to the truck, but when we reached it, Justin halted on the sidewalk.

"I'm not getting in with him," he said, cutting his gaze toward Gav.

"Fine," I said. "Then you can walk."

"What's going on with the kid?" Tobias asked as we climbed in. I got in the back with Gav, so Leo took my spot up front. I waited a second before closing the door, but Justin didn't budge. Tobias was looking back at me. I didn't know how to answer.

And then I didn't have to, because Gav jerked forward, sneezing, and sneezing again.

Tobias blanched and Leo flinched, and Gav's eyes went so wide and frightened he looked more like a little boy who needed his parents than like a guy who'd organized an entire town to save itself.

"Fuck," he said. "I'm sorry, I'm sorry." He fumbled with his scarf, which was wound tightly under his chin. As I reached to help him, his hands quivered, and he threw up his arm just in time to catch a volley of coughs. When they subsided, he pushed open the door and scrambled out, hauling the scarf up over his mouth and nose.

"I guess I'd better walk too," he said stiffly.

"Gav," I said, but he shook his head. So I got out as well. I wasn't letting him walk alone.

He kept coughing, on and off, as Tobias started driving. Leo must have explained what we were looking for. We strode along beside the car, Gav and me on one side and Justin on the other, jogging when we needed to catch up. A long series of condo buildings stretched across the streets just beyond city hall. At each one, Tobias stopped and Justin dashed inside to look around. It wasn't until the twelfth that he came back with a thumbs-up.

The door to the building's underground garage was jammed

open. Tobias parked the truck by the back, and we grabbed as much of our stuff as we could carry. It wasn't until we'd climbed up to the fourth floor, trying to put some distance between us and potential looters, that Justin mentioned our other problem.

"We're going to have to hang around in the same apartment as him, when he's like this?" he asked, gesturing toward Gav, who'd hung back a few paces behind the rest of us.

"I'll stay in the bedroom with the door closed," Gav said. "No one'll have to come near me."

Justin scowled, but he didn't say anything else. We dropped our bags in the living room of the condo we chose, and he turned back with Leo and Tobias to get the rest of our supplies. I followed Gav into the bedroom.

All the furniture matched the shiny black wood of the floor, the walls and comforter a contrasting off-white. The air was frigid. It felt as if we'd stumbled into a yuppie ice palace. Gav sank onto the floor next to the dresser, rubbing his mouth through the scarf.

"I know what you're thinking," he said. "Stop it."

He couldn't know, though. Because I hadn't been thinking anything. I'd just walked beside the truck and carried what I needed to and not let a single thought slip through.

It was getting harder to do that.

I opened my mouth and found that my throat had closed up. Everything felt closed up inside me, as if all my organs were trying to fold themselves into hard little balls. I swallowed and sat down across from him as he coughed.

He looked at me, the lighthearted tilt of his head at odds with the slump of his shoulders. I could see his jaw clenching and releasing. The effort he was expending to stay calm radiated off him.

He laid his fingers across my wrist and tugged gently. As if he didn't think he could ask for comfort. I shifted forward, and he wrapped his arms around me, pulling me in with a sharp little breath. He pressed his face against my hair as I settled into his lap. I hugged him, blinking hard.

"You're here," he said. "So I'll be okay."

I closed my eyes, but the tears I'd been fighting slipped out, streaking down my cheeks. I wanted to say that of course it'd be okay, *he'd* be okay, he could beat this. But I wasn't sure I believed it enough to say it like I meant it. And saying it like I didn't would have been worse than saying nothing.

The truth was, I didn't know anyone who'd survived the virus without some sort of extra immunity. If I could have taken some of my blood and just given it to Gav, maybe he'd be okay, like Meredith had been. But what Nell had done was more complicated than that, using procedures I didn't know.

"There's got to be at least one doctor left in this city," I said. "I'm going to find him, or her, and I'll make them do a transfusion like Nell did for Meredith. Since my blood's type O negative, they can use it for you no matter what type you are. It worked for Meredith."

If I could find a doctor who'd do it in the time we had. If there was a hospital somewhere that hadn't been stripped of the equipment we'd need. If there was anyplace left in the city with the electricity to run that equipment.

If, if, if.

If Gav hadn't been so stubborn. If I'd been more stubborn. I could have insisted that he either stay on the island or take the vaccine, and maybe all those other ifs wouldn't have mattered. Because he wouldn't have gotten sick in the first place.

I looked at the cold box, which I'd set down beside the bed, holding the priceless material that had dragged us all out here. The vaccine couldn't do a thing for him now. In that moment, I hated it.

Gav cleared his throat as if trying to hold back another cough. "We came here for a reason," he said. "I don't want to be the one who messes that up."

I eased back so I could see his face, still close enough that I could have counted the green flecks in his hazel eyes, and touched the side of his forehead. His skin was already warmer than it should have been, warmer than made any sense in the icy room.

"Looking for doctors is what we were already going to do," I said. "You're not messing us up. I've just got another reason now."

I slid down his scarf and kissed him. He hesitated for a second, and then he kissed me back. Afterward, he tucked his head next to mine. A moment later, he started to cough again.

This time, he couldn't stop. He shifted to the side, hacking and gasping, and I pulled my water bottle out of my coat.

"Here," I said. "You should drink something. And I'll see if I can get a fire going. It's freezing."

In the living room, the others were already standing around the fireplace. "We can go out and gather some wood," Tobias said. "There's lots of trees in the parks."

Leo nodded. "And we've got a whole building full of furniture."

"We should melt some more snow too," I said, and they turned around. "We're getting low on water. And we might as well check the other condos for food. If we're lucky, no one's bothered climbing all the way to the top yet."

In the bedroom, Gav sneezed. Justin's gaze darted to the closed door. "If we're not all like him in a week," he said, grimacing. Then he went still. "Hey. There were three containers of the vaccine. That means three doses, right? I could take it, and Tobias, and there'd still be one left."

One sample left. One chance, which we could lose as easily as glass breaking. To vaccinate two people who, if they were going to catch the virus from Gav, had already been as exposed as they would ever be.

"I'm sorry," I said, shaking my head. "But we don't even know if one will be enough. What if it turns out the one we keep is ruined from the time you took them out? We can't risk it. Gav will stay in the other room—I'll be the only one who goes in with him." I paused, remembering the pressure of Gav's arms around me, his breath in my hair. "And I'll find another coat, and use a different hat and gloves, so I'm wearing different clothes in there and out here. That way I won't spread it, either."

"He got to have the vaccine," Justin said, pointing at Leo. "If he did, we all should."

"I didn't know how hard a time we were going to have when I decided that," I said. "If I had . . ."

Would I still have asked him to take it? And Tessa?

"I would have said no," Leo said. "Like Gav did. Maybe I should have anyway."

Tobias dropped down onto the leather couch. "I'm with Kaelyn," he said. "That vaccine is more important than any of us."

"Seriously?" Justin said. When Tobias met his protest with a pointed stare, he threw up his arms. "You guys are crazy!"

"You can keep complaining, or we can do something useful," Leo said. He picked up our pots.

"Guess it's better than being stuck in here with him," Justin muttered.

It was easier to ignore the desperate ache in my chest when we were working. Leaving Tobias to guard the condo, the three of us tramped down the stairs and along the street until we came to a small park with a couple of benches and a swing set. As I scooped snow into the pots, Leo and Justin poked around the bases of the trees, picking up twigs.

"We're not going to get much fire out of this crap," Justin said after a few minutes. He eyed the trees, then reached up and yanked on one of the branches. With a crack, it split up the middle. After a couple more tugs, he broke it off.

"Not bad," Leo said. "How about this one?"

As he twisted his hands around another branch, footsteps rasped through the snow behind us. I turned.

A middle-aged man in a parka was coming across the street. The edge of a face mask poked above the top of his scarf.

He came to a stop on the sidewalk beside us. "Whatcha doing?" he asked. No greeting, no pretense of friendliness. His voice was casual, but there was a firmness in his stance that said he expected an answer.

I tensed, wondering what he'd do if we didn't give him one he liked. What he'd had to do to get that mask.

"Just gathering some firewood," Leo said, his tone light but careful. "Got to keep warm somehow, right?"

Justin took a step forward, dragging the branch he'd snapped off. "You got a problem with that?"

The man's eyes narrowed.

"Justin," I said. "It's fine."

"That's right," the man said. "You watch how you talk to people. If I wanted to make a problem, I would."

"Maybe *you* should watch how you talk," Justin said, raising the branch. "What we're doing isn't any of your business. So take off!"

I shifted between them, shooting a glare at Justin. The last thing we wanted was even more trouble. "I'm sorry," I said to the man. "He's just a kid."

"I'm not—" Justin protested, and I jammed my foot onto his toes before he could make the situation any worse. His voice cut off with a curse. The man's face crinkled as if he was smiling beneath his scarf.

"You get him to put a lid on it," he said. "All I'm doing is keeping an eye out."

And from now on, I suspected he'd be keeping an eye out for us too. I waited as he walked away. Even after he'd gone around the corner and disappeared from view, my arms stayed braced by my sides.

"That hurt," Justin said. "I was just—"

I spun around. "You were just screwing us over," I snapped. "You make that guy think we're a threat, you think he's just going to leave us alone? Now he's going to be watching for us when we're trying not to get noticed."

"Kaelyn's right," Leo said.

Justin's gaze darted between us. "Look," he said, "it's not my fault the two of you are too scared to stand up to a guy."

"It's not about being *scared*," I said. "It's about being smart. We are not the biggest fish in the pond here, and making like we are isn't going to prove anything; it's going to get us hurt—maybe killed. You know what you do when you're a little fish surrounded by sharks? You lie low and hope they don't see you, because they'll go after the most obvious prey. The only reason anyone was after us in the first place is we caught their attention. And it's not up to you to decide when we need to stand up for ourselves. This is my mission, those are my dad's samples, and you need to start acting like you know that. Or you can find some other people to tag along with."

By the time I'd finished, my throat was raw with the winter air. I wanted to turn away, to let the tension dissipate, but I couldn't, not yet. He had to know that the challenges and the posturing ended now. We had too much on the line to risk another mistake.

Justin's face had paled. He blinked, his mouth hanging open, and then he was the one who turned away. I drew in a breath, uncurling my fingers from my palms, feeling suddenly shaky.

"Let's get a few more of these branches," Leo said. He glanced at me and I nodded to show I was okay. As he and Justin went back to work on the trees, I left the pots I'd filled and grabbed a recycling bin I'd spotted on someone's porch. It was empty, and it looked clean enough, considering we were going to boil the water anyway. I carried it back to the park and packed it full of snow.

"Don't think we can carry much more," Leo said, hoisting a bundle of branches and sticks. "You good?" he asked Justin.

"Yeah," Justin said quietly. He stayed silent as we marched back down the street to the condo building. When we reached the door of the apartment we'd taken over, he hesitated. Leo went in, but I stopped and looked back.

"I'm sorry," Justin said. His gaze was fixed on the floor. "You're right. It was stupid. But you don't understand."

"I don't understand what?" I said.

He swallowed. "My dad—he was just going to see if there was any food left in the grocery store, and some guy shot him. I wasn't there to help him because he made me stay home with Mom, like some little kid. I don't want to be like that anymore, some kid who runs and hides. But I guess I didn't think; getting in people's faces isn't exactly the most mature move ever, either. I just get freaked out, you know, and I want to *do* something."

I leaned against the door frame. "I'm sorry about your dad," I said, meaning it. "I didn't know." He'd mentioned him, and I hadn't seen him at the colony, but it had never occurred to me to ask.

"Yeah, well. I guess I probably couldn't have done anything for him if I had been there."

I remembered Meredith's teary face as she asked me not to leave her behind. Pictured her here, amid the dead bodies and the looters. She'd been worried I was leaving her because I didn't think she was brave enough, but the simple fact was, I couldn't have lived with the guilt if I'd kept her with me and then hadn't managed to protect her.

"Whoever killed your dad, if you'd been there, they'd have killed you too," I said. "He probably made you stay home just because he cared about you and didn't want you to get hurt. You can't be mad at him for that, can you?"

"I . . . never really thought about it that way." Justin raised his head. "You still pissed at me?"

"Are you going to listen next time I say to back down?"

His mouth curved up. "Yeah," he said. "I'm going to work on that."

"Then I'm not pissed," I said. "But I am cold, and tired of

carrying all this snow. Let's get in there and see if we can make this place livable."

We stepped inside to the sound of Gav's coughing echoing through the bedroom door.

# TWENTY-TWO

Over the next few days we developed a routine. In the mornings, Leo and I would hike to a couple of hospitals or clinics, while Tobias and Justin scavenged through another few floors of the condo building. We all met back at the apartment to eat, and then the four of us headed over to city hall to look for a way in. Then another hospital. In the evenings, after dinner, Tobias fiddled with the radio and I prayed to hear Drew's voice.

All our efficiency hadn't helped us yet. Out of the dozen medical buildings we'd visited so far, Leo and I hadn't found one staff person. No medication, either. On the fourth day, we came across two bodies sprawled on the floor in a ward, bullet holes in their jackets, an icy glaze over their eyes.

We just kept going.

"Any luck?" Gav asked when I came into the bedroom to have lunch with him, a rasp in his voice that never quite left now.

"We're still looking," I said, forcing myself to sound optimistic, and started talking about how Tobias and Justin had managed to scrounge up another bag of food. I didn't mention the medicine cabinets they'd checked, all bare, which was why we didn't have even the most basic painkillers or decongestants to help Gav's symptoms.

When the rest of us headed out for city hall that afternoon, I looked around at the empty streets and darkened windows and tried to summon up a little of the hope that had carried me so far. Every time I stepped out into that wreck of a city, it got harder.

"Everything all right?" Leo asked as we tramped along the streets.

The question made me laugh. "Yeah," I said, even though it wasn't. Nothing was all right. Hell, even if we found someone who could replicate the vaccine samples, I wasn't convinced anymore that the vaccine would fix all I'd hoped it could. The world we used to have, the world I wanted back, was seeming more and more like a dream. I hadn't caught a glimpse of it here.

Even if we defeated the virus now, Leo couldn't take back the things he'd had to do. I couldn't go back to being a person who'd never seen someone die, who'd never stolen food and clothes and cars. Everyone still living had been changed—we couldn't have survived and not been. And even if we could change back, it wouldn't undo all the other damage the virus caused. Who was left to run the power stations? To stock the stores, now that the manufacturing plants were closed and the farms gone fallow and the transport trucks were stalled with empty tanks?

When we'd been on our little island, almost holding it together, I'd been able to imagine the problem was little too. But it wasn't just the island. It was the whole world.

I shoved those thoughts away as we reached the hall. The temperature had risen above freezing, the icicles over doorways dripping with a steady patter. We spread out, rapping on the doors and calling out to the people I still suspected might be inside and alive, then took turns trying to pound one of the boards on the broken windows loose. After an hour, no one had answered us, and the board hadn't budged. Finally, Tobias backed away, shaking his head.

The shrinking drifts of snow scattered around the courtyard revealed more than I wanted to see. The green sheen on a coat shielding a slumped back. A bluish hand and the cuff of a sleeve. Two socked feet, bent at painful angles. Because someone had wrenched off a pair of boots?

I winced and turned. "Let's go," I said, "before we bring out more scavengers." Two days ago, a couple of lurking figures had started trailing behind us on the way back. Wondering where we were staying and what supplies we had, probably. And whether they could take them from us. We'd managed to lose them by weaving through a series of apartment buildings and parking lots, but I wasn't eager to see them or anyone like them again.

We were halfway across the courtyard when an engine sputtered somewhere down the street. Close.

Leo froze, and I remembered his warning the last time we'd heard a car. Tobias reached for his gun. Justin started forward, almost eagerly, but I grabbed the back of his coat.

"Better not to get noticed," I reminded him. It would be a lot harder to lose a vehicle than to lose people on foot. I turned, searching for someplace to hide. The car was coming too fast, the sound of the engine thundering in the still air. My gaze slid over one of the half-buried bodies, and I found my answer.

"Play dead!" I said, already moving. I threw myself onto one of the higher drifts, shoved some snow over my back so it would look as if I'd been there awhile, and lay still. There was a brief shuffling around me that I hoped was the others following suit. I held my breath, the chill of the snow seeping through my scarf.

Possums could hold themselves like this for hours. Other animals too. My grandmother on my dad's side used to tell the story of her big family trip to South Africa when she was nine, rubbing the scar on the back of her hand while she talked. She'd seen a snake lying in the grass with its tongue hanging out, poked it a few times with her toe, and it hadn't looked anything other than dead until she'd crouched beside it and reached out to feel its scales.

I wasn't sure I could pull off a performance that convincing, but hopefully no one was going to come close enough to poke me.

The ground vibrated faintly as the car rumbled by. It slowed, and my pulse hiccuped, but the driver must just have been turning a corner. The noise of the engine rose again and faded gradually into the distance.

When I couldn't hear it anymore, I pushed myself upright. The others picked themselves off the ground, brushing bits of snow from their clothes. Justin was grumbling, but suddenly I felt like smiling for real. At least he was listening now. We'd managed to stay safe one more time, without having to fight, without being hurt. That was a sort of victory.

My mind slid back to Gav, waiting for us at the end of our walk, and my exhilaration dampened. It was a victory that didn't bring me any closer to saving him.

"You still haven't seen any phone books in the condos?" I asked Tobias as we set off.

"I'd guess they weren't sending out the printed ones anymore," he said. "Everyone just used the 'net."

A lot of good that did us now. "We need to find one," I said. "It might have the address for some of the private labs."

"Do you still think we're going to find doctors somewhere here?" Justin said, kicking at a chunk of ice.

"There are people here," I said. "Lots of people, considering. There has to be *someone* left with a background in science."

But we were running out of time. Gav was running out of time. I picked up my pace. "I'm going to look through the whole building myself when we get back."

In my hurry, I didn't catch the flicker of movement behind us until we'd climbed up the first two flights of stairs in the condo building. Fabric hissed against the wall somewhere below us, and I paused, the back of my neck prickling.

We had a shadow.

I made myself keep walking. When we reached our floor, I nudged Tobias's shoulder and continued past him up the next flight. The others looked confused, but they followed. On the fifth-floor landing, I pushed past the doors and backed several paces down the hall before I stopped.

"What's—" Justin started, and I jerked a finger to my mouth.

"We're being tailed," I said. "Watch."

We stood in a row, braced and waiting. A few seconds later, the stairwell door eased open a crack. Whoever was behind it must have seen us, because it stopped.

There was no hiding and no losing them, not when they'd followed us this far. We'd just have to hope they were peaceful.

"You want something?" I said. "Come out and we can talk about it."

The door twitched, and then yawned further open. A hooded figure in a long black coat slipped into the hallway.

"Don't be mad. I just wanted to see what you're up to."

The voice was a girl's, soft and squeaky. She took a few steps toward us, placing her heavy combat boots so carefully they didn't make a sound. Then she slid back her hood.

She was older than her voice had made me think—older than me, I guessed. Her nose was small and upturned, the mousy effect offset by the gray shadow smudged over her wide eyes and the maroon gloss on her lips. Light brown hair streaked with bleached highlights fell around her narrow face. She looked as if she should have been waiting in line outside a nightclub, not creeping after us through an abandoned building.

"I saw you at the hospital—at Mount Sinai," she said. "You looked . . . nice. Not like most people these days."

The hospital name sounded familiar, but I hadn't been paying enough attention to know how long ago we'd been at Mount Sinai.

"There are a lot of assholes around," Justin said, watching her as if he thought we might have to break into mortal combat. "We don't want anything to do with them."

The girl offered a smile that might have been amused or appreciative—it was hard to tell. "I'm Anika," she said, spreading her hands in a gesture of supplication. Her fingernails were painted the same color as her lips. "I don't want to barge in on you, but it's so brutal in the city right now. I've been on my own for weeks. You all seem like you're sticking together. I guess I hoped maybe I could stick with you. For a bit?"

She ducked her head with a nervousness that looked more coy than authentic.

Tobias opened his mouth, and then looked at me. Justin was frowning.

"You carrying weapons?" Leo asked.

Anika blinked with what appeared to be honest surprise. She turned out the pockets of her coat, then unzipped it and held it open so we could see she wasn't hiding anything under it other than a purple turtleneck and jeans tight enough that it would have been obvious if she'd had a gun or a knife tucked away in them.

"I could maybe even help you a little," she suggested as she zipped the coat back up. "I've been here the whole time—well, I've lived here my whole life. You're looking for things, I might know where they are."

My pulse skipped. Maybe she was just what we needed. Whether she was telling us the whole truth or not, she didn't seem dangerous. And there was just one of her and four of us—and we were armed, taller, and probably stronger.

It was worth the risk.

"All right," I said. "We're one floor down."

When we stepped into the apartment, Anika's eyes opened even wider, taking in the leather couch, the granite countertops, and the crackling fire. I noted with relief that all the food we'd scavenged was safely out of sight in the cupboards. The cold-storage box had stayed in the bedroom with Gav, all the better to make sure Justin wasn't tempted by it.

I was about to suggest we all sit down and talk when the sound of coughing carried through the bedroom door. Anika tensed, her head twitching toward the other room.

"You've got a sick one," she said.

"Yeah," I replied stiffly.

"It's okay," Tobias said. "He stays in the bedroom. We're really careful."

"I'll be back in a sec," I said, grabbing one of the bottles of boiled water we'd left to cool on the window ledge.

Gav was sitting cross-legged on the bed when I came in. He chugged half the bottle I handed to him and tipped his head against the wall, closing his eyes. Even though only a thin heat seeped through the walls from the living room, his fever was bad enough that he'd stopped wearing his coat. Since lunchtime he'd pulled off his sweater and tied it around his shoulders over his T-shirt. He looked leaner than it seemed to me he should, and I didn't think it was just because he'd taken off a layer of clothing.

With a ragged breath, he straightened up and swiped at his nose with the rag he'd been using as a handkerchief.

Anika's voice started to rise and fall on the other side of the door.

"You brought someone back?" he said.

I traded my outer clothes for the sickroom spares I had left on the dresser, and climbed onto the bed next to him. His arm slid around me automatically.

"A girl followed us back to the apartment," I said, keeping my voice light. "Says she wants to join our club. You think we should hold an audition?"

Gav cracked a smile. "Maybe we should just take her at her word. There seems to be a lot of turnover in this saving-the-world business."

I thought he meant Tessa and Meredith. He must have, because we still weren't talking about the fact that at some point in the next couple days, if I didn't find help, he wasn't going to be himself anymore. But for a few seconds, I choked up and couldn't speak.

I wrapped my arms around him and hugged him, and he squeezed me tighter, but after a moment his arms sagged. The coughing and the fever were sapping his strength.

"You think she's really okay?" he asked, more seriously.

"She might know something that could help," I said.

"Well, you'd better get out there before she's done telling her story, then," he said, "so I can hear it from you later. I don't want to be totally out of the loop."

"Of course," I said, kissing his cheek. "I'll bring the full report with dinner."

I could feel his eyes following me as I stepped out, his hunger to take part in what was happening a palpable weight on my back.

Anika was perched on the couch. Justin and Tobias sat on either side of her, Justin as if he were standing guard, Tobias as if he were afraid if he took his eyes off her she might disappear. Her hands flashed through the air as she spoke.

"And by the time Mom checked in to the hospital, they weren't letting visitors come in. That was when there were still people working in the hospitals to stop us, right? And they'd canceled all the classes at the college, and most of my friends had gotten sick or left town. But I didn't want to just abandon her, even if I couldn't go see her."

I grabbed a chair from the dining area and sat down by one of the living room's tall useless speakers. Anika's eyes flickered over to me and then back to the rest of her audience.

"Must have been rough," Tobias said. His face turned pink when she smiled at him.

"Yeah," she agreed. "The next thing I knew, people were trashing the hospitals left and right, and the doctors were freaking out and disappearing, and I don't even know what happened to Mom in the end. She was at Mount Sinai, but when I looked for her, I couldn't find her. So I've had to get by on my own."

"You look like you've been doing all right," Leo said mildly.

"I guess it could have been worse," Anika said. "I found a place like you have here, that no one seems to bother with, and Dad was kind of paranoid; he bought this camping stove and a bunch of fuel before the panic really started, so I've sort of been able to cook. I'm not, like, starving. But the people around here are crazy, most of them. It's scary. That's why I was so happy when I saw you."

"Who's the makeup for?" Justin demanded. "It's kind of weird, you going around like that."

"It's for me," Anika said. Her eyes narrowed for just a moment before she seemed to catch herself, and she tossed her hair with a laugh. "If you look older and like you've got yourself together, people don't bother with you so much. They go after the ones who look like victims."

I wondered what we looked like to her.

"You said the doctors were disappearing," I said. "Do you know if there are any still around, maybe in a smaller clinic or office that the looters could have missed?"

"If there are, they're keeping pretty quiet. But I could ask around." She cocked her head toward the bedroom. "That why you came all the way here from out east?" she asked. I guessed the guys had told her that while I'd been out of the room. "Because of him? It's a long way."

"We figured we had the best chance of finding someone who was still working on a cure in the big city," I said.

She shifted, her knee brushing Tobias's. He flushed darker. "I did hear something about a week ago," she said. "These guys were talking about a vaccine someone found, something like that? I don't know if it was real, but they sounded pretty worked up about it."

She glanced at each of us, her expression hopeful. Justin was staring at her, looking twice as suspicious as before, which was almost as bad as saying we knew all about the vaccine. Leo's mouth had flattened into a stiff line, and Tobias looked down at his hands. I held my face carefully calm, but my voice was stuck in my throat.

If someone had been talking about the vaccine here a week ago, when we were still holed up in that farmhouse, it could mean only one thing. The group who'd sent the people in the green van after us, who'd lied to us over the radio, had allies here too.

"If there's a vaccine, that'd be amazing," I said, hoping I sounded like this was the first I'd heard about it. "Who were these guys? Where'd you see them? Maybe we could find them and ask what they know."

"Oh, they were just guys," she said, lifting one shoulder and letting it fall awkwardly. "I don't know them. They were checking out some stores near the place I'm staying at. I only listened in because I heard one of them mention the vaccine thing."

"Did they say where they thought the vaccine was?" Leo asked.

Anika shook her head. "I don't think they knew. It kind of sounded like they thought someone might be bringing it here.

But like I said, they could have just been speculating. Maybe it's only a rumor."

My eyes met Leo's across the room and saw the worry I felt reflected there.

We hadn't outrun our enemies. We'd run right to them.

# TWENTY-THREE

I'd been spending my nights in the bedroom next to Gav. The others camped out in the living room by the fire, where it was warm, and Gav had tried to convince me to join them, but I wasn't going to leave him alone in the dark and the cold while the virus crept deeper into his brain.

"I want to stay with you," I'd told him, and when he started to protest, I'd looked him right in the eyes and said, "Shut up."

He'd stared at me for a second, and then, like I'd hoped he would, he'd laughed. He'd pulled me closer and kissed me and admitted, "I want you here too." And he hadn't tried to make me leave again.

The night after we met Anika, he dozed off quickly, but his arms and legs still twitched with the itches that never quite left him. I lay beside him, my eyes closed and my mind buzzing. I was all too aware of Anika's presence on the other side of the wall, an interloper in our midst. It'd seemed cruel to kick her out once night set in, and she'd offered to take us to a couple of government buildings that might have labs in the morning, but I wasn't sure how she was going to fit in with us yet.

Mostly, though, I was thinking about Gav. About how few nights like this we had left, before the virus gnawed into the part of him that controlled what he said and did and he started spewing out every unpleasant thing in his head, whether he meant it or not.

Dad hadn't managed to stay with Mom overnight after she got that bad. Would it be easier for me with Gav because I hadn't known him nearly as long? Maybe nothing he said would be able to sting too much.

Maybe tomorrow we'd reach someone who could help, and I wouldn't have to find out.

My thoughts were finally slowing, unraveling, when my ears picked up a faint squeak. The air shifted against the blankets. Someone had opened the bedroom door.

Burrowed under the covers, I couldn't see even when I opened my eyes. I lay quietly and listened. Footsteps brushed over the floor. With a click, a faint glow seeped around the edges of the blankets. A flashlight?

Our plastic bags crinkled. The footsteps moved around the bed and paused. I tensed.

The cold-storage box was sitting there at the foot of the bed.

I could have thrown back the covers and confronted whoever it was right then. But I wanted to know exactly what they would do. How far they would go.

There was a soft scraping sound as the lid was lifted, and an intake of breath. The seals snapped back into place. The light clicked off. And the box bumped the wall as it was lifted off the floor.

I didn't need more than that. I flung back the blankets, throwing my legs over the side of the bed. The figure with the cold box whipped around and ran for the door. I caught the sleeve of her coat, but not tightly enough. She yanked it from my grasp.

"Stop!" I yelled.

Anika's boots thumped over the floor to the apartment door. I charged after her. Sleeping bags rustled in the living room as the others roused themselves in a jumble of voices. "What?" "What's happening?" "Someone—"

Anika fumbled with the dead bolt. As I grabbed the handle of the cold box, trying to wrench it away from her, she jerked her arm toward me. Her elbow smacked me square in the forehead. My head spun, and my grip loosened. She pulled the box closer to her as she yanked on the doorknob.

But before the door had opened more than an inch, another arm shot out, slamming it shut. Anika flinched back, and froze.

A tall figure I dimly made out to be Tobias raised his hand. The low firelight caught the black shape of his pistol. His thumb rose and flicked off the safety with a click that sounded incredibly loud in the sudden silence. His voice came out strained but steady.

"I think you'd better give that box back to Kaelyn."

Anika lowered the cold box to the floor and released the handle. Leo and Justin came up behind Tobias, sleep-rumpled and frowning. I touched the spot where Anika's elbow had jabbed me and winced. Stepping just close enough to her to reach the cold box, I pulled it away and opened it.

Despite the scuffle, all the vials were intact.

"Kae?" Gav's voice wavered from the bedroom. "Everything okay?"

I exhaled and resealed the lid. "Yeah. It is now."

"They're going to end up finding you," Anika said. "It'd be better if you just let me take the vaccine. Then they won't be after you anymore."

"What 'they'?" Justin demanded. "What do you know about them?"

"The Wardens," she said. "Michael's Wardens." Her gaze slid over our faces, and her eyebrows rose. "You don't even know about Michael, do you?"

"We will if you tell us," I said.

When she didn't respond, Tobias shifted forward, the gun still pointed at her face. Anika curled her hands up into the sleeves of her coat and lifted her chin.

"I've never seen him," she said. "Apparently this guy named Michael came from all the way out in B.C., started going across the country after the virus hit, and he just sort of takes over places as he goes. Like here."

"How does one guy take over a city?" Justin asked.

Anika shrugged. "He's got food and generators and medical supplies, and he gives them to people who help him. The people who help him enough, he calls them Wardens. And then they—the Wardens—they keep an eye on the places he's been when he leaves."

"And he's in Toronto?" Leo asked.

"I don't think so, not right now. I don't hear everything—I'm not in with them like that—but it sounds like he's gone down to the States. The Wardens will be talking with him on their radios, though. And there's a whole bunch of them, and they've got cars and guns—you don't want to mess with them. They're looking for you and that vaccine."

"And you figured you'd get a reward if you brought them what they've been looking for," I said, watching her face. The desperation shone clearly in her eyes.

"I would have!" she said. "I would have been set. You want to be guaranteed you'll have enough food, you want to be in a building where the heat's running, you want one of those masks to protect you from getting sick, they're the only ones who have that now. Of course I want in."

My skin went cold. The guy who'd asked us what we were doing that first day when we'd gone out for firewood had been wearing a face mask. We'd been within talking distance of one of these Wardens, one of the people who would kill for the vaccine, and we hadn't even realized it. And if Justin had said even a little more, that guy might have realized who we were.

"You're stupid if you think you're safe here," Anika said. "You're just lucky I found you first. Going around to all the hospitals, shouting at city hall—I was guessing, but it wasn't a hard guess to make. Once they figure out you're in the city . . . you're done."

"Are you going to tell them?" Justin asked.

"I don't know," Anika said pointedly, glancing past the gun to Tobias's face. "Am I going to have the chance?"

Tobias went a little pale, but his hand didn't move an inch. He looked at me. Was it really that straightforward? I could give him the word and he'd shoot her?

My stomach turned. I didn't like what she'd done, but I could understand being that desperate to survive. She didn't deserve to die over it.

But we had to make sure we survived too.

"We're not going to hurt you," I said. Justin made a sound of protest, but he quieted when I glared at him. "We're *not* going to hurt her," I repeated to him, and turned back to Anika. "But we can't just let you take off, either."

Tobias lowered the gun slowly. "We could barricade her in one of the other apartments," he said.

Leo nodded. "That'd give us a chance to decide what to do next."

"And leave me to starve?" Anika said, her mouth tight. "Just shoot me now, okay?"

"No," I said. "We'd let you out, when we're ready to."

Justin sighed.

"We'll need a couch, or something heavy," Tobias started. His eyes flickered off Anika, and in that second of distraction she whipped out her hand.

She whirled around, a mist hissing from the tiny bottle she held. Justin leapt back, yelping and clawing at his face, and I staggered to the side, dragging the cold box with me, as a few droplets stung my eyes. Pepper spray. She must have had it lodged in her sleeve. Through a blur of tears, I saw Tobias coughing with his arm over his eyes and Anika tugging open the door, her slim figure darting out into the hall. I shoved the box toward the bedroom and ran after her.

The darkness of the hall was broken only by a faint haze that seeped from our open doorway. With my vision blurred, I couldn't see anything. Anika's boots scrabbled across the floor. She was already too far ahead. I took a few uncertain steps and heard the thud of the stairwell door closing. Sinking back against the wall, I swiped my sleeve over my eyes, again and again. In the apartment, Justin was moaning.

Leo appeared in the doorway. "Kae?"

"She's gone," I said.

"Are you okay?"

"Yeah." My eyes still smarted, but the tears were slowing. "It only hit me a little. You?"

"She missed me," he said. "I think Justin got the worst of it. Tobias is pretty bad too. He says water won't help much, so they're both just sitting there crying." He hesitated. "But we'd better get moving. She's probably running right back to those Wardens to lead them here."

"Right. Hell." I shuffled back inside.

Justin was crouching beside the couch, Tobias sitting in the armchair. "I'm going to kill her," Justin was saying, rocking slightly. "And then I'm going to kill her again."

"Just keep blinking," Tobias said. "The more you get the tears going, the faster they'll flush it out."

"Get the sleeping bags and the blankets," I said to Leo. "I'll start packing up the food."

"We're getting out of this freakin' city, right?" Justin said. "I am so sick of this place."

I paused. I hadn't even thought about where we were going, only that we had to get out of this building. "We can't *leave*," I said. "We'll find another apartment, not too close to here."

"Why?" Justin demanded. "Nothing useful here, anyway."

My throat tightened. The bedroom was quiet, maybe Gav had fallen back asleep, but the door still hung open across from us. He didn't have much longer. As long as we stayed, we might come across a person and the equipment to help him recover. If we hit the road... it would be like giving up on him for good. Giving him up for dead.

"If there are doctors and scientists anywhere, our best chance of finding them is still here," I said, lowering my voice. "We've got to change how we're looking, try other strategies, be even more careful than before, but we don't have anywhere else to go. Unless you want to head back to the colony and help with the planting?"

Justin made a face.

"I shouldn't have let my guard down," Tobias muttered. "She shouldn't have had the chance."

Leo hesitated, and then said, "It's the middle of the night. We're all tired and a little messed up. We can make a final decision later, right? Let's just get out of here while we can."

We had to abandon the truck. As we headed out to the garage, Justin stopped, his eyes still red, and said, "We told her. Anika. We told her about using the snowplow to get here."

"They'll be looking for it," I said. "Anywhere we leave it . . ."

Tobias turned his flashlight toward the street. Most of the snow had melted during the day, leaving the pavement bare.

"We wouldn't leave tracks," he said. "We can drive now, and then one of us can ditch it far away from the new place after we've found one."

We put more than a mile between us and the old building, leaving the shiny condos of downtown behind for concrete low-rise apartment complexes with rusty balconies. Tobias stayed beside the truck with the rifle and his pistol, while Gav slumped in the back, coughing weakly into the many layers of scarf he'd wound around his face. Leo, Justin, and I made our separate ways into the nearest buildings so we could check three places at a time.

It took seven tries before Leo returned with a crooked smile. "Not the nicest building," he said, "but it's got a fireplace."

We carried our things up as quickly and quietly as we could. The lobby and first floor stank of cat urine, though there was no sign of the cat responsible. By the time we'd climbed up six flights of stairs to the top floor, the smell had receded. We barged into the first apartment we found with an unlocked door. It was a two-bedroom, with a shabby polka-dot futon for a couch and stains on the rug. Gav walked straight into the nearer bedroom and crashed on the bed, his breath coming in rasps, while Tobias headed back down to get rid of the truck. The rest of us smashed up one of the rickety dining room chairs and sprinkled the varnished wood with our leftover twigs to get a fire going.

"We'll have to be even more cautious as long as we're still in the city," Leo said as the flames started crawling over the wood. "Someone should be watching the street at all times. We need to figure out an escape route in case these guys come looking for us."

He rubbed his face, his eyelids lowered, and I suddenly felt how late it was. I'd been running on adrenaline, but that was starting to fade.

"We can figure out an escape route in the morning," I said. "None of us is going to be thinking clearly right now."

"Still got to watch," Justin said. "I'll go first. Those assholes better hope they don't find me."

As he went out, I stepped into the bedroom. Gav looked asleep, but a moment after I lay down next to him, his arm slipped around me. He tugged my waist, and I rolled over to face him. His hand stayed on my side, his thumb tracing a slow loop, the pressure faint through my layers of clothing.

"Are we safe now?" he asked.

I'd only given him a sketchy explanation when I'd woken him to come down to the truck. I wanted to say yes, of course we were, but looking into his steady eyes, I couldn't bring myself to lie.

"I don't know," I said. And then I couldn't find any more words. Had he realized we were considering leaving the city?

I'd been trying not to think about what it would mean if we didn't manage to find someone here who could work with the vaccine. If we'd come all this way, gone through so much, but accomplished nothing. If Gav had gotten sick for nothing, and I couldn't even save him. I swallowed.

"Maybe we shouldn't have come at all."

Gav's hand stilled. "What?"

"You figured it'd be like this," I said. "That there wouldn't be anyone left to help. You always thought...And now—"

"Kaelyn." He touched my face, his fingers sliding along my jaw. When he opened his mouth to say more, he had to turn away instead, to cough against his shoulder. His arm trembled. I moved to get up, to find him some water, but he grabbed my hand, shaking his head as the coughs kept sputtering out of him.

After a minute, the coughing fit eased up. He shifted back toward me. His fingers returned to my cheek, brushing stray strands of hair away from my eyes. My skin tingled at his touch.

"I'm sorry," he said.

"It's not your fault," I said.

His breath hitched. "Not that. What you said before. I'm sorry.... I didn't believe you could do it. I'm sorry I didn't hide that as well as I wanted to. I guess, in a way, I didn't want to hide it, because I didn't want to pretend, because I thought I was right."

"Gav," I said, but he kept going.

"I wasn't right, okay?" he said. "I don't ever want to hear you say you were wrong to do this. I've had an awful lot of time to think the last few days. Everything was going to hell on the island anyway, even if I didn't want to admit it. We had to leave. And I really do believe, if there's anyone out there who can help us, then you'll be the person to find them. I fell in love with a girl who doesn't give up. So promise me. Promise me you're not going to stop trying, no matter what."

I found myself gaping at him, speechless.

"Say it," he said.

I cupped the back of his head and leaned close enough to press my lips against his. He kissed me back, but I could feel the tension in his arm that was still around me. I tipped my head forward, my nose brushing his cheek.

Gav didn't know how close I'd come to giving up completely when Meredith was sick. I'd never told him about standing on the edge of the cliff, planning the next step forward into nothingness. But I hadn't given up after all, and we'd made it through. I had to remember that.

"I won't stop trying," I said into the dark space between us. "I promise."

Only then did he relax. He kissed me again, and shrugged up the covers, and we fell asleep facing each other, our breaths mingling.

# TWENTY-FOUR

In the morning, with fresh resolve humming through me, I took over the front door watch from Leo and sent the guys on a building-wide search for a phone book. Tobias came to relieve me, carrying a thick softbound book.

"It's some kind of commercial directory," he said. "I figured it might be useful."

The directory turned out to be a jackpot—whole sections devoted to different sorts of laboratories. I paged through it, marking the most promising-looking locations in the map book. As soon as Leo came back from another scavenging run through the apartments, I grabbed him.

"We should go out and hit these two right now," I said, pointing to the ones that were closest. "We can be back before it gets dark."

We stuck to the side streets and walked quietly, listening for cars. One of our targets, a medical testing facility, had been looted, the doors busted open and the offices trashed. The other was a neurological research lab in a narrow stucco building that looked unharmed, but all of the windows were dark. No one answered when I knocked on the door.

"We just need one," Leo said as we headed back.

After dinner, as I sat on the couch planning the next day's targets, Tobias set the radio transceiver on the coffee table by the

244

sliding-glass door to the balcony. Leo and Justin snapped apart a couple more chairs and started feeding the fire. Tobias went through his usual process of calling out, switching channels, and calling out again. Leo had just tossed in the last piece when Tobias turned the dial, and a voice snapped through the speaker in midsentence.

"—there, please respond."

I dropped the map book and leaned forward. Tobias hesitated, his hand on the microphone, and then said, "We hear you. Who is this? Over."

The voice that answered was Drew's. "I'm looking for Kaelyn Weber. Who is this?"

Tobias offered the mic to me. I took it, my heart thumping. I'd been waiting for this moment since the first time we'd spoken, but suddenly I wasn't sure how much I wanted to know the answers to all my questions.

"Drew," I said, "I'm here. We've been trying to get a hold of you all week."

"I'm sorry," he said. "There's almost always someone in here monitoring the radios at the same time as me. Carmen's on a cigarette break, but I've probably only got a few minutes. You're not still in the city, are you? Tell me you left."

I was about to ask how he knew we had been in the city at all, but then I realized. Anika had gone straight to the Wardens, as we'd guessed she would. And Drew was right there with them.

There were so many other things I needed to say, but the words burst out: "Why are you with these people, Drew? What the hell are you doing?"

For a few seconds, the speaker gave me only a faint hiss. Then

Drew said, "I'm trying to figure out a way to help. Like I came here to do. You have to get in with the people who have power if you're going to make a difference."

He sounded almost like Anika. A sour taste rose in the back of my mouth. Before I could answer, he started talking again.

"What about you? The people they sent after you in New Brunswick—they found the bodies, Kae."

"I didn't want that to happen," I said quietly.

"Well, everyone here is gunning for you now. They're pissed. Hell, I'm glad you're okay, but I don't know what—" He cut himself off. "You didn't say where you are. Kaelyn, you left Toronto, didn't you?"

"We can't keep carrying the vaccine around," I said. "We have to find someone who'll know how to make more."

"So you're still here," he said. "Kaelyn, they're out looking for you *right now*. You're not going to find anyone here who can re-create a vaccine and wouldn't just turn it over to us anyway. When Michael came through, the first people he wanted on board were the ones with a medical background, and there's no one else left. I've been here almost two months; I'd know if there was."

I shook my head. I wanted to erase his words, but I couldn't. "So where are we supposed to go?" I said, my voice catching.

"I don't know," he said. "You could try— Right up until most of the communications went down, everyone was talking about how the CDC was working on the virus, trying to come up with a treatment. Michael thought they might still be at it—he started working his way down there three weeks ago, before he got word about you guys and the vaccine. I think—" His voice dropped. "Carmen's in the hall. Sorry. I'll try again tomorrow."

The transmission cut out, leaving only a dull hum of static. I felt as empty as it sounded.

Tobias switched off the radio and ran a hand over his pale hair. "The CDC," he said.

"What is that?" Justin asked.

Leo was the one who answered. "Centers for Disease Control and Prevention. When I was in New York, the scientists there were on the news a lot. It's in Atlanta."

Atlanta. My heart sank even further. This must be how Gav felt when I suggested continuing on to Toronto. How many more hundreds of miles?

"They obviously didn't do much," Justin said.

"They were trying," Leo said. "And . . . they have top-notch security there—they have to. They've got samples of all those deadly diseases: Ebola, anthrax, that sort of thing. So maybe the center wouldn't have gotten overrun like the hospitals here."

"Should we even trust this guy?" Tobias asked me. "I mean, I know he's your brother, but do you think he's right? There's no one here?"

My gaze slid to Leo, and he met my eyes, his mouth slanting down. I suspected we were both remembering our talk about how people changed.

Leo had changed. Drew had changed. Maybe in some ways for the worse. But whatever Leo thought, that didn't mean either of them was a bad person now. Drew had risked his life getting off the island so he could find a cure for Mom and for me. Both times on the radio, he'd been trying to protect me.

"Yeah," I said. "I believe him."

And I didn't want to leave him. If we waited, if we could talk to him tomorrow, would he be willing to come with us?

I let out a breath. I had no idea how far it was to Atlanta, but the distance couldn't be much shorter than what we'd already traveled. A trip that could have been two days and ended up taking two weeks. We had food, but we were going to have to find gas, and avoid Michael and his followers, and keep the vaccine cool as we headed farther south.

And there was Gav.

He didn't have two weeks. He didn't even have one. In just a few days, the hallucinations would come on, and we had no way to calm him down, no way of restraining him. But I'd promised him I'd keep trying.

We couldn't afford to wait for Drew.

"The truck," I said. "If we're going to leave, we'll need to drive. We can't walk to Atlanta."

Tobias frowned. "It's about a half hour from here on foot. If it's still there. I held on to the keys, but..."

But if Anika had told them about us, she'd probably told them everything. They'd have been looking for the truck too.

"Well, there's no point in going for it tonight," I said. "Drew said the Wardens are patrolling, and they'd be able to see the headlights from blocks away. We'll be a little less obvious driving by daylight. First thing tomorrow, we go get the truck, and if we can't use it, we start looking for something we can."

Gav woke me up so early only the dimmest dawn light was seeping through the bedroom window. He squirmed over on the bed, wrapped his arms around me, and pulled me close to him. For a minute I was glad. Happy to have a few extra waking moments with him.

He sneezed over his shoulder, and then he tucked his chin against the side of my neck.

"You are so, so pretty," he said. "And warm. And soft. It's nice. Did I ever tell you that?"

I started to laugh, but the sound caught in my throat. This didn't sound like Gav's normal teasing.

"The only other girl I was ever with like this," he went on, his breath whispering past my ear, "she was so skinny. All bones and angles. Not comfortable at all."

A twinge of jealousy hit me, wondering exactly what he meant by "like this." In bed together? What else had they done in that bed?

Then the rising horror overwhelmed it.

"Gav," I said softly.

"Wasn't the same anyway," he said, as if I hadn't spoken, and yawned. A few short coughs rattled out of his chest. "She was cute, and I thought I really liked her, but she always talked about the stupidest things, and then it turned out she liked Vince better anyway. The first day I came to your house, you didn't even want to let me in, and you were so *mad*, but you listened to me and you smiled and I knew. This is the girl. The one I want."

I turned in his arms and kissed his cheek. He looked at me, but there was a sort of vagueness to his gaze, as if behind his eyes he wasn't all there.

Because he really wasn't.

Sometime during the night, the virus had finally broken down that part of Gav that let him decide what he'd say and what he wouldn't, what was real and what was just impulse. I pressed my face against his coat and squeezed my eyes shut, holding back tears.

"I didn't know that," I said. It hadn't even occurred to me to think of Gav that way, that early on. My head had been too full of worries about the virus, with feelings for Leo I hadn't managed to let go of yet. How long had it taken me to see him?

"Even my parents," Gav said. "They were never interested in listening to me. Hardly even smiled, really. And now they're gone too. You're not going to leave, are you? You keep going out and I know you might not come back and I hate it. I want you to stay with me, Kae. I don't like being alone."

A sob broke out before I could clamp down on it. My jaw tightened. I swallowed and breathed, the tears slipping out and the taste of salt rising in my throat. "You won't be alone," I managed to say. "I'm staying with you. Don't worry."

"It's not really fair at all," he said. "Those guys, Leo and Tobias and them, they get to see you all the time, and I'm stuck in here, and I don't like that you're even *thinking* about them."

"I'm not," I said. "I'm only thinking about you."

"Leo—he says he's your friend, but *he's* thinking, I can see him thinking, all the time. He looks at you..." Gav stirred, suddenly restless. "It's not done yet. We haven't found any doctors, we haven't given them the vaccine. I should be helping, not lying around here. I—"

He paused and twisted to direct a coughing fit away from me. I grabbed the water bottle from the floor. When I turned back to him, he was sitting up. He drank and coughed and drank a little more, and then he pulled himself to the edge of the bed. His arms trembled with the effort of holding himself upright.

"We can go together today," he said. "You said we need to find a car. I'll help you look. I followed you all this way so I could help. Maybe we'd already have found one if I hadn't been so lazy."

I wiped my cheeks with my sleeve and gripped his shoulder. The heat of his fever radiated through his shirt. "Gav," I said firmly, "you haven't been lazy. You needed to rest, and you still need to, okay? When—when you've had enough rest we'll all go out together."

He hesitated, shivering, and then sank back onto the blankets.

"Probably not going to find anyone anyway," he murmured. "Those government pricks, they all ran off on us. Never could trust them. I knew it. I knew there was no point. We could have stayed where it was safe."

The words gnawed at me. Was that the truth, not what he'd said to me yesterday when he'd told me he understood why we'd had to come here?

I was probably never going to know.

"Try to go back to sleep," I said, picking up the now-empty bottle. "I'll get you some more water in case you need it. Okay? I'll be right back."

He lowered his head, his eyelids drooping. I eased out of bed, swapped coats, and slipped out the door.

The fire had died down to just a few tiny flames flickering over the embers, and a chill had crept through the living room. Justin and Tobias lay side by side in their sleeping bags in front of the fireplace. I padded around them to the window and the extra water bottles. As I edged back along the wall to the bedroom, I found myself evaluating the furniture.

The futon. If Gav got set on coming out of the apartment to help, we could hold the bedroom door closed with the futon. It looked heavy. I didn't think he was strong enough to push very much now.

And then I thought, *I am planning ways to trap my boyfriend inside a room to die.*

The apartment door opened, and Leo stepped inside. He stopped when he saw me. "The sun's coming up," he said. "I was going to wake up Tobias so he can check for the truck, wherever he left it. That's the plan, right?"

I nodded, not trusting myself to speak. The bottle wobbled in my hand. Leo's gaze fell to it and then rose to my face again, his brow knitting.

"Kae?" he said, and somehow the sound of my name broke the last shred of my self-control.

I dropped to the floor, clutching the bottle. My arms folded over my knees, and I mashed my face against them. My eyes burned, another wave of tears surging up and spilling out, hot and fierce. I gasped, choking down the sobs, not wanting the others to wake up and see me like this.

Leo didn't speak. He just walked across the living room and knelt in front of me, easing his arms around me. I resisted for a second, and then I let him draw me in so my head rested against his shoulder, my tears soaking into his coat. If I'd ever needed my best friend, it was now.

"If there's anything I can do," he said after a minute, his voice thick. "Anything at all, Kae, tell me and I'll do it."

But there was nothing he could do. Nothing he or I could do except sit there helplessly.

# TWENTY-FIVE

It occurred to me an hour later, as Gav dozed and I waited for Tobias to return, that there *was* one last thing I could do. I closed my fingers around the box of syringes I'd brought from Dad's lab. We weren't going to find a doctor in time to help Gav, that much seemed clear. But I could still give him some of my blood, with the antibodies it carried.

I didn't let myself think any further. I rolled up my sweater sleeve to wash the skin around the crook of my elbow. Then I sat down with one of the syringes, my hand in a fist, and studied my arm.

I remembered how Nell had slid the needle in when she'd taken blood for Meredith. It had looked so easy. But she was a doctor—of course it was easy for her. Gritting my teeth, I prodded the line of a vein with the needle tip, then pushed it in.

There was a stab of pain, and then a dull ache. I squeezed my hand tighter. The thick dark red liquid seeped into the body of the syringe. It would only hold twenty-five milliliters—a normal blood donation was almost twenty times that. I would be fine. I just wished I could give him more. But it was going to be hard enough convincing Gav to take one shot.

As I slid the needle from my arm, wincing, Gav shifted on the bed. Quickly, I stuck one of the adhesive bandages from the first-aid kit over the puncture and pushed my sleeve back down.

254

"Hey," I said, sitting on the side of the bed. Gav blinked at me and smiled in that new vague way that made my chest clench. "You remember how we helped Meredith when she was sick?" I said quickly. "We gave her some of my blood so the antibodies would help fight the virus. I'm going to do that for you too, okay?"

His smile dimmed. "No," he said. "You're not going to hurt yourself for me, Kae. No."

"It didn't hurt that much," I said. "And I've already done it. I just need to give it to you."

He shook his head, pushing himself back. "What kind of self-ish jerk would take his own girlfriend's blood?" he said. "I'm not that guy. I'm not."

"No, you're not," I said. "You're a guy who understands that his girlfriend needs to try anything she can to help him, and that she's going to feel guilty for the rest of her life if she doesn't do this. Right?"

His expression softened. "Guilty?" he said. "It's not your fault. It's this fucking virus. God, of all the things that could have done us in—"

"Gav," I said again, gripping his hand, "I need to do this. Please. For me."

He met my eyes, and then his gaze slipped away.

"Please," I said again.

"You have to try everything," he said, sounding resigned.

"You fell in love with a girl who doesn't give up," I said softly. The corner of his mouth curved up. I wondered if, in his virus-addled state, he remembered saying that to me.

"Yeah," he said, "I guess I did." He sighed. "All right. Go ahead.

But just this once, okay? I don't want you hurting yourself again. Ever."

"I got it," I said.

He turned his head and closed his eyes as I gave him the injection. With a twist in my gut, I watched my blood flow into his arm. It hardly seemed like enough. And maybe doing the transfusion this way, instead of using whatever serum Nell had created before, was completely useless.

But I'd tried. At least I'd tried.

I was so focused on Gav that I didn't notice the voices outside until I'd finished and he'd flopped down on the bed. Tobias had come back. What little hope I'd had in me deflated. He hadn't immediately announced it was time to go. Which meant he hadn't found the truck, not in working order anyway.

A few minutes later, Leo knocked on the bedroom door. "Tobias is going on watch, and Justin and I are heading out to see if we can find a car," he said. "The truck is gone."

There was a question in his voice—what about time? An image passed through my mind: joining them, barricading the bedroom door, then Gav hollering out the window for someone to let him out so he could look for me. I shook it away.

"I'll go too," Gav said, scrambling up. I grabbed his wrist. "I'm all right," he said, even as he wavered on his feet. "I can help."

"We're staying here," I said, tugging him back onto the bed. "We'll look at the map and figure out the best route out of the city. I'm too tired to do much walking," I added.

The last bit seemed to convince him. He leaned back against the wall and sneezed. "Atlanta, right?" he said. "Right. I always wanted to go to California first, if I ever got to the States. Sounded like a cool place. Maybe after Atlanta we could do California. Why not?"

"Sure," I said. "I'll get you some breakfast too."

"Ugh," Gav said. "I'm so sick of that canned crap. My stomach's all . . . ugh."

"I'll see what I can find," I said, hiding the trembling in my jaw with a smile as I got up.

He wouldn't eat the soup I brought, or even drink a cup of tea. His voice grew hoarser as he rambled on, and in the late afternoon he dozed off again, slumped over the pillow. I stayed with him until I was sure he was asleep, and then pulled the blanket up over him and went back into the outer apartment. I was in the kitchen, staring at our rows of cans and boxes and wondering what I could give him that he'd eat, when the others came in.

They were talking quietly, but an angry undercurrent ran through their voices. As soon as they saw me, they fell silent. I braced myself.

"What?" I said.

"We didn't find a car, not one we can use," Leo said. "Justin thinks we should leave now, anyway."

"For good reason!" Justin said. His eyes darted toward the bedroom door. When I crossed my arms over my chest, waiting for him to continue, he clenched his jaw. "I know what they get like, people who've caught it," he muttered. "He's going to go crazy soon, yelling and screaming, isn't he? How are we going to stop this Michael guy from finding us then?"

"They're still patrolling," Tobias put in. "When I was on watch, I went around to the side alley to take a leak, and as I was heading back, an SUV came down the street: black, tinted-glass windows. The guy driving rolled down his window and asked if I was on my own. I said yeah, acted friendly. He didn't look suspicious. But if they come by again and hear something..."

"So you want to walk?" I said, feeling cold. I wasn't sure Gav could, not far enough that it would matter. "You don't think we'd be kind of obvious, five of us wandering around with sleds full of supplies? Even if they don't drive right by us, we're going to leave a pretty clear trail, and it'll take us at least half a day just to get out of the city."

"There's not much snow on the sidewalks right now," Leo said. "We might be able to make it. If you think Gav's up to it."

"I don't know," I said. But I did. He could hardly stand up. Even if I could get him to eat, even if I supported him the whole way . . . "He's pretty weak. And it might not be easy to keep him quiet—"

"Then maybe we shouldn't take him," Justin said. His ears reddened.

"I already told him that's not happening," Leo said, touching Justin's shoulder, but Justin shook him off.

"What happened to 'the most important thing is the vaccine'?" he said, a whine creeping into his voice. "We know if we're going to find someone who'll make more of it, we have to leave, right?" He motioned to the bedroom. "And we know he's not going to get better. People don't get better. We're risking everything, and he—he might as well be dead already."

One second I was standing there with his words echoing in my head, and the next I was four steps across the room, my hands raised, my mind blank with anger. Tobias stepped forward and grabbed my arm, pulling me to a stop a few inches from where Justin stood. Justin backed away, looking terrified.

"Kae," Leo said.

My arms sagged, and Tobias let go. It was true. And that was why it hurt so much to hear it. But Gav wasn't dead yet.

"Would you say that if it was your mom?" I said. "Your dad?"

Before Justin could answer, there was a rap on the front door.

All of us froze. Tobias slid his hand into the inner pocket of his coat and withdrew his pistol. Had whoever was knocking heard us? Or were they just testing every door, moving on if no one responded?

The rapping came again, and with it a familiar girlish voice. "Open up, already. It's Anika."

Crap.

Tobias eased closer, and I looked around for a potential weapon.

"I'm not leaving," Anika said. "You're going to have to talk to me eventually. And I brought stuff you'd probably like to have sooner rather than later."

She didn't sound like she was bluffing—she knew we were here. I picked up the sharper-looking of the two carving knives in the kitchen and stepped toward the door.

"Who else is with you?" I asked.

"It's just me," she said. "I saw Tobias outside earlier."

"You saw me when?" Tobias said, and I realized the implications. He had only gone out those few minutes to relieve himself. What were the chances she'd happened to come by at the exact same time as the SUV?

"I was in the car," Anika said, sounding frustrated. "In the back.

I was supposed to tell them if I recognized anyone or saw anything that made me think I knew where you'd gone. But I didn't, right? You saw him glance at the backseat after you answered his questions? He was checking with me, but I shook my head. That's why he kept driving."

Tobias paused, and something in his face relaxed. I treaded past him to the door and peered through the peephole. All I could see was Anika's hooded figure directly in front of me, but there could have been others by the wall. I pressed my ear to the gap between the door and its frame. There was a faint rustle of fabric as she shifted her weight, nothing else.

"So why didn't you tell the guy?" I asked. "You told them everything else, didn't you?"

"You just don't get it," Anika said. "A couple weeks ago there was a kid—a *kid*—tried to hold me up for whatever food I had, with a shotgun he got who knows where. I don't have any feeling left in the fingertips of my left hand, 'cause I was stupid and fell asleep without mitts over my gloves one night, and it's so goddamned cold. And every time I go outside there are people coughing and sneezing and screaming, and I know that it could be me next. I knew if I could get in good with the Wardens, then I'd be okay. I just wanted to be okay again."

Her voice faded out.

"So why didn't you tell them about Tobias?" Leo said.

"It wasn't okay," she said softly. "When we got to the condo and saw you'd taken off, one of the guys said I should have come to them sooner. He shoved me into the wall—my shoulder still hurts when I move it. And then they made me go around with them looking for you all night, and the next day, and today. They only let me sleep a few hours at my place last night before they came by to get me again."

"We feel so sorry for you," Justin said, with blatant sarcasm.

Anika went on without acknowledging him. "I started thinking, I'm not really any safer with them than I was with you. You've got guns, you've got food, you've got the vaccine. And you let me in without expecting me to pay my way. You didn't hurt me even when I tried to screw you over." She paused. "I'm sorry about the spray."

Justin snorted.

"We also have a whole bunch of people who want to hurt *us* on our tails," I said. "We're not exactly safe."

"Yeah," Anika said, "but if Michael gets the vaccine, I don't know if I'll ever get to use it. You want everyone to have it. I don't want to be scared of getting sick anymore."

"You're not getting any vaccine until we find someone who can make more," I said. "I don't know how long that's going to take."

"That's okay," Anika said. "It's better than never."

*It might be never,* I thought, but I didn't say it. I didn't trust her. I couldn't imagine letting the cold box out of my sight while she was around. But she sounded like she believed what she was saying.

She believed in our way of doing things over the methods Michael and his people used. She believed in me.

Tobias hadn't put away his gun, but his expression was torn. Justin shook his head. Leo just looked back at me evenly, as if he trusted that whatever decision I made would be right.

Maybe she could help us. Maybe she'd screw us over again. There was no way to know. But they were all waiting for me. I had to decide.

She could tell us when the Wardens might patrol next, what their habits were, help us figure out a route through the city so we could avoid them. She might even know where to find a car.

I remembered, suddenly, the moment when we'd stood in the harbor across the strait from the island, with Tobias and his truck. We hadn't trusted *him* then, either. He'd been party to a catastrophe far worse than anything Anika had created. But without him, we wouldn't have made it anywhere near Toronto. We might all have been dead by now.

I reached out and, ignoring Justin's squeak of protest, opened the door. No one rushed at us with guns raised. There was only Anika, standing with her arms wrapped around a bundle of what looked like little bottles, her face pale beneath her dark hood.

"Thank you," she said, holding out the bundle. "I brought this for you. I know it doesn't make up for what I did, but I thought I should at least try. It's medicine. For your boyfriend, Kaelyn."

Leo eyed the package as I took it from her. "Medicine from where?"

"A veterinary clinic," she said. "I don't think many people have tried that. The first one I went into was still totally stocked. My grandfather was a vet—I looked through one of his old reference books. There's nothing that seemed safe that's supposed to kill a virus, but I found sedatives. If they'll calm down a cat or a dog, they should work on a person, if you give him enough."

An animal sedative. I should have thought of that. If we could be sure Gav would stay calm and quiet, he might not be able to walk, but he'd be perfectly safe in a vehicle.

If we could get a vehicle.

Anika looked at me hopefully, and I was struck by the knowledge that, under her layers of makeup, she was only a year or two older than me. In the lives we'd lost, we would both have been hanging out in cafeterias with friends and arguing with parents who were still alive and not worrying about whether we might die tomorrow. But this was what we had.

"Thank *you*," I said. "There is something else you could do. Something that would make up for everything. Do you know how to get us a car?"

A slow smile spread across her lips. "Yeah," she said, her eyes brightening. "You bet I can do that."

## TWENTY-SIX

Anika said she'd bring the car "sometime" the next day. By the late morning, we were all on edge. Justin started barking about her being late when Tobias came up from his turn at watch. Hearing him, I left the bedroom to settle things down.

"We want her to be careful," I reminded Justin. "If she's not, we're all screwed."

"She'll come," Tobias said.

"You just want her here because you think she's hot," Justin said, and Tobias blushed. He was standing strangely, his hands in his pockets, his shoulders stiff.

"If you're so worried," I said to Justin, "why aren't you down there keeping an eye out for us? It's your watch." And then he flushed too.

He hurried out the door, and I was about to turn back to the bedroom when Tobias said, "Kaelyn, can I talk to you for a sec?"

When I said, "Sure," he turned and stalked into the second bedroom.

"What's going on?" I asked, following him.

"I want you to tell me, honest to God, what you think," Tobias said. He let his hands fall from his pockets to hover, clenched, at his sides. "When I was down there on watch, I started... There's this spot..."

His control broke. His right hand leapt to the back of his neck, and he closed his eyes as he scratched at the patch of skin that must have been driving him crazy. My heart sank.

"Tobias..." I said, and then I didn't know what else to say.

He forced his hand down again, grimacing. "It's been nagging me for maybe half an hour now." His mouth twitched. "Do you think— Have I got it?"

"We've been so careful," I said. "You haven't been anywhere near Gav."

Then I stopped. Because he had been. At the very beginning, in the car. Gav had sneezed and coughed after we'd left city hall, before he'd gotten out, with nothing shielding his face.

"Leo was there too," I said. And Leo was looking perfectly healthy, and not at all like he was hiding some secret itch. "He's fine. It could still be nothing."

"Leo's had the vaccine," Tobias said.

"We don't even know—" I started, and cut myself off. If Tobias was sick and Leo wasn't, then maybe we did know. As well as we ever would, without mass testing.

Tobias swallowed audibly, and guilt welled up inside me. He was terrified, and I was thinking of him as a test subject.

"Maybe I should stay back," he said. "I'm putting you all at risk...."

"Don't be ridiculous," I said. "Gav's coming, and we *know* he's sick. Just... just make sure you keep your scarf tight over your mouth and nose the whole time we're in the car. And if that spot's still bothering you, put some snow on it—the cold might help."

"Are you sure?" he said. "I mean, I'd get it—Gav's your boyfriend, and I'm nobody."

"Tobias," I said firmly, "we are not leaving anyone behind. We came this far together, and we'll keep going together. Okay?"

His eyes flickered with what looked like relief. "Okay," he said, and loosened his scarf to pull it up over his nose.

Leo glanced up as I came back down the hall. I tried to study him surreptitiously, pausing for a second outside Gav's room. He looked a little tense, but his hands lay easy and open on his legs where he sat by the window, and his expression seemed unguarded.

"Everything all right?" he asked me.

"I think so," I said, and then, before I could stop myself, "You've been feeling okay, right?"

The momentarily puzzled look he gave me dissolved all my fears. Then understanding dawned in his expression. "Yeah," he said. "I'm fine. No worries."

A shiver of excitement raced through me, as awful as I felt for Tobias. For so long, we hadn't known. I hadn't known if all the danger we'd faced bringing the vaccine from the island had been worth it. But maybe I'd just gotten my proof.

"Are we leaving yet?" Gav asked when I came back into the bedroom. He was sitting propped up against the wall, but his face looked washed out, and even his sneeze was weak. He was still refusing to eat. I couldn't see that my attempted blood transfusion had affected him at all. The brief excitement drained out of me.

"The car's not here yet," I said.

He rubbed his knee absently. "Are you really sure we should go? I don't like this place much—it smells and it's cold—but it's better than wandering around, isn't it? Unless we go back to the island."

"We've talked about that," I said, sitting next to him. "It's not safe to go back to the island. And we still have to take care of the vaccine."

"We were going to take it to Ottawa and that didn't work, and we were bringing it here and that didn't work either," he said. "It's just going to be the same thing in Atlanta, isn't it? And we're going to be even farther from home."

*We don't have a home anymore*, I wanted to say. The world that had been our home was gone. But I didn't think this virus-afflicted version of Gav would understand.

"You're right," I said. "Our other plans didn't work. But I think—I really think Atlanta could be the right place. We have to try."

I brushed my fingers over his cheek. His skin was burning up.

"I don't want to go anywhere," he said. "I'm tired. You dragged me this far, Kaelyn, but don't you think it's enough? This is crazy. The vaccine probably doesn't even work. There's no doctors to help us. They all took off. We should too. We should go home. We were happy there. I was, anyway."

My eyes got hot. "I was too," I said.

He turned away, coughing. His whole body shook. I rested my palm on his back, wishing I could send him strength through my touch.

Feet clomped past the door. "I heard something!" Tobias said.

Gav straightened up and shifted his weight onto me. He crossed his arms behind my neck, pulling me close. "We could let them go, and we could stay," he murmured. "It doesn't have to be you. They can take the vaccine. Then it'd just be the two of us, like it was supposed to be. You told me, before—you said—"

The front door burst open. "She's here!" Justin called. "Let's move!"

Gav nuzzled my nose with his, and an ache spread through my chest.

I could do it. I knew, in that moment, I could. I could tell the guys to take the cold box while I stayed here with what was left of Gav until the end, the way he wanted.

I let the idea hover in my mind for maybe half a second, and then I pushed it away.

What Gav had said about the vaccine wasn't true. I knew as well as I ever would that it probably did work. And what I'd said to Justin that first day in the city, that *was* true. It was Dad's vaccine. It was my mission. My responsibility to see it through. Leo and Tobias and Justin—they were counting on me to know what to do, to keep them going. Just like Gav had been counting on me to keep going, before he'd gotten this sick.

"We've got to leave, Gav," I said, taking his hand and intertwining my fingers with his.

"No," he said as I stood up. He sat there looking up at me like a petulant kid. My stomach knotted, but there wasn't time for this. I had to make him come, now.

Even if that meant being cruel.

I let go of his hand. "I have to," I said. "I want you to come with me. If you won't, I'll have to go without you. You'll be here on your own."

If he'd called my bluff, I'm not sure how far I would have taken it. To the apartment door? Into the hall? At some point I would have turned around and come back. But he didn't make me. Panic flashed across his face, and he scrambled to his feet, swaying.

I adjusted his scarf to cover his lower face and wrapped over it the second one I'd brought, so there were four layers of fabric between his breath and the air. Then I slung my bag over my shoulder and grabbed the cold box. Leo opened the bedroom door.

"You okay?" he said. "Justin and Tobias have brought everything down. We're ready to go."

"I need to sit down," Gav said, his voice muffled by the scarves. I pulled his arm over my shoulder and walked him into the living room.

"Come quickly," I said. "You can sit in the car."

"So bossy today," Gav muttered, and I saw Leo bite back a smile.

"Here," he said, taking Gav's other arm. "You can lean on me too if you need to."

We made it down the stairs in fits and starts, stopping so Gav could rest against the wall and breathe at every landing. By the time we reached the first floor, he was coughing a little with every step.

Outside, a few flakes of snow were drifting past the lobby doors. Tobias was standing on the sidewalk, beside a black SUV with tinted windows.

"Well, what did you think I was going to get?" Anika was saying from the driver's side. "I knew where to find the keys for this one. They'll all think one of the other Wardens took it out. If you'd come on and get in, we'll be out of the city before they realize anything's wrong."

Tobias started to argue, but I cut him off before he could finish the first word.

"It's fine," I said. "This is what we have—too late to change it now."

I didn't even feel surprised. It made sense that she would have stolen from the Wardens to get what we needed, just like she'd once tried to steal from us for them.

As the others tossed our supplies into the back, I sat Gav down on the edge of the backseat and pulled out the bottle of water I'd dissolved four of Anika's sedatives into. I'd stirred in some powdered orange-drink mix we'd found, to try to hide the taste. Gav eyed it suspiciously.

"It'll help the coughing," I said. "Your throat's got to be pretty sore."

His nose wrinkled, but he shifted his scarves and took it. "Drink as much as you can," I said.

He gulped down several mouthfuls before stopping with a gasp. "Ugh," he said. "That's awful."

"Yeah, well, medicine doesn't normally taste good," I said. "Let's get in. You can have the window seat."

I helped him shuffle across to the opposite side of the car. The hatch banged shut behind us. Justin and Tobias squished in after me, and Leo scrambled into the front with the map book. It was a tight fit. Gav ended up half on my lap. He tipped his head against the back of the seat, shuddering. A seat-belt receptacle was digging into my butt, but all I cared about was getting out of there.

"Okay!" I said. "We're all in."

We eased down the street amid the snow. Tobias twisted around, peering first out the side window, then out the back. His hands stayed tight in his pockets. There was a dark splotch on the back of his scarf that I guessed was from melting ice.

We passed stores, banks, a church with shattered windows. Gav squirmed against me. His eyelids were drooping.

"I feel weird," he said, and then something else I couldn't make out. I took his hand in mine.

Anika slowed down as we edged around a streetcar stalled in the middle of the road, and I gritted my teeth with impatience. As she pressed the gas again, Tobias stiffened.

"A car just came around the corner a few blocks back," he said. "Heading this way."

"It's probably nothing to do with us, just some other Warden business," Anika said. "As long as they don't see who's driving, we're good. Here, we have to turn now; they'll go right by."

The SUV slid a little on the snow as she took the left, but she managed to hold it steady. Justin and I craned our necks toward the back window. I watched the road behind us, waiting for the other car to pass by. All I could hear was the growl of our engine and Gav's ragged breath.

A navy blue truck cruised into view. Instead of passing, it turned onto the street after us. My heart skipped a beat.

"They're following us," Tobias said.

"Fuck!" Justin said. "We're screwed."

"No," I said, over the thudding of my pulse. "We're not screwed unless they catch us. We just won't let them do that."

"How the hell are we going to stop them?" Justin demanded.

The engine roared as Anika put her foot to the gas. She took another turn at full speed, skidding, and nearly plowed into a streetlamp. Gav's head bumped against mine. He coughed faintly and mumbled, but his eyes were drifting shut.

"I don't know how they figured it out," Anika said. "I swear, I was so careful."

"It doesn't matter," Tobias said. "Maybe we can outrun them. I think there's only the one vehicle chasing us."

"If they have a radio, they'll be telling the others," Leo said.

I peered out the back again. The truck had come around the corner behind us, only a couple of blocks away now. I could make out two figures through the windshield. The one on the passenger side leaned out his window, pointing a narrow object at us.

"They've got a gun!" I said. A shot ran out, painfully loud, making a metallic ding as it hit the back of the SUV. Anika yelped. The four of us in the backseat ducked down, me sliding my arm across Gav's back to keep him still.

"They're going to kill us!" Justin said.

He was right. Another shot crackled past us, puncturing a stop sign we were whizzing by. They couldn't aim well, not while driving, but when they got closer they'd start hitting their mark. I doubted they cared about keeping us alive.

"What should I do?" Anika squeaked. "What the hell are we doing?"

I didn't know. The truck's engine gunned behind us, and it occurred to me that this was going to come down to us dying, or them. The question was only which of us it'd be. And I knew I didn't want it to be us. I just couldn't see how to save us.

As we took another wobbly turn, I hugged Gav close, and remembered. A few days ago we'd evaded one of the Wardens' cars by playing dead. Dead as a possum.

Dead as a snake that wasn't really dead.

My breath caught. Tobias had put the rifle in the trunk, but I was sure he had his pistol. He wouldn't be able to aim any better than the guys in the truck while we were moving. But we could stop, pretending to be giving up, and then, as they came closer, strike when they didn't expect it.

I could tell him right now to gun down two strangers who, in the end, were just trying to survive. Like we were.

I'd told Anika we weren't like Michael's people, but maybe there weren't so many differences, when it came down to it.

A bullet scraped over the roof, and I winced. I thought of a thumb rubbing the scar on the back of a hand. And something in my brain clicked.

*Not every bite has to kill.*

"Tobias," I said, "if we stopped, they'd stop too, and get out. Do you think you could shoot both of them, before they'd have a chance to react?"

"Stop?" Anika said, but Tobias was nodding, his jaw tense.

"I could do it," he said.

I caught his eyes. "Not to kill them," I said. "Just…just so they can't shoot us, or keep coming after us. Can you do that?"

"What?" Justin squawked. "But—" I elbowed him before he could go on. Tobias hesitated, staring back at me. Then a hint of a smile lit up his face.

"Yeah," he said. "I bet I could do that too." He cocked his head toward the front. "Stop the car."

"For real?" Anika said.

"Stop the car, Anika," I said, and she hit the brake.

We slid to a halt, bumping against the snow-covered curb.

Tentatively, I raised my head. The flakes were falling thicker now, but I could still easily make out the truck behind us. I hoped Tobias could see clearly enough for what he needed to do.

He rolled down his window, the cold air rushing in. The blue truck ground to a stop about twenty feet back. Tobias shifted, leaning closer to the door.

"Keep the engine running," he said, drawing out his pistol. "You have to drive as soon as I say so."

He eased his arm along the edge of the open window. Outside, the two men had gotten out of the truck. One still carried the handgun he'd shot at us with, but they were both grinning.

They thought we'd stopped because they'd scared us. They probably also thought that if we wanted to fight back, we would have by now. That was the most important part, if they were going to let their guard down so Tobias got his chance. They had to think we were helpless.

"Please don't hurt us!" I yelled out the window. "Just tell us what you want, and you can have it."

"All right," said the one who'd been driving. They sauntered closer, scanning the car. "Let's have you all come out, and we'll talk about this properly."

The last syllable had hardly reached my ears when Tobias threw himself partway out the window and fired.

The man with the gun jerked back, his arm going limp. The gun dropped from his hand as he clutched at his shoulder. Before the driver could do more than flinch, Tobias's pistol crackled again. The driver stumbled, blood blooming across the knee of his jeans.

"Drive!" Tobias said, yanking himself back inside. "Drive, fast!"

Anika didn't need to be told a second time. She slammed on the gas, and the SUV lurched forward. I gazed out the back as we raced down the street. The driver fumbled for the pistol, dragging his injured leg, but he hadn't reached the gun by the time we whipped around another turn and left them behind.

"They won't be able to follow us like that," Tobias said. "And if we're lucky, anyone they called is a good ways off."

The sound of the shots echoed in my ears. I'd thought it wouldn't matter nearly as much, knowing we'd left them alive, but my heart was still pounding, nausea curdling in my stomach.

I did the best I could, I told myself.

"Thanks," I said to Tobias, and the corners of his eyes crinkled with a grin.

The SUV thumped over a crumpled cardboard box, and we pulled onto the freeway. The snowflakes fell faster, coating the windshield a second after the wipers brushed them away. Filling our tracks.

"I can hardly see," Anika said.

"You don't need to," Leo pointed out. "There's no traffic. Just keep going."

I held Gav's sleeping form against me and thanked Mother Nature for working in our favor, just this once.

A small cough broke from Tobias's lips. He covered it up by clearing his throat, but his face went white. I glanced at Leo in the front seat. He still hadn't shown a single symptom.

"So we're heading to Atlanta?" Justin said.

I sagged back, taking stock. We were all alive. Leo could still dance. Justin might still rejoin his mother eventually, and I might return to Meredith. Someday we might even see Nell and everyone else on the island again. Maybe I hadn't found what I'd hoped for, maybe the world was horribly messed up and would never again be the way it used to be. But the people in it were still worth fighting for. We hadn't lost everything.

"Well, we can't go back now, can we?" I said.

Leo met my gaze in the rearview mirror. "No," he said, as if he knew I meant more than just Toronto. "I don't think we can."

"All right," I said. "Then we go forward."

# ACKNOWLEDGMENTS

I owe many thanks:

To Cyn Balog, Amanda Coppedge, Saundra Mitchell, Mahtab Narsimhan, and Robin Prehn, for their insightful eyes in pointing out what I was doing wrong in the early drafts, and just as importantly, what I was doing right.

To my editor, Catherine Onder, for her thoughtful guidance in shaping the later drafts into a story I'm proud to share with the world.

To Deborah Bass, Ann Dye, Tanya Ross-Hughes, Dina Sherman, Hayley Wagreich, and the rest of the team at Hyperion, for their skill at turning simple documents into beautiful books, and at getting those books out into the hands of readers.

To Melanie Storoschuk and the rest of Hachette Book Group Canada, for their perseverance in helping the book reach its audience here in my home country.

To my agent, Josh Adams, for his incredible dedication to seeing this series grow and for keeping track of all the important details I'd otherwise forget.

To Jacqueline Houtman, for generously offering her time and knowledge so I could verify that my science at least mostly made sense.

To the readers of *The Way We Fall*, for sharing their enthusiasm for the book and making me even more pleased to be able to present the next part of the story.

To my family and friends, for their love and support over the years.

And to my husband, Chris, for standing by me through both good times and bad, and never letting me lose sight of why I'm on this journey.